THE TIGHT WHITE COLLAR

The Tight White Collar is primarily the story of a man who had a dream, and of the people who prevented his dream from coming true. Christopher Pappas, whose dream was to be the best teacher who ever taught, wanted to teach truth, selflessness and justice in a small town in New England called Cooper Station.

But he was a "native," and he was married to a woman named Lisa who refused to accept the conventions. And then Anthony Cooper came home and in Lisa he found a reason for staying alive.

When Chris was first offered a job as teacher in the Cooper Station high school, only one woman, Doris Delaney Palmer, opposed him. Doris said that Chris and Lisa were "undesirables," but in her heart she was frightened because while Lisa and Chris had made a mistake which they admitted to the world, Doris herself had made a mistake and could not ever tell her husband about it.

Cooper Station was filled with people who faced and solved an issue. This is the vivid and moving story of these people; of Chris and Lisa Pappas and of those who were for and against them, told with the same narrative power and penetrating insight into character and motive that made *Peyton Place* one of the outstanding best-sellers of all time.

By the same Author

PEYTON PLACE
RETURN TO PEYTON PLACE

The Tight White Collar

Grace Metalious

THE BOOK CLUB
121 CHARING CROSS ROAD
LONDON W.C.2

FIRST PUBLISHED IN GREAT BRITAIN IN 1961 BY
FREDERICK MULLER LIMITED

Printed and Bound in Great Britain by
The Hollen Street Press Limited London W 1

1

SOMETIMES, just once in a great while, the seasons run in a perfect cycle in northern New England so that when you have grown old the memory of perfection is so sharp and clear-edged that you look back and say to yourself, Yes, *that's* the way it was. You remember that you were young and that at the end of summer, just before school opened, everyone you knew had a cellar full of vegetables put up in glass jars because summer had put forth just the right amounts of sun and rain. In autumn the apple trees were so red and so swollen with fruit that the branches dragged on the ground and your mouth watered when you thought of biting into a McIntosh because you knew what the sharp tang would be like against your teeth and how the juice would feel running down your chin. The foliage was brighter than it had been since anyone could remember and under your feet the leaves crunched louder and the bonfires sent up a sweeter, smokier smell than they had ever done before. There was snow on the ground at Thanksgiving and you remember best the smell of cranberries and mincemeat and butter and how it felt to come in out of the unfriendliness of November and into a bright warm kitchen where something was always going on. By Christmas Eve there was enough hard-packed snow on the roads that you could go carol-singing in a horse-drawn sleigh and your mittens were bright red and your nose ran a little and over everything there was the smell of freshly cut spruce. In January there was a blizzard that knocked down the power lines and closed the school for three days. Then you stayed home, warm and safe in front of the fire, and read *Snowbound* to your little brother and it wasn't at all like reading it in school because this time you *felt* all the words instead of just saying them out loud, and that night you ate canned food for supper because no one could get out to the stores. The thaw set in at the end of the month and everyone who was older than you said it was unhealthy but you didn't believe it and you looked forward to the next day because maybe tomorrow you wouldn't have to wear overshoes to school. But then it was February, bleak and snowy and not much fun at all because now you were looking forward to spring, and sleds and skates had become tiresome. You were not surprised when March came in like a lion and went out like a lamb because you had heard that it was so in school and you forgot all the years when it had not been true. In April the rains that would bring the blossoming of May ripped at the rivers and streams until winter melted clear out of sight and then it was the time of gentleness. Purple violets poked their little heads suspiciously out of the ground and the more daring crocus rose defiantly out of patches of now harmless snow. Bare ground was covered overnight with a soft green fuzz and on the trees the new leaves were the colour of lettuce, so tiny and tender-looking that you wanted to pick a handful to put into your mouth. The forsythia bushes were like young girls at a party with their yellow skirts all spread out, fresh and crisp and new-looking. Even the pines discarded their black winter faces and turned now, washed and green, towards the sun. You walked in the woods where the pine needle floor was still soggy from the recently gone frost and if you were very lucky you found a lady's-slipper with its colour going all the way from shell-pink to deep rose and you felt singled out and special all

8

day long because this was a Practically Extinct Flower and you had found one. You put your blossom in a glass of water and set it on your bureau and you could not believe that the flower would be dead by morning.

One year spring came with gentleness to a town called Cooper Station. It was the spring that Anthony Cooper came home after ten years away, and after he had come to the top of the last hill before the long slope down into town he parked his car at the side of the road and looked down at Cooper Station. The town looked like something, or the reflection of something, in the bottom of an enormous green cup.

Like something I dreamed, thought Anthony, or like a picture on a calendar or on a Christmas card.

The sun shone warmly on pink brick and white wood and it filtered down through the leafed trees to make patterns on the shadowed sidewalks. It reflected itself in the front of the shops on Benjamin Street, the main thoroughfare, where even the First National was painted white and had small-paned windows. Anthony noticed that the marker at the town line was still a plain black post with the name of the town painted in white block letters on a cross-piece. There was no huge billboard such as is found at the entrance of many towns and which, in this case, might have read, WELCOME TO COOPER STATION. WORK, PLAY AND LIVE IN OUR TOWN, for the simple reason that Cooper Station did not welcome just anybody. If a man wanted an obvious Chamber of Commerce welcome he had to go north for another ten miles, beyond the camouflaging hills, to where there was a gigantic curve in the river, and there he would find the city of Cooper's Mills. There he would find the factories, the tenements, the sixty-watt light bulbs in the soiled beer joints, the Canucks and the Catholics. But Cooper Station was different. It was made up of the people who profited from the existence of Cooper's Mills and who could, therefore, afford not to live there.

For a moment Anthony felt some of the old bitterness which had caused him to leave Cooper Station in the first place, but then he merely shrugged and put his car in gear. He had not come home to champion lost causes. He had come home to die.

"And I intend to do it with dignity and in peace and quiet," he said aloud as he turned his car off Benjamin Street and into Smith Road.

Much later, Anthony would say that he had given up the idea of dying because he never found the time for it. He had been home less than six weeks when, as he put it, all hell broke loose.

"Ferguson, would you hate it so if Nate didn't go into the mills? There is Benjamin, and if I didn't know better myself, I'd swear that he'd been born under a spinning machine."

"Nonsense," said Ferguson. "The mills are for both boys. Believe me, it'll take two of them to run them if we keep on going the way we are now. Nathaniel wasn't named after his grandfather for nothing. He'll learn. Just as Benjamin did."

"Just because a child is named after his grandfather doesn't mean that he is cut from the same piece of cloth," said Isabel. "And believe me, there are times when I'm very grateful for that fact."

Ferguson rattled his newspaper nervously. "That's enough, Isabel," he said.

"I should be the one to say what's enough," said Isabel angrily. "I've had more than enough of your father and you and Benjamin with your foul-mouthed companionship with the mill-hands and your nights away from home swilling beer with them, waiting for the moment when you can go to the greasy embrace of some factory girl. Nathaniel's different, and you're not going to make him into another image of yourself."

"Isabel!" roared her husband. "That's enough!"

"You needn't shout in pain because the truth hurts so much," Isabel said. "I've known for a long time. But you leave Nate alone. He's not like the rest of you."

"You'll be the one to leave Nathaniel alone," replied Ferguson. "He'll learn."

But Nathaniel did not learn for a long, long time. When Benjamin, who had been named after Isabel's father, was twelve years old he could completely dismantle a knitting-machine and put it back together, while Nathaniel, even at sixteen, did not only know where to begin but always ended up with parts and pieces left over.

Benjamin, so everyone said, was a true chip off the old block—the same block that had fashioned Old Nate and Ferguson. When he was twenty years old he got a girl in trouble and for a while he was afraid that there was going to be hell to pay, but his father and grandfather fixed it so that very few people found out, and the few who did were made to keep their mouths shut. The

15

girl's name was Laura Ford and she was the daughter of the Cooper Station high school principal, Edward Ford, who did not relish a scandal any more than did the Coopers. Laura and Benjamin were married in the Congregational Church and then shipped off to England where Benjamin would supposedly study British manufacturing methods. Later, Benjamin looked back fondly on the months he had spent in London. He had become involved almost immediately in a love affair with an Algerian dancer who performed in a Soho night-club, and he had drunk a river of champagne and had lost a considerable amount of money at cards. Since there were no Algerian dancers in Cooper Station and champagne was served only at big weddings and cards were played for small stakes on Saturday nights in the back of somebody's garage, Old Nate and Ferguson paid gladly for Benjamin's English diversions. Their only prayer was that Laura would produce a child who would be born dead or, failing that, one who would be as small and sickly as herself so that both Cooper and Ford faces could be saved in the two towns. Laura came through with flying colours. Anthony had weighed less than five pounds at birth and for a time it was doubted that he would live at all. Ferguson sent a distraught Isabel to London to accompany the frail mother and "premature" baby home.

When Benjamin returned to Cooper Station and stepped into the mills beside his father, Nathaniel was allowed the delicious delusion that perhaps he would never have to go into the mills at all.

"You see, Nate dear, things always work out for the best," said Isabel. "Benjamin and your father will run the mills with Grandpa and in a little while I'll talk to your father about building that greenhouse you've always wanted. And then, when Anthony is grown, he'll be able to step in with Benjamin. Everything is going to work out for the best."

Benjamin was everything that Old Nate and Ferguson had been in their younger days. After Old Nate died, Nathaniel kept more quiet than ever and tried to make himself blend into a background of obscurity. He was enrolled at Harvard, where, because his father insisted, he majored in business administra-

16

tion, but he carried a minor in botany and he was happy. Benjamin, on the other hand, had never even bothered with high school. He hated books, loved the mills and was encouraged in both emotions by Ferguson.

To Isabel, making sure that Nathaniel heard, Ferguson said, "Nobody needs a college education to count money. You can either count to a million or you can't, and there's nothing a tight white collar will do for you but choke you and leave a red mark around your neck."

A year later Laura died and six months later Isabel followed. Benjamin closed his house and with Anthony moved across the street with Nathaniel and Ferguson.

"Bad things come in threes," said Ferguson. "Grandpa and Laura and Isabel. Now it'll stop for a while."

But less than a year later, while standing in front of a knitting-machine at the mills, Benjamin fell forward.

"Nathaniel!" he screamed, just before he died.

Everyone in both towns said that Benjamin had died calling for his brother and that it was an omen telling that Nathaniel would come to stand in his brother's place. But for ever after, Nathaniel wondered if perhaps Benjamin had not called to his absent grandfather, screaming for the old man to get him out of another scrape.

Ferguson did not mince words with his one remaining son.

"It's up to you, Nathaniel," he said. I'm not getting any younger and somebody has got to look after things. You'll have to go into the mills as soon as you're through school, and it's going to fall to you to see to things after I'm gone. You won't get any help from Anthony, I can guarantee you that. Takes after his mother's side, that boy. Frail and empty-headed as they come. None of Benjamin in him at all. This house'll be yours, Nathaniel, and the running of the mills. Benjamin's house belongs to Anthony now, but this one is yours. For you and the wife you'll bring here some day and for your sons."

Nathaniel looked around him. He looked at everything. He looked at the mills and he looked at the people. He looked at the house where he had been born and raised. And he tried to think, to find a way out.

17

"Don't ever get the idea, Nathaniel," said his father, "that your grandpa and me and Benjamin ran the mills. Get that idea out of your head. The mills ran us. Just like they'll run you. And don't forget, too, when you look around, that everybody you see depends on you. Without you, there'll be no Cooper's Mills. Every worker in the factories has a family. Without you there'll be no bread for them. Your grandpa built Cooper Station. He built it to live in, for when he wanted to get away from the mills for a little bit. Without you there'll be no reason for Cooper Station to be here. Nate, son, when you get very tired, look at your hands. Look at them and remember that you hold the lives of thousands of people in them. It's not easy, Nate. But, then, none of us ever said it was. It's the way things are, if you're a Cooper."

From the top of the hill where he sat, Nathaniel looked down at the mass of red brick for which he was supposed to do the thinking, and he shivered suddenly.

So, it's impossible for man to reason without God, is it? he thought angrily. His eyes turned heavenward and his fingers snapped the new green vine he held. Defiantly, he looked at heaven and shouted:

"All right, You've got all the aces. You call the turns, but I'll never believe a damned word about justice and mercy. A big, magnanimous God! Well, tell me Your reason for Robin. What possible reason could You have for her? And what about Margery?"

Nathaniel squeezed the sides of his head in an effort to shut out the memory of a night now almost ten years old. The night he had gone to Margery and she had turned on him, screaming.

"Get away from me!" Margery had shouted, pushing at the hands that touched her with love. "Don't touch me!"

Impossible to reason without You? said Nathaniel to the silent sky. Far more impossible to reason with a God who'd bitch me up the way You have. I'm here. Where are You?"

Nathaniel Cooper turned and began the slow trek down the

hill to his car. Never had he felt such loneliness, such complete emptiness and exhaustion.

I hope Anthony won't linger after dinner, he thought as he climbed into his car. I've got a Guardian meeting to go to.

3

THE Cooper Station high school stood in an open field at the end of Laurentian Street. This was the oldest street in Cooper Station, named by Old Nate in memory of the place where he and his wife had spent their honeymoon. The school was a beautiful new building, all brick and glass and completely fireproofed, and almost everbody in Cooper Station regarded it as the town's monument to free education and its tribute to the American Way. Sometimes there was talk of building the same kind of school in Cooper's Mills, but this kind of talk always trailed off into vagueness and finally halted altogether until someone brought up the subject again. The people who usually brought up the subject were Dr. Jess Cameron, Nathaniel Cooper and Thomas Averill, the owner of the *Twin Town Clarion*. For a while, everyone would be enthusiastic about the idea of a new high school for Cooper's Mills, then the subject of higher taxes would come up at town meetings and the excuses, old and tired and very much used, would begin.

"After all, the Catholics over there have their own school, so it hardly seems worth while to go to the expense of building a new public high school."

"Most of the kids at the Mills don't really want to go to high school anyway."

"And most of them who do go never finish. I mean, they quit as soon as they're sixteen years old and go right into the factories.

I mean, the kind of education we give our children here would be sort of wasted there."

Besides being the newest, finest school building in the state, the Cooper Station high school had been provided with an auditorium and several smaller meeting-rooms which provided facilities for all important town activities since the town hall was old, draughty and inadequately heated.

As Nathaniel Cooper walked towards the lighted school building where the Cooper Station Town Board of Guardians was having its regular monthly meeting, he thought of the rather uncomfortable dinner he had just finished. It was always awkward to have dinner with a relative one hadn't seen for ten years, he supposed. And Anthony certainly hadn't been the best company.

He drinks too much, thought Nathaniel, remembering the way Anthony had gulped four Martinis before dinner.

"Just put in the gin, Nate," Anthony had said. "And then whisper Vermouth. That's all. Whoops! Here, let me do it. You said Vermouth too loud."

Margery had been nervous.

"I watched for you, Anthony," she had said. "When you wrote that you were coming and didn't say anything about having anyone meet the train, I figured that you'd be driving. Is everything all right over at your house?"

"Wonderful," Anthony had said. "The place is so spotless that it looks as if Mother's ghost had been busy cleaning for a month. And Cooper Station hasn't changed a bit. Nobody can fart but that it doesn't make the front page of the *Clarion*. I hadn't been in the house three minutes when you called up and I'll bet everyone in town knows I'm here."

"Well, I don't know what we'll do from now on," Margery had said worriedly. "I've had Marie over there, but she cleans for Jess regularly and I just borrowed her from him."

"Don't worry about it, Margery. I'll be fine. I don't want anyone underfoot all the time anyway."

"Anthony?"

"Yes?"

"How are you feeling?"

21

"Good Lord, Margery, stop fussing. I'm fine. I just came home to rest and get some work done."

"Nate wrote to your agent, Anthony."

"Margery," Anthony had said savagely, nervous breakdowns are very fashionable among writers. Didn't you know?"

The last of the Coopers, thought Nathaniel sourly. Oh, well, it's probably a good thing. Maybe the line's been around too long as it is.

Besides Nathaniel, the Cooper Station Town Board of Guardians was made up of James Sheppard, a relative newcomer to the town who had been elected by what almost everyone regarded as a fluke, and Doris Delaney Palmer, the wife of Adam Palmer who was the president of the Palmer Soap Company of Boston. The Guardians, as they were called, acted in a supervisory capacity over all social and educational matters that concerned the town. The Board acted as trustees for the town hospital, a fact which had driven Jess Cameron to outrage more than once for, except for Nathaniel who believed in leaving the job of hospital administration to those who knew what they were doing, the Board, more often than not, fancied itself wise beyond wisdom and insisted on arguing about the price of X-ray machines when, as Jess put it, they should have busied themselves with rolling bandages. The Cooper Station library was also a victim of the Town Board of Guardians with the result that the small library contained a surfeit of books about Tibet while the works of Sigmund Freud were regarded as suitable reading for foreigners who planned eventually to work in insane asylums and therefore not fit for the eyes of God-fearing northern New Englanders. Nathaniel Cooper had given up in his efforts to buck the ladies who served with him on the Board long ago and until the election of Jim Sheppard, Nathaniel's attitude had been one of to hell with it.

"Not that I expect to see the works of Henry Miller on the shelves of the public library," he told Margery, "but perhaps now we can put in something besides the limp mutterings of Frances Parkinson Keyes."

The library, which had been given to the town by his grandfather, was Nathaniel's pet project while Doris Delaney Palmer's was the Administration of Funds for the Poor. Doris loved the poking and prying that was involved with such administration and it was a point of pride with her that she handled every town dollar as if it were her own. The end result of Doris's way with money was that more than one family had lived on oatmeal and beans rather than ask the town for a dime and every year, at town meeting, Doris always delivered the accounting of funds with what some people considered pardonable pride.

"You have to hand it to Mrs. Palmer," they said. "Knows where every cent is every minute of the time."

But although the Funds for the Poor might be where Doris did her best work, it was at the selection of school-teachers that she really shone. She relentlessly questioned and probed into the life of every man or woman who applied to Arthur Everett, the school superintendent, for a position in the Cooper Station schools.

"After all," Doris was fond of saying, "we *are* paying their salaries and when a person is going to be in charge of our young people, we just can't be too careful, now can we?"

Doris preferred teachers who had graduated from the state university, were married to people who had also attended the university and had the good taste to restrain themselves to one child.

"They make the most suitable teachers," she said. "They are settled but not harried and they seem to fit right into things."

"It beats me how the hell you find anybody dumb enough to apply for a job here in the first place," said Adam Palmer. "Not with the money you pay."

"Adam, to a dedicated school-teacher there is no such thing as money," said Doris.

"Well, then, I guess I can see why you'd never make a teacher," said Adam.

"Adam," said Doris severely, "it's coarse to discuss money with such obvious interest."

"You're right," said Adam grandly. "I shall leave the obvious interest to you, on the first of the month, when you examine the bank statements."

23

Adam Palmer was the only man in Cooper Station who was wealthier then Nathaniel Cooper, a fact which gave Doris unlimited hours of pleasure. She could not understand what she called "Adam's kotowing" to Nathaniel.

You could buy and sell the Coopers a dozen times over," she told her husband often and angrily. "What makes them so special anyway? Why, that Anthony is totally worthless, off in New York doing heaven knows what. And as for Margery and Nate, well, if I couldn't do better than produce an idiot——"

"Why don't you shut up, Doris?" said her husband. "Just try to remember that there were Coopers around here when my grandfather was still stirring up hog fat and lye in his barn and long before any of the Delaneys had got off the boat."

"And you should see the way he high-hats me at Town Guardians' meetings," continued Doris as if Adam had not spoken. "I've known Nathaniel Cooper for fifteen years and he still calls me Mrs. Palmer. Well, he needn't think that I'm going to Mr. Cooper, sir, him like one of his mill-hands."

"Good evening, Mr. Cooper," said Doris Delaney Palmer when Nathaniel walked into the room when the Town Board of Guardians meeting was to be held.

"Evening, Mrs. Palmer," said Nate. "Mary. Jim. Arthur."

Mrs. Palmer's smile never wavered. That bastard, she thought savagely, I'll fix him. And that Jim Sheppard, too. Jim never had any business getting on the board in the first place. Callie Webster should be sitting in his chair right this minute.

Mary Welch, the town librarian, had come to make her usual futile plea for money and Arthur Everett waited impatiently until she had gone.

"Well, let's get to it," he said briskly. "I've got to go to a meeting up the Mills when I finish here." Arthur Everett always spoke briskly when he was unsure of himself. "We've got to get the new teacher question out of the way. As you all know, there is a vacancy in the history department caused by the resignation of John Colbath. I'm recommending a young man named Christopher Pappas to fill that vacancy." Arthur took a deep breath, the way a man might if he just stepped under a cold shower at seven o'clock in the morning. "Here are Pappas's

24

records," he continued, not looking at Doris, and tossed a sheaf of papers down on to the table in front of Nathaniel.

"Arthur," said Nate, whose head felt a little heavy from the Martinis before dinner, "I've been looking at papers of one sort or another all day. Can't you just tell us about this fellow? Then we can vote and get it over with."

"You're recommending *whom*?" demanded Doris Palmer.

"Christopher Pappas," said Arthur Everett and sighed inwardly. I knew it, he thought, I knew she'd never stand for it.

"Do you know who Christopher Pappas is?" cried Doris, turning to look at Nate.

"Well, from what Arthur's said," replied Nate, "I gather that Christopher Pappas is a male teacher."

"I'll tell you about him," said Doris. "He's that Greek fellow from the Mills. Born and raised there. And he got a job teaching down at West Farrington, the Lord only knows how. He was there for less than a month when he just upped and quit his job. No reason, just like that, he upped and quit. He'd signed a contract and everything. He was committed to teach for the whole school year and he just quit." Doris fixed her eyes on Arthur Everett. "Everyone knows about Christopher Pappas," she said. "And I, for one, would like to know whose bright idea it was to suggest a man like that for a position here in Cooper Station."

James Sheppard balanced a yellow pencil on two fingers and looked up at Doris Palmer.

"Mine," he said calmly.

"Mr. Sheppard," said Doris, "must I remind you that the welfare of our children depends on us and that is not a responsibility to be taken lightly. After all, we are being asked to approve a *teacher*, not a garbage collector, and——"

"Mr. Pappas is a teacher," said Jim Sheppard.

Doris Palmer quivered with outrage. "Some teacher!" she cried. "Do you know what he's doing now? He's living in a shack up at the Mills with that wretched wife of his and their two brats and he's teaching physical education at the School for the Feebleminded over at Marmington."

Jim Sheppard put down the pencil he had been holding.

"The Pappas family is not living in a shack," he said quietly.

25

"They live in a house which they rent from Eben Seton for thirty-five dollars a month. The Pappas children are not brats, but attractive, well-behaved, intelligent children. And Mrs. Pappas is far from wretched."

"She's not even decent!" shouted Doris Palmer. "She was pregnant before she ever got married. Everybody knows it."

"You don't know that for a fact, Mrs. Palmer," said Jim Sheppard. "And even if it was true, I don't imagine that Lisa Pappas is the first woman around here to have found herself in the same circumstances."

"For God's sake, Arthur," said Nate wearily. "Will you please tell me about this man so that we can vote and get it over with?"

Arthur Everett looked at Doris. She might not be a Cooper, but Arthur knew that she was not without a certain power with many people in town. People who admired Palmer soap and Palmer money and who were not without influence when it came to a question of Arthur's job.

"Well, Nate," said Arthur, "Pappas is a good man. Honour student at the state university, two years' experience with excellent references. It was Jim, here, who suggested that we consider him, but it was Ed Bailey, the head of the education department down at the university, who really talked me into recommending Pappas for this job."

"It would seem to me, Mr. Everett," said Doris Palmer angrily, "that Cooper Station has a superintendent with remarkably little backbone when someone we don't even know can talk him into suggesting an undependable foreigner to teach in our town."

"Christopher Pappas made a mistake on the job at West Farrington," said Arthur. "He was younger then and he was an idealist and he couldn't take interference in his work. Besides, Pappas isn't a foreigner. He was born right here in this state. Right next door to Cooper's Mills."

"Where were your parents born, Mrs. Palmer?" asked Jim Sheppard.

Doris Palmer's whole body trembled. "Mr. Sheppard," she said, "you forget yourself."

"The hell with all this," said Nate rudely. "Let's hear the rest of it, Arthur."

26

"Well, it was a culmination of a lot of things with Pappas," said Arthur. "For one thing, there's a fellow down there on the school board. Name of Hammond. Hammond had a daughter, a senior, the year Pappas started down there. The girl was failing American History and Pappas sent a warning home to her parents. Old Hammond blew his top. Went down to the school to see Pappas and told him he'd better pass his daughter or else. Like I said, Pappas was young. He asked Hammond or else what. To make a long story short, the girl failed the next exam and Pappas gave her a fifty for the quarter. Mrs. Palmer was mistaken when she said that Pappas taught for less than a month. It was just short of three months that he was there. There were a few other things, too," Arthur went on, this time openly nervous.

"Like what?" insisted Nate.

"Ridiculous things," said Jim Sheppard, sorry for Arthur Everett. "There were a few pinheads in West Farrington who claimed that Chris Pappas was a Communist because he told the kids that some of the greatest writers in the world were Russians."

"They were," said Nate.

"And Pappas also said things such as the Puritans had run away from intolerance only to become intolerant themselves."

Nate smiled. "Pappas," he said. "God's Angry Man. Might do this town good to have someone like that around. I vote that we hire this fellow."

"I'm with you," said Jim Sheppard.

"Thank you, gentlemen," said Arthur Everett gratefully.

"Just a minute!" cried Doris, "I won't stand for this!"

"You've been outvoted, Mrs. Palmer," said Arthur as gently as he could. No matter what else you could say about Doris Palmer, she was a fighter. He only hoped that she was a good loser.

Doris Delaney Palmer grabbed her gloves and handbag from the desk in front of her.

"I don't care," she said. "You haven't heard the end of this. Maybe none of you cares what happens to our schoolchildren, but I do. And I'm sure that the citizens of this town will agree with me."

"Mrs. Palmer," said Nate, at the end of his patience, "you have

27

been outvoted. At the close of this meeting, Mr. Sheppard and I will sign our names to a contract hiring Christopher Pappas. You may join us or not, as you like, but Christopher Pappas will teach in the Cooper Station high school next fall."

Later that night, Arthur telephoned Christopher Pappas.

"Well, Pappas," he said, "the Guardians approved you, but you're going to have a time of it. Mrs. Palmer is dead set against you. She wouldn't sign your contract along with Jim and Nate Cooper."

"I'll make it, Mr. Everett," said Chris Pappas. "I'll do such a good job that she won't be able to stay set against me."

"That's the spirit," said Arthur. "Good night, Chris. Good luck."

The school superintendent hung up slowly. Poor bastard, he thought, poor, stupid bastard to break his heart for three thousand dollars a year.

4

LISA PAPPAS lay on her back in the bed next to her husband. She was naked and Chris's hands travelled over her in a pattern that had not deviated in almost ten years.

Now that it's over, thought Lisa, I wonder why I wanted Chris to get this job so badly. Three thousand a year isn't going to do much for us with the kids and all the bills.

Sometimes Lisa could pretend that Chris was not touching her at all. Then it was as if she were someone very tiny, hiding in an undiscovered corner of herself while a stranger performed a ritual over a body she did not know. When she could do this, it wasn't so bad. She could think her own thoughts with most of her mind, leaving just enough of her brain free to dictate the right moments to moan and the proper time to make her body writhe and undulate.

He'd damn well better do a good teaching job this time, thought Lisa, after the way I begged Ed Bailey to recommend him and the year I spent working on Polly Sheppard. If he louses up this job he might just as well plan on going back to a job in the mills.

With this thought, something in Lisa stopped functioning so that she could no longer pretend that she was not being touched. With something like a thud, she felt herself back in bed with the broken spring in the mattress that always poked into her back and with Chris, who hadn't taken a shower that day.

Lisa Pappas was born Melissa Anne St. George in the town of Cooper's Mills and the first sentence she could remember hearing as a child was, "For heaven's sake, Lisa, remember who you are!" To everyone but her mother, Irene, it was obvious who Lisa was. She was the only daughter of a Canuck named Wilfred St. George who, until the time he had run off with a waitress from a beer saloon when Lisa was five, had been employed as a loom-fixer in the factories. As for Irene, who worked as a secretary in the main office of the mills, the town regarded her as just another Cooper's Mills girl who had gone away for a few years and had returned with a lot of fancy ideas, the main one being that she thought herself a cut above everyone else in town. But, Cooper's Mills opinion notwithstanding, there was something different about Irene. Her father, Alcide Chaput, had not been a mill-hand. He had been a gardener, and a good one. When Irene was twelve years old, Alcide had packed up his family and left Cooper's Mills to take a job as caretaker and gardener on the estate of a family named Durand who lived in the southern part of the state. Sometimes Irene looked back on the years she had spent with the Durands as the happiest in her life, but at other times she wondered if perhaps she would not be more content with her lot now if she had not had a five-year taste of luxury and gentility.

The Durands provided Alcide and his family with an attractive, well-furnished cottage which stood just inside the spike-topped iron gate that barred the entrance of the main driveway leading to what Irene's mother, Marie, called the Big House. Marie thanked God on her knees every morning and every night for the good fortune He had chosen to bestow on her. Her cottage was finer than the houses of the well-to-do in her village in Canada, and Alcide had vast acres of grass and shrubs and flowers to care for so that he was always busy and, therefore, always happy. And Marie herself was entrusted with the care of all the dainty clothing of Mrs. Durand and her twin daughters, Felice and Marianne. A regular laundress came to the Big House twice a week to do the ordinary washing but Marie did all the pretty, lacy underwear and pressed the ornate party dresses and sewed tiny buttons on the cuffs of expensive white gloves. But best of all

30

were the advantages for Irene, advantages beyond belief to Alcide and Marie.

The Durands hired a tutor for their twin girls and since Mrs. Durand thriftily believed that it was just as easy for a man to teach three children as two, Irene was admitted to the classroom.

Also, Mrs. Durand, perhaps remembering a rather wretched childhood of her own, did not believe in any child around her wearing hand-me-down clothing, so whenever she bought dresses for her own children, she bought exactly the same thing for Irene. The Durands treated Irene Chaput almost like a member of the family. Almost, because of course there were areas where Irene could not go. One of these was the huge blue, white and gold bedroom of Mr. and Mrs. Durand. Sometimes Irene would come to the Big House early, ready and waiting for lessons to begin, and she would stand in the upstairs hall listening to the sounds from the Durand bedroom. She would hear the deep voice of Mr. Durand, the voice that always, no matter what he said, had laughter running just beneath its surface. Then would come the excited shrieks of talk and laughter from the girls and the gentle, smiling voice of Mrs. Durand. In the morning there was always the delicate clink of china coffee cups under the talk and Irene wondered if the family drank coffee late in the afternoon, too, because she knew that Mrs. Durand and the girls always had a sort of party when Mr. Durand came home. Irene had never seen nor overheard what went on at one of these afternoon get-togethers but she knew they happened because every day, at four o'clock, Mrs. Durand came into the classroom and said, "That will be enough for today, Mr. Chatterton. Come, girls, you must bathe and change. Father will be here in less than an hour."

The girls always left in a swirl of colour and chatter, each of them with an arm around Mrs. Durand, and then Irene and Mr. Chatterton would pick up the papers and notebooks and put them away. One afternoon, after Felice and Marianne had left the classroom with Mrs. Durand, Mr. Chatterton smiled at Irene and said, "My dear, has it ever occurred to you that you and I spend a great deal of our time living in the middle of a very French eighteenth-century household?"

In three years Irene had never heard Mr. Chatterton make

31

a joke or say anything except in the utmost seriousness. She did not think of Mr. Chatterton as a human being, like her father for instance. He was a Teacher, and, therefore, above all things that might appeal to lesser mortals such as jokes and laughter.

"What do you mean?" she asked.

"Come now, Irene. I spent all last week discussing the eighteenth century with you and the girls. Don't tell me that you've already forgotten all about Louis the Fourteenth and Marie Antoinette and the Revolution."

"But what does all that have to do with us and the Durands?" she asked stupidly, unable to reconcile this smiling stranger with the familiar disciplinarian who turned to ice daily at every misspelled word.

Mr. Chatterton sighed and put his fountain pen back in his pocket.

"I was just wondering when and upon whom the guillotine will fall this time."

"What a terrible thing to say!" cried Irene, and was immediately and thoroughly frightened. One did not, after all, contradict a Teacher.

But Mr. Chatterton did not reprimand her. He merely smiled his tired smile and smoothed back his hair with his hands.

"Good afternoon, Irene," he said. "I'll see you in the morning."

"Yes, Mr. Chatterton," she said.

When Irene was sixteen years old it had become fashionable for people with money to see to it that their daughters learned Something Practical, so a woman named Miss Comstock was brought into the Durand household to teach the girls the intricacies of shorthand and typewriting. There was a great deal of laughter about the new lessons in the blue, white and gold bedroom. Sometimes Felice and Marianne were allowed to call on Mr. Durand at his office and the three of them would make jokes about the girls taking Mr. Durand's dictation and answering the telephone. But Marie and Alcide Chaput did not make jokes about Irene's education. To them it was unbelievable that Irene would some day be equipped to actually work in an office somewhere.

"The Durands are more than good to us," said Alcide.

"The Durands are going to be saints in heaven one day," said Marie. "You mark my words."

The world came to an end for everyone on the Durand estate three days after Irene turned seventeen. On that day the police went to Mr. Durand's office and arrested him and the sheriff came to the Big House with papers of attachment. Mrs. Durand was found in her rose-coloured bathrobe with her life flowing out of her wrists in red-ribbons and the twins sat on the edge of the bed in the blue, white and gold bedroom and screamed.

Irene sat in the classroom and tore strips of paper from the pages of her notebook and Mr. Chatterton smiled and said, "The guillotine has fallen on all of us."

Much later, Irene wondered at her lack of curiosity. Nobody had ever really told her what business Mr. Durand was in but somehow she had thought that it had something to do with stocks and bonds. She had gone to his office one day with the twins and she had seen the lettering on the door: DURAND ENTERPRISES.

"What's enterprises, Mr. Chatterton?" she had asked the next day.

"You know better than to ask me that, Irene," replied Mr. Chatterton sternly. "If you want to know the meaning of a word, and know it so that you'll never forget it, you must go to the dictionary and look it up."

The dictionary said that an enterprise was any projected task or work; an undertaking. Irene could never remember where she had got the idea that Mr. Durand's undertaking had to do with stocks and bonds because it turned out that Mr. Durand was the biggest bookmaker in northern New England. He was also the owner of several floating crap games and the proprietor of the most aristocratic whore-house in Boston.

Alcide and Marie and Irene went back to Cooper's Mills and Alcide got a job in the factories as a sweeper. They bought a small house on the outskirts of town where Alcide could have a garden, but life and hope and trust had gone out of the lives of Irene's mother and father. Within a year of Mr. Durand's arrest Alcide was dead and Marie followed four months later. Irene was left alone in the little house and the only thing she was grateful for was that the Durands had made her learn shorthand and typewriting. She got a job in the main office of the mills and two years later she married Wilfred St. George. She married him because she was lonely and because he was a loom-fixer and, as everyone in Cooper's Mills knew, loom-fixers were the highest-paid factory workers of all.

What fascinated Wilfred St. George about Irene was that she was always so clean. Her clothes, her hair, her fingernails were always spotless. She wore little white gloves every time she stepped a foot out of her house and they always looked as if she never touched anything. But most of all Wilfred was intrigued because Irene would not sleep with him. He pleaded, got angry, threatened her and finally stopped courting her altogether, but still Irene would not budge from her pedestal of chastity.

"She is made of steel, that woman," Wilfred complained to his fellow-workers. "Her virginity is attached to her with chains of cast iron, and every Goddamned chain is labelled Marriage!"

In the end Irene won, as she had known she would, and she and Wilfred were married in church, by a priest, and Irene wore her white gown proudly, as a symbol of purity, which was more than she could say for most brides in Cooper's Mills.

It did not take Wilfred long to discover that while it might be fun to escort a lady in white gloves to the rather limited social functions of Cooper's Mills and show her off as a prize to his friends, it was quite another matter to be married and have to live with one.

Irene was a nag. She complained about the rim of dirt under Wilfred's fingernails and who, asked Wilfred plaintively, could help having dirty fingernails when he sweated his arse off fixing machinery all day long? Tell him that, he demanded. And by God, when a man finished his day's work he wanted to go home and have a good supper waiting for him but if he were married to a lady, God help him, he could just wait around until seven-thirty to eat what his wife called dinner and then, mind you, only if he had taken a complete bath in a tub of hot water. And not only that, but while it was one thing for a man to stop for a few beers after work it was quite something else again to have to wait for a drink until after the Goddamned bath and then to have to sit down in the parlour and drink gin out of a thin-stemmed glass.

"I tell all of you, my friends," said Wilfred to his fellow-workers, "don't ever marry a lady who works in the main office."

Now, Corinne, who waited on table at the Happy Hour Café, there was something else again. Corinne had a smile almost as big as her rump, and her rump was something a man could put his hand on without feeling a corset beneath his fingertips. She had a pair of knockers on her that could choke any man, even big-mouthed Wilfred St. George, and if a man like Wilfred St. George with money in his pockets said, "Wanna go for a ride, honey?" Corinne always had a smile and a "Sure, honey," to give right back. It made a man feel big to be around a woman like Corinne. It made him feel especially big if all he had at home was a pale, thin wife and a pale, thin daughter who threw up after every feeding. It was a relief to be able to go to the Happy Hour and swing Corinne up off her feet when, if a man did the same thing at home to his little girl, the child's mother said, "Stop that, Wilfred! You'll upset her stomach!"

Wilfred stood it all until Lisa was five and then one Friday, pay-day, he took Corinne and his old Ford and left his job, his wife and Cooper's Mills. He finally settled in Bridgeport, Connecticut, and got a job in a factory there but he never let Irene know where he was and he never saw his daughter, Lisa, again.

For a little while after Wilfred left, Irene was the town martyr and she played the part to the hilt. She was the woman wronged, deserted, abandoned and left with a small child to bring up alone. A woman who worked hard every day and kept her house and her child neat and clean. Everybody in Cooper's Mills marvelled at Lisa, so sweet and well brought up, regular little lady, the town said. But after a year or so the tragedy of Irene and Lisa became part of the town's everyday life and nobody exclaimed or sympathized any more. Lisa grew up, alone for the most part, because her mother was so busy all the time with her job at the mill office. It was only if Lisa did anything the least bit wrong that Cooper's Mills remembered. If Lisa's white gloves were dirty or if she forgot and said "ain't", then Irene would get that frozen look on her face and her lips would tighten and she would say, "For heaven's sake, Lisa, remember who you are!"

Lisa could not remember just when her mother had given up

the battle against loneliness and poverty and dirt. She only knew that by the time she was sixteen, Cooper's Mills had dismissed Irene with the most final words of all.

"She drinks," said Cooper's Mills of Irene.

And it was true. She did.

At sixteen, Lisa was a slim, pretty girl with long brown hair, big hazel eyes and more self-reliance than is either usual or expected in girls of that age. She had learned the first step on the road to maturity on the day she had gone to the school nurse in tears, terrified that she might be bleeding to death, and she had never attempted to discuss anything with Irene after one abortive attempt.

"Don't be common," Irene had said, wrinkling her delicately boned nose at the idea of anything physical. "For heaven's sake, Lisa, remember who you are!"

Lisa was never very sure who she was. At school, she was just another Canuck kid, brighter than most, but the daughter of mill people all the same, while at home she was the very ladylike daughter of a *grande dame*.

"Lisa, cut that sandwich up into quarters before you wrap it up to take to school."

"But, Mama, none of the other kids——"

"I don't care about the others," cried Irene, immediately enraged. "And don't call me Mama. For heaven's sake, Lisa, remember who you are!"

"Yes, Mother."

"Lisa! Don't sip your coffee so that I can hear you, and don't spill any of it in the saucer!"

"But it's hot and I couldn't help it, I——"

"Lisa, a lady does not make excuses. For heaven's sake, Lisa, remember who you are!"

"Lisa, break your roll up into smaller pieces."

"Lisa, sit up straight."

"Lisa, don't chew your fingernails."

"For heaven's sake, Lisa, remember who you are!"

It was not until she was sixteen and fell in love with Christopher Pappas that Lisa thought she knew who she was at last.

Christopher Pappas was the son of two people to whom everyone in Cooper's Mills referred as the Greeks Who Run the Fruit Store on Main Street. If you worked in the mills and you wanted a pound of grapes, a package of cigarettes, a newspaper or a magazine you sent one of your children to the Pappases' store.

"Run down to the Greeks and get me a pack of Luckies," you said. Everybody did.

Their first names were Aphrodite and Costas and they worked eighteen, sometimes twenty, hours a day in the store where they sold everything from condoms to pomegranates. Chris was the eldest of six children and really the only one who counted to Aphrodite and Costas because the other five were girls. Aphrodite wanted her son to go to college to become a dentist but Costas, although he did not know it, echoed the words of Ferguson Cooper.

"It don't take no four years at no college to learn howta count money," said Costas in his heavily accented voice. "Whaddya want, huh? We gotta good business here, but no! It ain't good enough for my son, huh? No. My son, he's gotta have a job where he can wear a white collar allda time. I tell you somethin', boy. A white collar can get Goddamn tight, especially when your kids are bawlin' from empty stomachs."

Chris did not want to be a dentist as his mother wished, nor did he want to go into the store with his father. He didn't know what he wanted except that it was to get away from his foreign-talking, foreign-acting, foreign-thinking parents and away, far, far away from Cooper's Mills.

California, thought Chris wistfully. Or Alaska. I'll bet it's clean in Alaska with all that snow and ice.

The first things he ever noticed about Lisa St. George were that her white socks were always spotless and that sometimes he could discern the outlines of hard little nipples under her sweater. At sixteen, Chris was almost six feet tall with a head of dark, curly hair and a pair of very large dark eyes. He also had the swarthy complexion and fine lips of his ancestors and it was inevitable that he be classified as "tall, dark and handsome", by the girls who attended the Cooper's Mills high school.

"And on top of everything else," said many an envious classmate, "he's gotta go and be elected captain of the basketball team and be a senior when he's only sixteen."

The fact that Chris was in his last year of high school at his age was due to the fact that he had received a double promotion in the fourth grade and had never lagged behind since, but others in his class had a different interpretation of the facts.

"A brain," they said.

"Yeah, but you can't hold that against him," said his defenders. "He's O.K. anyway."

Chris never really asked Lisa for a date, in the beginning. It was just that both of them always seemed to be in the library in the evening and when the building closed at nine o'clock, Chris would offer to drive Lisa home. Sometimes they stopped for a Coke at Durocher's drugstore, but more often Chris would drive to the outskirts of town and park by the river. There was so much to talk about, things that neither one would have dreamed of discussing with anyone, and that came so easily between the two of them.

"You know something?" asked Lisa.

"No. What?"

"Well, I mean, did you ever think of praying the same way you'd think about throwing a stone into a lake?"

"Do you mean something about circles? The way one circle gives way to another and another?"

"Yes. It just keeps making circles, the stone you throw, I mean. And you never really know where the circles end."

"Well, at the edges of the lake, I imagine."

"Yes, but what if it's a great big lake?"

"Well, how big?"

"Well, as big as the whole world, for instance."

"Well, that's space, I guess."

"Chris, do you think very much about God?"

"Not any more than anybody else, I guess. I guess that it's just—— Well, what I mean is that God is something everybody has to make up his own mind about. That's all."

"But does it scare you, Chris? Sometimes doesn't it scare you a little? I mean, about being here and everybody being alive and nobody really knowing why."

"Gee, Lisa, to tell you the truth I never really thought much about it one way or the other."

After about three months, everyone at school took it for granted that Lisa and Chris were going steady and Lisa suddenly found herself accepted by a whole new group of girls. This was the group that went in for smoking, drinking warm beer out of cans and heavy petting. On Monday mornings the girls in this group got together in the Ladies' room at the high school and compared notes and Lisa listened, fascinated, to the remarks that bounced back and fourth between the white-tiled walls.

"Listen, before I go out with him again I want to hire a good referee."

"Well, you know Bobby after he's had a few. Then he says that his name is not Bobby at all—but Boddy!"

"How do you spell that, dear? Body or Bawdy?"

"If my mother knew about Jim! I mean, his mother belongs to the Ladies' Aid and everything, with my mother, and they, all the ladies, I mean, think that Jim is an absolute saint. Good God!"

"Last night Don bet me a dollar that he could make me moan before he was done with me and you know what? I had to pay him!"

"Lisa, I'll bet Chris is really something when he gets going. I mean, those dark Latin types just seem to smoulder and smoulder until they catch fire."

"He's wonderful," said Lisa and felt that she was dying a little because she could never come right out and admit that Chris had never even kissed her.

"Come on, Lisa, tell."

Lisa tried an enigmatic smile but her thumping heart and aching facial muscles told her that it did not work.

"That's private," she said. "I'm no kiss-and-tell girl."

During all the nights she stayed awake after leaving Chris, Lisa wondered wretchedly why he had never even tried to kiss her good night. She was afraid that it was because she was unattractive, cold-looking, and to be cold was worse than anything according to the girls in the Ladies' room at school. But, perhaps it was because she was behaving as her mother had always taught her to behave. Like a lady. And maybe boys didn't go for ladylike types. Look at her own father. He hadn't wanted to live with a lady. He'd run off with a beer joint waitress. Lisa tossed and turned and got up and looked at herself in the mirror and went back to bed and wept.

As for Chris, he lay awake with a thumping heart and an ache in his groin.

It was all craziness, he thought. He didn't even have guts enough to kiss her, let alone anything else. If he kissed her she might get scared, and if she got scared she wouldn't go and park with him by the river and then he'd have to be content just to look at her in school.

Finally, in the spring, Lisa failed a French exam and, as she said to herself later, it was well worth getting a poor grade for the semester and the devil from her mother because that evening, in the parked car by the river, Chris put his arms around her as she wept and then he wiped her eyes with his handkerchief and then he kissed her for the first time.

"God!" he said fervently, "I've wanted to do that for so long."

"I was afraid that you didn't want to do it at all," whispered Lisa.

They kissed with the soft, dry kisses of inexperience but as the weeks went by Chris began to experiment with all the things he had heard and read about. He explored the soft, warm inside of her mouth with his tongue and his hands found the buttons on her blouse, the hook of her brassière, and both of them trembled uncontrollably when he caressed her breasts.

"Beautiful, beautiful," whispered Chris as his lips found her tight little nipples.

"Please," said Lisa. "Please." And she did not know why she begged him, nor for what.

To Lisa and Chris, as to many young people in the United States and to the majority in northern New England, the idea of sex was not an entity in itself. Sex was the hand within the glove of love. The words, "I want you", existed for Lisa and Chris only as words to be spoken after "I love you", because if one loved, deeply and truly, then sex was all right. It was justifiable and could be enjoyed without guilt.

40

"Lisa, I love you."

"And I love you, Chris."

"How much?"

"All there is, darling. All there is."

"Darling, do you want to?"

"Yes."

"Oh, honey, I want you so much."

"And I want you."

"Honey, sometimes with girls—I mean, I read in a book that sometimes it hurts a girl the first time."

"I don't care. I love you. I belong to you."

"Not in the car."

"No. Not in the car."

"Outside? On the ground?"

"Yes."

Chris had been graduated from high school less than a month and was working in the fruit store with his mother and father when Lisa told him that she thought she might be pregnant.

"Oh, my darling," said Chris, "you'll have to go to the doctor's at once. Tomorrow morning."

"I can't," said Lisa, suddenly frightened. "If I go to Dr. Dorrance he'll run right to my mother and tell."

"I could take you to Boston or some place like that. Nobody knows us down there. I haven't got much money, though."

"No, wait. There's Dr. Cameron over at Cooper Station. In fact, there's two of them over there. The old one and the young one. I'll go see the young one. He wouldn't tell on anybody. At least, I don't think he would."

"Honey?"

"What?"

"If you are, you're going to have to tell your mother anyway. We'll have to get married."

"Nobody *has* to marry me, Christopher Pappas," cried Lisa, crying out in her fear and uncertainty, crying out because she knew she loved Chris and Oh, God, what if he didn't really love her and was just trying to do the right thing now that she was caught. "Nobody *has* to!" she said.

"Honey," he said against her cheek. "Honey, I didn't mean it that way. I only meant that we'll be getting married sooner than we expected to, that's all. I love you, darling. I love you with all my heart and soul and brain and body."

"Darling," she whispered, and was quiet again. "I love you, too."

"Then nothing else matters," said Chris, feeling the old, old words on his tongue without even knowing that they were old. "Nothing matters at all as long as we have each other."

"We'll get married and find a darling little apartment," said Lisa. "And I'll fix it up so that you'll have the nicest home in Cooper's Mills. And then we'll have the baby and neither one of us will ever have to go home to different places again. We'll be married and we'll never have to be separated ever, ever again."

Lisa went alone to Cooper Station. Chris had to work in the fruit store that afternoon and besides, as Lisa said, people might think it funny, the two of them walking into the doctor's together and everything. She drove carefully and well, as Chris had taught her to do, on the road to Cooper Station.

I am carrying Chris's child, she thought as she drove. I am carrying Chris's child under my heart. We have mated together and I am fulfilled. He loves me and I love him and this child will be the fruit of our love.

Lisa had read hundreds and hundreds of confession magazines and the words and phrases which filled her mind now were those of not quite forgotten stories.

I am carrying a love child, she thought happily. And everyone knows that love children are the most beautiful children of all, because they were conceived in love.

She hummed to herself as she parked the car in front of the Cameron house.

The brass plate on the front door of the old house said: *Dr. Gordon Cameron* in script and below that, in the same script but with the letters sharper and newer-looking, *Dr. Jess Cameron*. A white card over the doorbell said: *Walk In*.

Lisa rang and went through the door into the carpeted hallway. To her left was a waiting-room filled with leather-upholstered chairs, potted plants and tables covered with magazines. To her right was the living-room. From where she stood,

42

Lisa could see the big, comfortable-looking chairs and the enormous brick fireplace. She noticed that the carpeting in that room covered the entire floor from one wall to another. It was the first time in her life that she had seen a room where the rug was not surrounded on all four sides by a border of bare, painted floor. The Cameron living-room was prettier than any picture she had ever seen in any magazine and now she could imagine what her mother meant when she spoke of the beautiful house that had been owned by the Durands.

I'll fix our living-room just like this one, thought Lisa, and could hardly wait for the afternoon to be over so that she could get back to Cooper's Mills to tell Chris.

She was still standing there, staring into the living-room, when the door at the far end of the hall opened.

"Well, hello there," said the woman who came towards her. "You're an early one, ain't ya? First one in today." Then she stopped and eyed Lisa suspiciously. "Say, don't I know you?"

Lisa whirled around. She knew who the woman was, all right. Everybody knew. She was Marie Fennell and everybody in Cooper's Mills knew about Marie. Maybe they even knew about her in Cooper Station. Maybe the whole state knew about Marie.

"I never saw you before in my life," said Lisa coldly.

Marie Fennell seemed to sag with a sudden weariness. Nobody's ever goin' to forget, she thought tiredly. Never.

"Doctor'll be right with you," she said. "Young Doc that is. Other one's over at the hospital." She indicated the room to the left. "Go on in and have a seat."

"Thank you very much," said Lisa and hoped that she sounded like Irene when she said it.

Imagine, thought Lisa. Two doctors in a nice place like Cooper Station having someone like Marie Fennell in their house. It was awful, that's what it was. Just plain awful.

She was half-way through a magazine when Jess Cameron put his head through the door.

"Hi," he said. "Come on in."

Why, he's not *young* at all, thought Lisa, feeling outraged. He must be *thirty* if he's a day! She told herself that she had a good mind to get up and leave right now. But the thought of gossipy Dr. Dorrance in Cooper's Mills stopped her.

"Sit down," invited Jess after she had stepped into his office. He indicated a chair next to the desk and Lisa sat.

Just wait until I tell Chris, thought Lisa angrily. Why, he's old enough to be my father and probably talks more than any ten old women put together.

Jess Cameron sat behind his desk and unbuttoned his coat. He lit a cigarette and removed the cap from his fountain pen and took a white card from a drawer.

"Now," he said, and smiled at her. "What's your name?"

"Melissa Anne St. George," she replied primly.

Jess tossed his fountain pen down and leaned back in his chair.

"Now don't tell me that every time I talk to you I have to say all that," he laughed.

Suddenly he did not seem old at all, and Lisa laughed too.

"No," she said, "that was just for the record. You may call me Lisa if you want."

"I want," he said, and picked up his pen again. When he had finished writing her name on the card he looked up. "Well, Lisa, what seems to be the trouble?"

"Trouble?" she asked, And then she smiled. "Oh, no trouble, Doctor. I mean, I'm not sick or anything. I'm going to have a baby."

Jess Cameron looked down at the card in front of him and did not move.

I knew it, he thought. I knew it the minute I saw her. But I'm never going to get used to it. Never. A child herself, and now this.

As soon as he was able, he looked up at her. "Is that so?" he asked conversationally.

"Well, at least I *think* so," said Lisa and blushed a little. "I haven't come around—I mean, I haven't menstruated for three months."

"Yes," said Jess. "Well, that's usually a pretty good indication of something or other. Let's find out."

While Lisa was undressing in the other room, Jess put out his cigarette.

Christ! he thought. Seventeen years old. I wonder if the boy will marry her quietly or if there'll be a stink. I hope to hell he's no one from around here.

Lisa lay on the narrow table and suffered what she later described to Chris as agonies of embarrassment while the doctor poked and prodded and put his cold stethoscope on her.

He was nice, though, she thought later. He didn't stare at her at all while his hands were on her. Finally he straightened and, keeping his back to her, went to the small sink in the room and pulled off his rubber glove.

"You may get dressed," he told her.

When she had her clothing on and was seated next to his desk again, he said, "Lisa, you're going to have a baby all right. In about six months, I'd say."

But he sounded so sad, thought Lisa. And all she wanted was for him to be as happy as she was. She began to figure mentally.

"It must have happened practically the first time we were together," she said at last.

"Lisa, listen to me," said Jess. "Does he—does the father know?"

"Well, yes. I mean, he's not sure but neither was I until just now."

"Is he willing to marry you?" asked Jess.

"Of course he's willing to marry me," cried Lisa angrily. "He *loves* me and I love him. With us, Doctor Cameron, it isn't a question of *having* to get married. Oh, I've heard plenty about girls and boys *having* to get married, but not Chris and me. We *want* to get married."

"Tell me this boy's name," said Jess tiredly. "His name, where he works. Everything."

"His name is Christopher Pappas. He is seventeen years old and he works for his father and mother in the fruit store at Cooper's Mills," said Lisa as if she were reciting a lesson in a classroom. Then she added, "He lives in the house behind the store with his family and his father and mother hate me and my mother hates Chris."

Jess shielded his eyes with his hand as he wrote. "Does he get paid for the work he does for his parents?" he asked.

"Of course," said Lisa proudly. "He gets sixty cents an hour.

45

That's what men get when they first go into the mills, you know. And Chris's folks pay him the same thing because they want to keep him at the store."

"I see," said Jess. "Lisa," he said, "you tell this boy tonight. Tell him that you were here and that we're sure."

"Well, of course I'll tell him," said Lisa, not understanding the man at all. "He's just dying to hear. I promised that I'd stop by the store and let him know as soon as I was sure myself. We even worked out a sort of code in case his mother or father is around. If one of them is there and I am, I'm to ask him for a package of Wrigley's spearmint gum, and if I'm not I'm to go to the fountain and order a small Coke. So now, of course, I'll order the gum. If one of his parents is around, I mean."

"And Lisa," said Jess, as if she had not spoken, "if you run into any trouble at all, either with the boy or his family, you are to come back here to me at once. Do you understand? At once."

"Yes, sir," said Lisa and all of a sudden she felt like crying. She didn't feel warm or excited any more at all. "Yes, Doctor Cameron," she said and walked out of the door.

Chris reacted as Lisa had known he would.

"I'm glad," he said. "I love you and you love me and we're going to have a baby. So what?"

He put his arm around her shoulders and said again, defiantly, "So what?" as if daring the world to tell him so anyway, and Lisa was overwhelmed with love.

The trouble, when it came, was between Irene and Mrs. Pappas.

"A child!" screamed Irene. "You, Lisa? A child? With this *nobody*? This *shopkeeper*?"

Lisa, Chris and the two mothers sat in Irene's living-room. Lisa held Chris's hand and looked around and she could hardly believe that just that morning she had thought that this room was perfectly comfortable and attractive. She supposed that it was still all right, in its way, but it just wasn't the kind of room she liked any more. The wallpaper had a dark tan background with small, lighter tan figures printed on it. Lisa had often wondered what the figures represented. Sometimes they looked like rose arbours in a garden and sometimes like the faces of old men, and sometimes like church windows. The furniture was covered

46

with maroon plush, like the seats in the coaches on the Boston and Maine Railroad, and Lisa, sitting one of her mother's living-room chairs, felt slightly sick and a little scared.

"If she's that way," said Mrs. Pappas, "it's because she led my Chris on so he didn't know what he was doing. How many times have I told him, 'Chris,' I said, 'Don't play around with no tramps.'"

"Lisa isn't a tramp," said Chris quietly. "She's a nice girl."

"Led him on!" yelled Irene so loud that Lisa almost said, "For heaven's sake, Mother, remember who you are!"

"Led him on! Let me tell you something, Mrs. Pappas, my Lisa wasn't brought up like that. She's a good, decent girl. A young lady."

"Brought up! Huh! With you in a beer saloon every chance you get, tell me how good she was brought up?"

"You filthy foreigner," cried Irene. "You in that cockroach-infested store of yours, raising up a son to violate a young girl."

"He didn't," said Lisa and began to cry. "He didn't do that. I love him."

"She's a little tramp!"

"If he were any good she wouldn't be in this fix!"

"She asked for it. Her kind always does."

"God only knows how many other girls he's done this to!"

"My Chris never had no girls! He always stayed home or in the store minding his own business until that little hot britches kid of yours started in twitching her tail at him!"

"Enough, you vile-tongued harridan!"

"Ain't you somethin' with them big words, huh? Yeah, yeah, Mrs. High and Mighty herself. Can't even hang on to her man. You drunken bum!"

"It is always the ignorant," said Irene, calm at last, "who look down upon their better-educated neighbours."

"Educated your arse! That's a good one. Educated by a pimp like old man Durand. Well, all I can say is that you learned good, Mrs. Fancy Pants. Real good. And you taught your kid all the things you learned from that crook."

Lisa and Chris were married. In church. With double rings and a priest and three organ selections because Mrs. McGovern, the organist, always played three selections at all weddings for which she was paid five dollars. Irene stayed on after the ceremony just long enough to wish the newlyweds luck and then she headed for the Happy Hour Café. People at the Happy Hour knew Irene for the lady she was. At the Happy Hour, no one ever said a mean word to her. They listened to her stories by the hour and they never questioned a word.

The Pappases did not put in an appearance at the wedding at all, and Cooper's Mills wondered and whispered.

"Wonder where Irene kept the shotgun hid all during Mass?"

"It won't last a year. Marriages like that never do."

"Well, it's too late now. Imagine, a priest and everything. They can never get a divorce now. It's too late."

"I never thought Lisa was that kind of girl."

"Well, it don't surprise me none."

"A regular little hot pants bitch."

"And Chris Pappas. What a sonofabitch he turned out to be. And him so smart in school and all."

"It's a wise child knows its own father. I wonder if Lisa's kid'll know."

"She's beginning to show already."

"I noticed."

Chris and Lisa rented a two-room apartment on River Street in Cooper's Mills. The apartment was in a building that had the subtly decayed quality peculiar to buildings in the manufacturing towns of northern New England. There was no real reason why the board of health should have condemned the place, for the building had the required number of exits and the proper number of fire extinguishers in the halls, but there was a feeling of age about the place, a feeling of rottenness that came from the sagging of hidden sills and mildewed clapboards, and over everything, there was the smell of aged wallpaper and faulty drains.

Lisa and Chris had an apartment in the back of the building so that they had a view of the river, and sometimes Lisa sat in front of her kitchen window and pretended that she was in a palace and that the river was the Rhine and that Chris was not going to come home from the job he'd taken at the factories after his folks put him out, but that he would be returning from an afternoon of hunting on his own private game preserve.

When it was time for the baby to be born they had to put the new crib against a wall in the kitchen and then there didn't seem to be room to turn around anywhere, but Lisa and Chris didn't mind. Living together, being married, was just like playing house except that the game never ended and neither one of them ever had to leave to go somewhere else. Jess Cameron delivered the baby, a girl, three days after Thanksgiving, 1941, and Chris took Lisa from the hospital on the same Sunday morning that the Japanese bombed Pearl Harbour.

"I'll have to go," he told Lisa. "I guess everybody will before it's over."

"Yes," said Lisa, not caring, really, about anything that was happening some place as far off as Hawaii. "But not today, darling, not today."

"But soon," replied Chris, unsmiling, "very soon."

"For heaven's sake, Chris," said Lisa, "can't you think of anything besides a silly old war some place? We've got a brand-new baby to think about. You don't plan to rush off to Pearl Harbour this minute, do you?"

Chris looked down at the little face inside the pink bunting.

"No," he said at last. "Not this very minute."

5

Years later at the State University, a professor in the education department had asked Chris why he wanted to be a school-teacher at all.

"There has to be a reason, Chris," the professor had said. "All of us have to have a reason and a good one, too. One that will stand up when the going gets rough as it always does sooner or later. No one goes into this racket because of the money because there's no money here. And that crap about doing one's bit for mankind is also pretty lame. If a man has a big yen for that sort of thing he could join the Salvation Army and have a much easier time of it. Tell me, Chris. What reason are you going to give yourself?"

"It was the war," said Chris. "I decided during the war."

"Yes, but I didn't ask you *when* you decided. I asked you *why*."

But Chris could not tell him. At first he hadn't been able to tell Lisa, either. When he had decided that he wanted to become a teacher he had simply written her a V-Mail and told her of his plans. Her answer had come back that she thought it was wonderful and that with the GI Bill there wouldn't be any problem at all and wasn't it terrific that at last they'd be able to get out of Cooper's Mills.

"I'm so proud of you, darling," Lisa had written. "You'll go to

50

college and become a teacher and everything is going to be wonderful."

But it wasn't the threat of Cooper's Mills and the factories that had influenced Chris. It was something else, something that had taken a long time to happen and end and crystallize into decision, and Chris couldn't tell anyone because he couldn't remember exactly when or how it had come about.

The town, he remembered, could have once looked like a great many of the towns in northern New England except that there wasn't much of anything left of this particular town that looked like anything at all. It had been late afternoon and they had been trudging through the countryside since before dawn. They were lost. The lieutenant knew it, Sgt. Christopher Pappas knew it, the whole Goddamned platoon knew it. There wasn't a sign of regiment, battalion or company anywhere. The road curved on, uneven with frozen ruts. The men had ceased to be tough infantrymen, eager for another crack at the Germans. They were ugly and tired and beginning to turn on each other.

"Listen, Lieutenant," said Chris, "you can see they're fagged. It might be a good idea to stop for chow."

"After we get around the next curve," replied the lieutenant.

So they marched on over the broken road. Chris listened to the scrape of combat boots against the rough ground and he heard the mutterings of the men behind him.

Suddenly the road straightened and sloped downward and there was a little town in front of them. Or what was left of a town. Every building that had not been destroyed altogether had some part of it smashed; roof or window or wall.

"For it's Hi-Hi-Hee for the Field Artilleree——" sang the lieutenant under his breath as he looked around.

They all gathered at the foot of what had once been the main street.

"Let's eat," called the lieutenant and the men headed for what was left of the town church. There were only three walls standing but these offered some protection from the cold wind.

"Gonna snow again," said one of the men.

"So what're ya bitchin'? We'll all go skiing." He pronounced it "sheeing" and laughed at his own joke. "Get it?" he asked

51

when no one else laughed. "She. You know. She. Dame. Female. Broad."

No one even smiled.

"Why don't you shut up, O'Brien?" asked one of the men.

O'Brien shrugged and sat down on the hard ground.

They opened K-rations and ate. They smoked. And during the half-hour that they sat there no one had anything to say. Chris looked at the broken walls of the church and wondered if once the spire had risen straight and white and plain or if it had been topped with a gilded cross.

Lutherans, aren't they? he asked himself. Aren't most Germans Lutherans? Anyway, it doesn't feel as if anyone had ever burned incense or genuflected here.

"Off your butts," called the lieutenant.

The men stood up and fell into a semblance of a rank and started to walk.

Chris heard the artillery ahead of them now, very faintly, from miles ahead, but he knew it was there.

When the next curve in the road straightened, they saw a small settlement of six or eight houses spread out before them.

Peaceful, thought Chris, as if the war had never passed this way at all.

Smoke came from the chimneys of the houses and somewhere a dog barked.

"Jesus!" muttered the lieutenant. "Just like Currier and Ives."

"Like Vermont, right around Thanksgivin'," said someone else.

"I can't help thinkin' that my old woman would say that it's a hell of a way to the nearest store," said another.

"You, Kenyon," the lieutenant signalled a man. "Come over here."

Kenyon was a corporal and, according to the lieutenant, the best Goddamned scout in the United States Army.

"Go take a walk around and see what you can see," said the lieutenant.

Kenyon made his way carefully towards the first of the little white houses while the men who stayed behind waited tensely, hands suddenly pliant and ready for action on their rifles. When

Kenyon returned he did so quickly, walking upright, not bothering to tread carefully nor to take cover.

"Nobody there but farmers," he reported, "cookin' supper. And let me add that what they're cookin' smells a helluva lot better and more appetizin' than what we just ate."

The lieutenant was chewing his thumbnail. His eyes darted from one farmhouse to the next and Chris Pappas felt a sudden hatred, tinged with pity, rise within him.

The lieutenant is going bugs, thought Chris. He's at the point now where he sees a fugitive German soldier in every farmhouse and he lives in a world where every *hausfrau* is a traitor. Poor bastard. He can't even look at a scene full of peace without thinking of the war.

"Too Goddamned good to be true," muttered the lieutenant.

"I'm tellin' you, Lieutenant," said Kenyon, hurt.

"I know, I know," said the lieutenant. "I'm not doubting you, Kenyon, it's just this Goddamned feeling I've got."

"The Artillery passed this way," said Kenyon, "and even they left this place alone."

"I know," repeated the lieutenant and turned to Chris. "Come with me," he said. "The rest of you wait here."

Kenyon was deeply and gravely offended and it showed on his face.

"To hell with him," he said to the man next to him. "If he can't depend on me any more to hell with him."

They moved slowly and as Chris followed the lieutenant he smiled inwardly at the sight of the big, brave American officer advancing on a peaceful farmhouse with his rifle clutched in both hands and a tight look around his mouth.

How many years of civilization went before us, thought Chris. How many years of teaching and preaching have come to nothing now that we walk over each other's countries with the sole idea of killing one another. We're supposed to be *men*. Hundreds of thousands of years went into making us into men and now look at us. Waste. Thousands of years—millions and millions of brains. For *this*.

The lieutenant paused before he kicked at the door of the first

53

farmhouse to motion to Chris. Stay back and to one side, his hand said. Cover me.

Chris crouched under a window and hated the lieutenant in earnest now. The officer had infected him with fear and suspicion. He had smashed the shell of civilization from around him and made him into an animal whose only thought now was to preserve himself.

An old woman came to the door. She wore a dress of flowered, lavender material and a black knitted shawl was wrapped around her shoulders.

The lieutenant addressed her in excellent German which Chris did his best to follow with what he remembered from high school and what he had picked up overseas.

"I am an officer in the American Army," said the lieutenant. "Who besides yourself is in this house?"

Chris peered cautiously through the window over his head. There was no place for anyone to hide in that room except behind a curtained space which might have concealed a closet or another small room. Chris almost giggled. Even if there was no one in this house there might be someone in one of the others. He wondered if the lieutenant was going to go through this performance at every one of the other farmhouses.

"No one," said the old woman in a voice as cold as the look she gave the lieutenant. "My only son was killed in France. I am alone."

The curtained space in the room was very still. Too still? Again, Chris damned the lieutenant. The virus of fear was running through every vein in his body, poisoning him.

Chris never knew what it was that made the lieutenant so sure that the old woman was lying, nor what extra perception told her that the American officer knew. In the next second she had thrown the door wide and hurled herself towards the lieutenant. He threw her to the floor in one vicious motion and his aim never wavered as he fired twice into the curtained space. Two German officers fell forward as Chris watched and the flowered curtains billowed gracefully around them. The old woman lunged for the lieutenant's gun and the lieutenant took deliberate aim and shot her.

Later, Chris had a girl friend in Germany. Her name was Margretha and her husband had been killed by the Russians. Chris brought her cigarettes and sugar and chocolate for her little girl. In return for these gifts, Margretha slept with him, cooked whatever food he brought and tried to create a small island of comfort and peace for him in her house. The child's name was Christine and Margretha often laughed with Chris about this.

"There you see?" she told him. "Christopher and Christine. They go together like the American ham and eggs."

Often, during the weeks that Chris lived with Margretha, he took the snapshot which Lisa had sent of his own daughter out of his wallet and studied it carefully.

"I'll get mixed up," he had laughed with Lisa before leaving for overseas. "Whatever shall I do with *two* Lisas to think about?"

"You're not to call her Lisa," Lisa had said. "We'll call her Midget because she's so little and cute."

Chris looked at Christine in Germany and at the snapshot of Midget and saw that between the two children there was actually very little difference. They were of an age, the offspring of young parents, and both had been born under the shadow of war. Christine was blonde, blue-eyed and pure Aryan, her mother said, and Midget was dark-haired and had brown eyes exactly like her father's.

The children! It came to Chris after a long, long time of thinking.

It's the children who are not different!

Adults, nations, languages, customs and habits were all opposite one from the other. But not the children. He had seen them in England, Holland, Belgium, France and Germany, and children were children. Small, untaught, unformed, born in hope and often destroyed by grown-ups who could think no more clearly than those whom they attempted to mould. Untaught. The word clung to Chris's mind as a spider-web would have clung to his hand. Untaught. Children were born gentle. It was the people who taught them who pointed out the ways of greed, destruction and decivilization.

Now if it were up to me, thought Chris, if I were a teacher . . .

55

It was not until after he got home that Chris told Lisa the story about the war and about the old woman in Germany and about how he had come to realize that the problems of the world could be solved if one taught the children early, often and thoroughly.

"Well, for heaven's sake," Lisa had said, horrified. "He didn't have to shoot that poor old woman, did he?"

After that, Chris never told the story to anyone. It all sounded much too melodramatic and Chris never wanted people to think that he dramatized anything. But most of all he did not tell because he wasn't sure himself if he taught because he really believed the things he had told himself or because of the feeling that came over him sometimes in a classroom. A feeling that he could not bring himself to admit he felt.

Power.

I'm doing this all by myself. I'm moulding their minds. Shaping their thinking. Forming the children in my image.

Sometimes, in the years that followed, Lisa Pappas was occasionally reminded of the years she and Chris had spent at the university. Then she would shudder and think, That hell hole, and push remembrance determinedly from her mind.

The town of Denton, where the university was located, was in the central part of the state and was a pretty town by the standards of northern New England with its old-fashioned lamp posts, ivy-covered brick buildings, small-paned windows in old houses and its general aura of age and stability. But the end of the Second World War and the advent of the GI bill of Rights caught Denton flat-footed and unprepared for the influx of student veterans. Almost overnight the town and the university found themselves in the position of having to make provision not only for hordes of new students, but for students who would arrive with wives and children and furniture. Hastily, they cleared a vast tract of land a quarter of a mile out of town and there they erected row upon row of old Army barracks and converted them into four-room apartments, and they called this place College Road Housing for Student Veterans. There had been neither the time nor the inclination to paint the buildings so they stood now, the same olive-drab colour as they had been on Army posts throughout the country, and the walls that had been slapped together to divide the apartments were made of the thinnest plywood. It soon became a standing joke on College Road for families already situated to warn new-comers about the walls in the College Road Apartments.

"Don't put your bed against the wall of the apartment next door," they said and laughed.

"Nobody on College Road makes love without an audience of at least four," they warned.

Christopher Pappas moved his family into No. E16 College Road on a hot, wet Saturday in August and Lisa took one look at the drab, uniformly painted cream-coloured walls, the old-fashioned ice-box complete with galvanized drip pan and the two-burner electric plate, then she sat down on a packing crate and burst into tears.

"I'll never be able to stand it here!" she wept against Chris's shoulder. "It's so ugly."

And even Chris, who was wildly enthusiastic about starting his courses, had to agree to that. Over Lisa's head he could see out of the window to the bare gravel space between the barracks in which he would live and the one opposite. There was no grass, not a single bush or flower.

"It's ugly all right," he said to Lisa. "But listen, honey. This is the beginning for us. Time will pass quickly, you'll see, and in no time at all I'll be a teacher and we'll move away to some place beautiful with lots of grass and trees and flowers."

But the years of Chris's education were slow, painful ones and often Lisa thought bitterly of the ideas she had held on "college life" before coming to Denton, ideas and images culled from a hundred magazine stories and as many movies. Where were the convertibles, the secret bottles of liquor, the gay young men and their wild girl friends? The answer was simple, realized Lisa. College life as she had dreamed and read of it was lived in the big fraternity and sorority houses on campus by people not much younger than she who were not tied down with College Road apartments, husbands, bills and children.

But the years did pass and by the time Chris was a junior at the university, Lisa had found a sort of escape from reality for herself. She discovered that if she read all the time and concentrated on what she read her brain would not stray into the uncomfortably real ugly world of College Road. She had started on murder mysteries but she had soon tired of violence and sameness and then she had begun on what Miss Huntoon, the head librarian at the university library, called "the Classics".

While she drank her morning coffee, Lisa read. She left the dirty breakfast dishes on the table and went into the living-room where she lay on the sofa and read. Sometimes, at noon, she felt it difficult to stop reading long enough to warm up a can of soup for Midget and Chris and she resented having to leave a book for all the other duties.

I have a very good mind, Lisa told herself. I'll bet I could write a book if I had the time. I should have had a career of some kind. I'm much too intelligent to be a slave to a sinkful of dirty dishes.

When she was not reading, Lisa sat still and stared into space. She imagined herself as a brilliant authoress, ballet dancer, opera singer, artist, and in all her daydreams the wonderful, talented people of the world sat at her feet and looked up at her in adoration. Then, inevitably, something would happen. Midget would come crashing into the room, or a neighbour would poke her head through the door or Chris would come home from class and Lisa was back in her cream-coloured living-room with the space heater that baulked and the second-hand furniture.

I'm trapped, she thought angrily. Trapped with a husband and a child and poverty, and I can't get out.

Lisa began to wonder about things that she had always taken for granted, like sex. She read countless stories in which women experienced indescribable joy during the act of love and she wondered why she never felt this emotion with Chris.

In the beginning, it was one thing, she thought. Then it was new and different and that's all that made it exciting.

At first, when she had realized that Chris no longer excited her she had blamed it on the fact that perhaps she had inherited her frigidity from her mother, but now she looked at her husband with new eyes and fastened a new label on him. Unsatisfactory.

She was not to blame. Chris had very little imagination and he was Unsatisfactory.

It seemed to Lisa that her whole life hinged on one sentence and that sentence was, "When Chris graduates and starts teaching."

Well, what of it, she thought. What then? Teachers don't make any money. We won't be a hell of a lot better off than we are now.

By the time Chris was a senior the situation was almost unbearable to both of them.

"I don't know what's got into you," Chris shouted, "but whatever it is, you'd better get rid of it and fast."

"Don't you talk to me like that! Just who do you think you are?"

"I'm your husband, Goddamn it, and I'll talk to you any way that I find necessary. I don't mind your trying to improve yourself, but I'm damned if I'll let my wife sit on her backside all day while my daughter goes hungry and the house goes to pot."

"There are things vastly more important to me than housework," cried Lisa. "I've never been anything but a slave to you since we got married. I never realized before that I have a brain. Well, now I do and I intend to use it and I should think you'd be proud of the fact that I'm trying to keep up with you instead of letting myself get into a rut."

"Listen, Lisa," said Chris and made an effort to lower his voice. "I loved you before you went on this learning kick. You're smart enough for me. All I want is for you to be the way you used to be."

"I'll bet!" said Lisa. "You loved it when you were the sun and the moon and I was nothing but the good old solid earth that revolved around you and whatever you wanted."

"For Christ's sake, you don't even know what the hell you're talking about!" shouted Chris and stamped out of the apartment.

I'll leave him, thought Lisa. I'll take Midget and walk out of here right now.

Walk out to where? Back to Cooper's Mills and Irene and the beer bottles and the gossip? Never. Well, where then? Lisa knew the answer even before the questions were complete in her mind. Nowhere. I'm trapped.

A few weeks later she discovered that she was even more trapped than she had thought. She was pregnant and, weep and rage as she might, she stayed that way. Little Chris was born two weeks before Chris graduated from the university. The afternoon of the graduation exercises was the first time Lisa was able to go out after the birth of the baby and as she stood in the warm June sun and watched Chris, she began to hope again. She heard his name, Christopher Pappas, and she heard the words of the hard-earned degree, Bachelor of Arts, and she heard the special words, *magna cum laude,* and she thought: Now things will be better. We'll be able to get away from this wretched place and start again. Little Chris must have been an omen. A new baby, a new diploma, and a new life.

Christopher Pappas was offered and accepted a position to teach social sciences in a town called Devon, and after he and Lisa had seen the town there was something like enthusiasm between them for the first time in years.

"It's lovely here," said Lisa.

And it was. They rented a small house and met their new neighbours and settled down to live.

"Live!" cried Lisa a few weeks later. "Is this what you call it? Living? I'd like to see anybody else in this town living on twenty-five hundred dollars a year!"

There was never enough of anything. Lisa had to plot and scheme for a whole month to find enough money to buy one pair of shoes for her children. She had to scrimp on food and clothing and neither she nor Chris had been to a dentist in over five years. But Chris was happy. The Devon high school was small but well equipped and as far as he was concerned, he'd have been content to spend the rest of his life there. Neither the members of the P.T.A. nor the principal interfered with his teaching methods and there were enough bright students enrolled in the school to make his job exciting to him. If it hadn't been for the money, he and Lisa might well have remained in Devon, but at the end of his second year there, the school board at West Farrington offered him a position teaching fewer classes for more money and Chris, weary of watching his wife pinch every penny and hopeful that a few hundred dollars would help ease things, accepted.

He knew from the first day he began to teach at West Farrington that he would never make it through the year.

"I'm hamstrung," he told Lisa. "I can't teach with both hands tied behind my back and lies rolling off my tongue."

At first Lisa, remembering the hard-earned degree and the miserable years at the university, argued with him. "Go along with them," she said. "How can that hurt? Just say yes and humour the damned board and keep your job."

Chris just looked at her hopelessly. "I can't," he said, and one Friday afternoon, after he had been teaching for three months, he came home and said, "Let's start packing, Lisa. I've had it."

Lisa was too tired to fight. "All right," she said.

They left West Farrington the next morning and arrived in Cooper's Mills that same afternoon.

"Ha!" said Costas Pappas, not bothering to conceal his triumph. "So you fin'ly got sick of wearin' a tight white collar, huh? Was chokin' you a little, huh? Come on, Mr. School-teacher man, cheer up. Come on out back and I'll give you a little drinka oozu and you're gonna feel better. I'll even give you a job in a store."

"No thanks, Pa," said Chris quietly. "I'm not going to work in the store. Tomorrow I'm going to get a job in the mills."

"You was always a Goddamn fool," said his father. "Go ahead. Go get a job in the mills. Go ta hell if you want. I don't give a damn no more."

Lisa and Chris rented a house from Eben Seton and Chris began a new job at the factories. He had been there for six weeks when a call came from the head of the State School for the Feeble-minded at Marmington.

"You'll never be able to stand it," argued Lisa. "You're not trained to teach idiots."

"The teachables aren't idiots," said Chris. "And anyway, it's teaching, no matter what they are. I can't stay in the mill, Lisa. It's either teach or starve. It's all I want to do."

"Well, go ahead then," said Lisa angrily. "But you'll hate it

c   61

worse than West Farrington, you'll see. At least there you were dealing with adults. Maybe they weren't too bright, but at least they were adults and not feeble-minded kids."

During the weeks that followed Chris thought often of Lisa's words and there were times when he was sure that he'd never stick it out, for at Marmington he had come to what must surely be the most despairing moments of his life.

It was the end of a long day and Chris began to pick up scattered balls and bats from the baseball field at the State School. A few feet away, a group of ten boys ranging in age from eleven to nineteen years stood and watched him.

Ten of them, thought Chris. Ten boys. Too many of them for one team and not enough for two so that one kid always has to watch the others. I wonder what Goddamned nitwit thought up this system.

At the State School for the Feeble-minded, it had been decided that ten pupils at a time were all that one sensible adult could manage. The system had been inaugurated many years before and it had never occurred to anyone that there were times when the pattern was wrong. Except to a few teachers, of course, and in the eyes of the trustees, teachers, for the most part, were notorious idealists with no idea of system, pattern or efficiency.

Chris had once spoken to Cyril Haskell, the head of the school, about the way things were run.

"Sir," Chris had said, "it seems to me that it would make more sense if a few more children were allowed in the classrooms and on the playing fields. The way it stands now, I get to help only ten kids a day, while for those ten, eighty or ninety others have nothing to do but hang around the buildings all day long. I've noticed a good many of these children trying to organize games of their own but they have no supervision, and——"

"Pappas!" roared Mr. Haskell. "That's enough! Sit down!"

That good old-fashioned school-teacher ring of authority, thought Chris. I wonder if I'll ever have it.

"Pappas," said Mr. Haskell more gently as soon as Chris had seated himself, "there are a few things that you'll have to learn if you're going to get along here." He held up one forefinger.

"Number one," he said. "The people here to whom you refer as kids, children, pupils and students are none of these. They are patients. They are sick, weak, mental deficients, mostly unteachables, so get that through your head." He held up a middle finger. "Number two. The places you refer to as buildings and houses are neither. They are wards." His ring finger joined the other two. "And number three. While you are working here stop referring to yourself as a teacher. You are here as a rather well-paid keeper and that's all. That fancy degree of yours from the university doesn't amount to *that* in this place." He snapped his fingers and then his hand came down and he put it in his pocket as if storing it away until it was needed for further use. "A keeper, Pappas. I guess that's why, as far as teachers go, we don't get exactly what you might call the cream of the crop around here."

A keeper, thought Chris wryly. Well, I asked for it. Nobody is going to forget West Farrington in a hurry. And yet, I know I was right. Maybe I shouldn't have just walked out as I did, but basically I was right.

"I don't imagine that I have to remind you that you're lucky to have a job in any branch of education," said Mr. Haskell.

"No, sir," said Chris. "You don't have to remind me."

Chris finished picking up the baseball equipment. Just a little while longer, he thought doggedly. Just a little while longer and then I'll be able to get the hell out of this place.

One of the boys, a huge hulk eighteen years old, followed Chris as he walked towards his car.

"Papp," he said, "Papp?"

Chris turned to look at him. The boy walked with his enormous head jutted forward, his big shoulders hunched. He had very heavy, loose lips and they were always wet and he had an IQ of fifty-nine.

"Papp, kin we play tamorra?"

Chris put a hand on the boy's arm. "Sure, Kevin," he said. "You be very good tonight when you go back to the ward and we'll all play again tomorrow."

As Chris drove towards Cooper's Mills he thought of them all. The ones who stammered and drooled, the others who wanted to

stand right next to his elbow every single minute as if seeking a
kind of warmth or friendship, the ones who forgot, sometimes,
and wet themselves and the ones who fought and broke things
and masturbated in the back of the classroom.

I *can't* stay, he cried silently as if in silent apology to all those
who had learned to trust him. I have to think of myself and Lisa
and the kids and the State School is a dead end. I can't get stuck
here. I mustn't. There's too much to do.

6

DORIS DELANEY PALMER did not believe in wasting time. All her life, whenever she had wanted anything, she had fixed an unmoving eye on her ultimate goal and had proceeded towards it until her purpose was accomplished. Now her desire was to keep Lisa and Chris Pappas out of Cooper Station and she went about this the way she had always done everything else; quickly, finally and thoroughly. On the day after the Town Guardians' meeting at which Chris Pappas had been engaged to teach at the high school, Doris went to see her attorney, Richard Strickland, and asked him to draw up a formal petition of protest against the young school-teacher. Richard Strickland was shocked and disturbed.

"Just what do you expect to accomplish with this?" he asked.

"I'm going to get it signed," replied Doris.

Richard Strickland's eyes narrowed a little. "How come you've got the axe out for Christopher Pappas?" he asked.

"I do not have the axe out, as you put it, for anyone," protested Doris. "It is simply that I have a responsibility to the parents and children of Cooper Station and I fully intend to see that that responsibility is fulfilled."

"Doris, I've been your lawyer for fifteen years and I think that during that time I've always given you fairly good advice. Now I'm advising you to leave this thing the hell alone. Pappas has a valid contract signed by the majority of the Guardians and the petition you want me to draw up won't change a thing!"

Doris's hands trembled a little with an outrage she tried to keep hidden.

"Pappas was elected by Nathaniel Cooper who has never had a thought in his head that didn't concern either his mills or his idiot child and by Jim Sheppard who should never have been elected as a Guardian in the first place. I'm the only one of three who thinks of the welfare of our children and, as I pointed out to you, I fully intend to do a good job of it."

"There are a few other things you're forgetting," said Strickland. "Pappas was graduated with honours from the state university and he was so successful at his first teaching job that another town offered him a three-hundred-dollar raise for their school."

"Pappas also walked out on that job," said Doris with heavy sarcasm. "He is also a foreigner from Cooper's Mills and is married to a girl who was three months pregnant before the wedding."

Richard Strickland sighed. "Two mistakes, Doris," he said. "Should anyone hold two mistakes against a man for the rest of his life?"

"Mistakes are one thing," said Doris. "Irresponsibility is something else again. Cooper Station is a nice, clean town full of respectable people. We certainly don't need people of the Pappas' ilk here and especially we don't need a man like that teaching our children! There must be some way to stop this outrage."

"Well," Richard Strickland sighed again, "you could try to get a petition for a referendum. I don't recall that it's ever been done but twenty-five per cent of the voting population of the town can petition for a referendum in which the townspeople could overrule any specific action of the Town Board of Guardians. It all goes back to the day when all the affairs of the town were decided at town meetings. Seems nobody was willing to give up the idea entirely that the townspeople should control their own affairs."

"Then draw up a petition for a referendum," Doris said.

"Listen here, Doris," said the lawyer, "most people don't want to get mixed up with anything like this. You'll never get enough people to sign it. Why don't you just forget the whole thing?"

"I have no intention of forgetting anything," said Doris and then smiled a little. "I don't imagine the citizens of this town will be unwilling to sign the petition when I finish talking with each and every one of them."

"All right," Strickland said, "I'll have it for you tomorrow. I just hope you know what you're doing."

"I know precisely what I'm doing," said Doris and marched out of his office.

Next day, Richard Strickland met Jess Cameron on Benjamin Street.

"Seen Doris?" he asked the doctor.

"No," replied Jess. "Should I?"

"You'll have to hang on to your hat when you do," said Strickland. "She's on the warpath again."

If there's one thing Richard loves more than the law, thought Jess, who was very tired, its a cliché.

"Which warpath is it this time?" he asked aloud.

"She's got a petition for a referendum that she's going to circulate around town," replied Richard.

"A referendum for what?" asked the doctor.

"She wants the townspeople to reverse the decision of the Guardians to hire that new school-teacher they approved the other night, Pappas."

Jess felt himself tighten with anger. "But Doris can't——" he began and then checked himself quickly.

"Doris can't what?" asked Strickland curiously.

"She can't possibly be so inhuman as to try to keep a man from making a living for himself and his family."

The lawyer shrugged. "She doesn't care if he makes a living," he said, "she just doesn't want him making it here in Cooper Station."

"I see," said Jess.

"Well, I don't," replied Strickland. "But you know Doris once she gets set on something. Remember the time she didn't want that Jew fellow opening a clothing store here? You notice he never did get into town."

"I remember," said Jess. "But that time nobody bothered to

67

fight her. Maybe this time she's bitten off more than she can chew."

"I doubt it like hell," said the lawyer. "I've known Doris for years and she's always managed to get what she goes after."

"Well, she'll never get my signature on her damned petition," said Jess. "I'm a little tired of Doris wearing her respectability like a mink coat."

"Well, I suppose she's entitled," said Strickland. "Doris has always been a good woman with the interests of the town at heart ever since she moved here."

Like hell, Jess wanted to say as he watched the lawyer climb into his car and drive away. He remembered a story his father had told him about Doris Delaney Palmer and he wondered now as he had then about the woman.

If the truth were known, he thought, I don't imagine that Doris could afford to talk about anyone else in the world.

Jess was even more correct than he imagined. If the whole truth had been known, Doris would never have been able to live in Cooper Station in the first place.

Doris Delaney was born in Belfast, Ireland. By the time she was fifteen years old she had a pair of full, pointed breasts, a tiny waist and a set of well-flared hips. She had also learned to read and she knew that she was never going to be satisfied with being a housemaid for a wealthy Irish family. Getting to the United States was one of the first goals Doris set for herself and it took her three years to save and borrow enough money for a steerage-class passage. When she was eighteen she landed in New York, sure that everything good that the United States had to offer would soon be hers. Doris had the lovely dark hair, the clear blue eyes of the Irish and a brogue that was as thick as good carpeting. Within two days she had secured a position as chamber-maid with a wealthy family named Justine who owned a town house on fifth Avenue in New York City. Doris learned her new duties quickly and well, and within a month Mrs. Justine promoted her from the upstairs of the house to the main floor.

"You are a good girl, Doris," said Mrs. Justine, "and a smart and pretty one. I shall teach you your new duties myself so that you'll never be able to use the excuse that you've forgotten anything important. You will have to serve tea on our at-home days and you'll have charge of the front door on Tarkington's day out. You must be neat and well groomed at all times and Doris, with that brogue of yours, I'd rather you spoke as little as possible. Do you understand?"

"Yes, ma'am," said Doris and thought, How I hate you, you fat bitch. "I understand."

Mrs. Justine nodded in satisfaction. "Just smile that pretty smile of yours," she said. "That is all that will be necessary."

"Yes, ma'am, said Doris and smiled.

Doris wore a black uniform with a little white apron which she tied tightly around her little waist and a narrow starched ruffle on her black hair. Her lips were naturally red and her cheeks pink and when Mrs. Justine had lady callers they always commented on Doris's looks.

"Oh, she'll do," said Mrs. Justine deprecatingly.

"And she's so quiet and well trained," said the ladies.

"Yes," agreed Mrs. Justine modestly. "I trained her myself."

Doris smiled sweetly at all the ladies and kept her eyes demurely downcast, but she listened to every word and every inflexion and at night, in her room, she sat on the edge of her bed and repeated what she had heard until the sound of Ireland began to erase itself from her voice.

When the Justines had gentlemen callers, the men never said much to Doris. They just looked, and more than once Doris had to brush away a searching hand as she made her way from the butler's pantry to the drawing-room. But she learned to do it in such a way that the gentlemen were never insulted. Her smile and her gentle, repulsing hand seemed to say, "But sir, I am nothing but a lowly housemaid. If I weren't, things might be different, but I have to think of my job." The gentlemen always seemed to understand.

The Justines had three children, two girls named Pamela and Patricia, ages fifteen and seventeen, and a son, George, who went to Princeton. The girls, however, went to school in New York and lived at home and Doris copied their talk and their mannerisms and when no one was about she sneaked into their rooms and tried on their clothes. In the end, of course, she got caught. George Justine, home from school for the week-end, found Doris in Patricia's room, wearing one of Patricia's good dresses and posing in front of Patricia's full-length mirror.

"What have we here, my pretty maid?" he demanded as he came up behind her.

Doris whirled. "I didn't think anyone was home," she said weakly.

"A lucky thing for you they aren't," replied George sternly, "or you'd be out on the streets, bag and baggage."

Doris sized him up shrewdly and decided against playing the frightened housemaid.

"I suppose you're going to tell," she said boldly. "Well, go ahead. I won't have any trouble finding another family to work for."

"Oh ho," said George. "You won't, will you? You think it would be easy to go somewhere else without a reference from my mother?"

Doris looked up at him. "I'll be my own reference," she told him.

"You are a saucy one, aren't you?" said George. "And I imagine that you think you're quite special and very attractive besides, don't you?"

"I'm just as attractive as some of those girls with skimmed milk complexions that I've seen you bring here," said Doris.

"You little hellion!" said George and laughed as he pulled her into his arms.

Doris kicked him in the shins. "Just because I work here don't think that you own me," she told him angrily.

George held on to his shin. "Well, I'll be damned," he said.

"So now you can go tell your mother," said Doris. "I don't care. But anyone who wants a kiss from me has to ask me."

George laughed again. "All right," he said, "I'm a reasonable man. May I have the pleasure of kissing you, your Highness?"

"Not until after I get out of this dress," said Doris. "Now turn your back."

George did so at once, but Doris made sure that she was in a position where all George had to do to look at her was to raise his eyes and look into the mirror that faced him from the opposite side of the room. She let him see part of one leg and the tops of her breasts as she struggled back into her uniform and when she told him it was all right for him to turn around she saw that the back of his neck was pink and that he was breathing rapidly. He reached for her at once.

"Not in here," she said. "Someone might come in."

"Nobody's going to come in," replied George. "You promised."

"I never did. But I will anyway. I have to dust the library in a few minutes. You come in there as if you were looking for a book and then I will."

George dropped his arms reluctantly. "All right," he said. "I'll come down in a few minutes."

"Are you sure?"

"Yes, I'm sure."

Doris smiled up at him and her lips were very red and moist-looking.

"Please hurry," she said.

"Oh, I will," said George, more breathless than ever. "I sure will, Doris."

But by the time he entered the library, George had calmed himself to the point where he could take Doris in his arms quietly and expertly as befitted a Princeton man. He kissed her on the mouth without bumping her nose or doing anything else awkward and Doris never moved.

"Is that how they teach you to kiss at that fancy school of yours?" she asked him.

"I've kissed some of the finest girls in New York," George said. "And I've never had any complaints."

"Humph," said Doris and turned away from him.

"I suppose you know plenty about kissing," said George, following her about the room as she dusted.

"More than you do," she said.

"All right then, show me."

She put down her duster at once and put her arms around his neck. Her breasts pressed into his chest and she moved gently against him and then he felt her tongue against his teeth.

"My God!" he whispered when it was over. "My God!"

71

"And I've never been to Princeton," said Doris. "I learned everything I know from books."

"There aren't any books that teach you things like that," said George, still unable to control his breathing.

"Oh, yes there are."

"Where?"

"You'll tell if I let you know."

"No, I won't, Doris. Honestly, I won't."

"There are books like that right here in this room."

"You're crazy," said George. "If you think my mother would allow books like that in this house you're stark, staring crazy."

"All right," said Doris. "Don't believe me then," and she went on dusting.

"Just show me," demanded George.

"No, I won't. You think I'm crazy and you don't believe a word I say so I'm not going to show you anything. Besides, you'll tell."

"Doris, I swear I won't tell, and I don't think you're crazy and I do believe you. I swear it."

She looked at him for a long time, then went to the humidor that sat on a corner of Mr. Justine's desk. She rummaged through it for a moment and finally brought out a small gold key. Then she went to the locked bookcase directly behind the desk and unlocked the doors.

"There," she said.

"I knew you were crazy," George said in disgust. "Those are my father's books on economics and law and things like that. After all, he is a stockbroker and that's his library of business books."

Doris smiled. "Take a look at one."

It took George Justine only a few minutes to realize that his father, Theo, was the owner of one of the most extensive pornographic libraries in existence. His face grew whiter and whiter as he picked up one book after another and his hands trembled violently.

"Have you looked at all of these?" he asked at last.

"I've read every single one of them," said Doris.

"My God!" said George weakly. "Does my father know?"

72

"Don't be such a fool. Of course he doesn't know."

"How did you find out about the key?"

Doris smiled. "I know a lot of things about this family," she said. "Little things that none of you would want outsiders to know. I wasn't really worried when you caught me in Patricia's dress, you know. If you'd said you were going to tell and had gone to your mother, I don't think she would have fired me."

"What kind of things?" demanded George.

"Oh, you'd be surprised," said Doris.

"Tell me at once."

"Oh, things like your sister Pamela lets that friend of yours, Edward Duckworth, open the front of her dress when the two of them are supposed to be out looking at the garden."

"I don't believe you!" cried George.

"Well, don't then. But it's true just the same. Ask her if you don't believe me. Ask him."

"You know very well that I'd never insult either of them with such a question," said George.

"Don't then."

"You're nothing but a disgusting little sneak," said George. "I don't know how I could ever have thought that you were sweet and pretty."

"I am sweet and pretty," said Doris. "It's just that I'm alone in the world and I have to look after myself."

George did not even glance at her as he stamped out of the room and Doris smiled and hummed as she picked up her duster and finished her work.

For the most part, Doris had judged George Justine correctly. He could not keep away from the locked bookcase in his father's library and now he took to coming home from Princeton almost every week-end.

"He's a fine boy," said Mrs. Justine. "He loves his home and his family. Why, just look. Other boys his age have nothing on their minds but carousing about every week-end and George comes home to his family."

But when the Justines went out on Saturday evenings, they could never get George to accompany them. He always pleaded a heavy study schedule or a headache and as soon as the family

73

was out of the front door he made his way to the library. Doris smiled and waited and, as the weeks passed, a terrible anger grew in her. For if George Justine could not keep away from his father's books, he could and did keep away from Doris.

She smiled at him and posed in front of him and as often as possible she managed to be in the same room with him, but George never smiled back and all he ever said to her was either "Good morning, Doris" or "Good night, Doris."

You bastard, she thought viciously. You blue-nosed bastard. Just you wait.

But summer arrived and George prepared to go north to Bar Harbour with his mother and sisters and Doris was still as virginal and untouched as the day she got off the boat. It was the only time her shrewdness had failed her and it was the last time in her life that she ever misjudged a man. Never again did she allow herself to become over-confident nor make the mistake of over-playing her hand.

"You'll spend the summer here," Mrs. Justine told Doris. "You and cook and one of the other girls. And you must all take very good care of Mr. Justine. He gets very upset at times when the family is away and I want all of you to make things as pleasant as possible for him."

Doris had counted heavily on the summer at the shore and she almost wept with frustration. On the morning that the family left, George Justine stopped her in the hall of the second floor.

"My father knows," he said.

"Knows what?" demanded Doris.

"You know what," whispered George angrily. "He saw one of those books in my room."

"You're a fool, George Justine," said Doris.

"He knows that you know, too."

"I knew you'd tell."

"I wasn't going to take all the blame by myself," said George. "He asked me how I'd found out and I told him."

"Isn't that nice," said Doris sarcastically. "What is he going to do? Throw me out?"

"I don't know. He didn't want to do anything until Mother and the girls had left."

74

"You bastard," whispered Doris viciously.

George stood up straight. "You brought it all on yourself," he said sanctimoniously. Then he turned and went downstairs to join his mother and sisters.

Days passed and Doris waited nervously for the axe to fall, but Mr. Justine neither said or did a thing. Towards the middle of July she began to breathe more easily and think that perhaps Mr. Justine had chosen to ignore the whole episode. But one hot night she was in her third-floor room, dressed in a thin wrapper and brushing her hair, when there was a knock at her door. She opened it quietly and Theo Justine stepped into her room.

"Keep still," he ordered. "If you make a sound, I'll have you thrown out into the streets, bag and baggage."

"What is it?" whispered Doris.

Theo Justine leaned back against her closed door and his eyes grew heavy as he looked at her.

"Take off your clothes," he said.

Doris stepped away from him, more in surprise than in fear.

"But sir," she protested, playing for time to think. "I'm just a young girl. A good girl. I've never been with a man before. Please, sir. Don't make me. What would Mrs. Justine say?"

"Shut up," said Theo Justine. "I'm not going to hurt you and Mrs. Justine is in Bar Harbour. Do as I say. Quickly."

As Doris began to slip the wrapper off her shoulders she heard him turn the key in the lock, but he never moved away from the door. He stood and leaned against it, his arms straight down, his hands flat against the panels, and only the sound of his quickened breath betrayed the fact that he was in the room at all. Doris stood nude before him and as his eyes travelled over her, she watched him.

The old bastard, she thought in sudden exultation. All he wants is a free look. Well, it's not going to be as free as he thinks it is.

"Turn around," said Theo Justine and Doris turned slowly, letting him admire her, and the sound of his breathing filled the whole room.

During the weeks that followed, Theo Justine came to Doris's room more and more often and as time passed she grew more and more bold with him. She still followed his panting orders, but more slowly now. "Aren't you tired of just looking, Mr. Justine?" she would say. "Wouldn't you like it all?"

"Adultery is a sin," rasped Theo Justine. "I've never been with any woman other than my wife since we married."

Doris smiled and moved her body on the bed.

"But you'd like to be with me, wouldn't you?"

"I can't," whispered Theo. "I can't."

Doris laughed out loud and turned over on to her stomach, then she began to contract and relax the muscles in her buttocks until they quivered and she listened to Theo's harsh whisper.

"Turn over, Doris. Please turn over. Please, Doris."

She made him beg and plead, often until tears streamed down his cheeks.

"What'll you give me if I do?"

Theo did not answer her. With a great cry he fell on her and struggled and fought his way into her and Doris tasted blood where she had bitten through the shoulder of his dressing-gown. When it was over, it was Theo who wept. Doris held his head cradled against her breasts and listened to him sob, and even with the throb of pain that burned between her legs, she smiled up at the ceiling.

The next morning there was an envelope with a hundred-dollar bill in it that had been slipped under her door sometime during the night, and as August came to a humid end there was a neat stack of bills under the stockings in Doris's dresser drawer. Theo came to her almost every night now, and every time he swore to her that it would be the last, but Doris had learned well from his supply of hidden books. She made love to him with a perfection that was in itself almost a perversion and Theo could not keep away from her.

By the time September came and the family returned, there was a new quality to Doris's smile. It was self-confidence and power and it even showed in the way she stood and walked.

"I must say," said Mrs. Justine crossly, "that a summer in the city didn't hurt you a bit, Doris. You're blooming like a rose."

"Thank you, ma'am," said Doris demurely.

"Theo my dear," said Mrs. Justine. "You look exhausted. I

76

know I should have insisted that you leave business to join us at the shore. Just look at you."

Doris filled Theo's coffee cup and smiled when she saw the way his hand shook.

One evening, towards the end of October, Theo Justine was alone in his library. Mrs. Justine had gone to a concert with the girls and George had not come home for the week-end. Doris waited until the rest of the household were in bed, then she went downstairs. She faced Theo across his desk and she did not mince words.

"I'm pregnant," she said.

Theo put his head in his hands. "I knew it was going to happen," he said.

"Well, it's too late to feel sad now," said Doris briskly. "What are we going to do?"

He raised his face. "We?" he asked stupidly.

"What do you think?" demanded Doris. "Surely you don't expect me to cope with this thing alone?"

"I can't do anything," protested Theo. "I have my family to think of."

"I'm not asking you to leave your silly family," said Doris. "I'm just telling you that I have to be looked after and that someone is going to have to support the baby."

Theo might have been a fool in many ways but he was also a businessman. He knew when a deal was in the offing.

"How much?" he asked at last.

"Fifty thousand dollars," said Doris bluntly.

"You're crazy," he said.

"No, I'm not. But you very possibly may be if I decide to open my mouth."

"No one would ever believe you," said Theo.

"Maybe not everyone," said Doris. "But enough people would to make things ugly for you. Your wife, for instance. And your children. And I might even decide to get a lawyer or go to the newspapers."

"Who'd believe a little Irish housemaid?"

"We can try to find out if you'd like."

Theo Justine sighed. "I'll have it by the end of the week," he

77

said. "And as soon as I hand it over to you, I want you out of my house."

"That's what you say now," said Doris with a sly little smile. "But there'll be nights when you'll be sorry I'm not here."

"Get out of here," said Theo.

He paid her in cash and Doris left the Justine house in the middle of the night. From the moment she left she covered her tracks well. She opened an account in an obscure bank, keeping just enough money with her to see her through the months to come, and she left New York for Philadelphia. She found a small apartment and took very good care of herself during her pregnancy, not for the sake of the child soon to be born, but for her own. She posed as a widow and oddly enough people in Philadelphia believed her just as had the people at the bank in New York. The baby, a boy, was born in the spring and Doris began to make plans at once. When her son was six weeks old, she left Philadelphia and returned to New York. She rented a cheap room and withdrew her money from the bank and she waited for a dark, rainy night. It came at the end of the second week in June and Doris dressed her son in clothing she had bought in a cheap, crowded store. She wrapped him in a blanket and carried him through the rain to a Catholic church three blocks from her rooming-house and when she got there she fed him and waited until he was asleep. Then she got up quietly and left him lying in the corner of a dark pew. Within an hour she was on a train bound for Boston, her few belongings packed in one suitcase that was lined with over forty-eight thousand dollars in cash. By the time the train arrived in Boston, Doris had washed all remembrance of New York, the Justines and her son from her mind. None of that had ever happened. She was twenty-one years old and her life was just beginning.

Doris Delaney never got through the locked door of Boston society, but with her looks, her smart address and her new wardrobe, she managed to attach her self to the fringe that dwelt right outside. She met Adam Palmer at a charity ball at the Copley and made up her mind to marry him.

Adam Palmer was a good businessman but he was notoriously lacking in the ways of the world. Doris posed now as an orphan

78

who, although fixed well enough financially, was totally alone in the world. Adam was first sympathetic, then very sorry for her and at last in love with her. Within three months of the charity ball at the Copley, he asked Doris to marry him.

"I know I'm much older," he said apologetically, "but I'll try to make you happy."

"Oh, Adam, my dear," said Doris gratefully.

"You'll like Cooper Station," Adam told her. "It's a nice town, a pretty town."

Doris had counted on remaining in Boston and was startled at this announcement.

"But, Adam, what about your business?"

"Oh, it practically runs itself now," he said comfortably. "I come down on the train and spend a day or two here every week, but the rest of the time I go up home and putter around. There's breathing room in Cooper Station which is more than I can say for this place."

Doris shrugged mentally. Perhaps it was better this way, after all. Adam would never be upper crust in Boston and maybe it was better to be a big fish in a little pond like Cooper Station than to be no fish at all.

"Oh, Adam," she said softly. "You've made me so happy."

"I love you, Doris," he said. "You'll never be sorry."

They were married in Boston and went to Niagara Falls for the wedding trip and Adam Palmer treated his wife as if she were made of fragile china that might shatter under his clumsy touch. Doris did nothing to offend his strict New England sensibilities. She wore a nightgown that covered her from head to foot and she shivered as if in fear when Adam tried to touch her.

"Oh, Adam, Adam," she cried. "I'm so frightened!"

"I love you, dear," he repeated over and over. "I'd never harm you."

At last she let him force his knee between her thighs and then she tightened herself against his onslaught. When at last he penetrated her, she gave such a cry of agony that Adam Palmer never doubted for a moment that he had deflowered a virgin.

Doris Delaney Palmer did well in Cooper Station. She joined the Congregational Church and became attached to various clubs and committees. Within five years the town elected her to serve as a Guardian and the mantle of respectability that Doris wore perpetually fitted her as if she had been born with it in place. Within ten years, there were many people who never stopped to remember that Doris had been born elsewhere, so completely did she suit Cooper Station. The only person who ever wondered about Doris was Dr. Gordon Cameron. She had come to him because she suffered from acutely painful menstrual cramps and, in the course of his examination, the doctor had seen the episiotomy scar that gave her secret away. But he kept silent. Afterwards, as he filled out a card, he asked casually, "Have you ever been pregnant, Mrs. Palmer?"

"Of course not," said Doris, but her hands had begun to sweat. "Why do you ask that?"

Dr. Gordon Cameron smiled. "There's nothing unusual about that, is there?" he asked. "A lot of married women get pregnant. I just wondered if perhaps you had ever been so and then perhaps aborted."

"Not that I know of, I'm sure," said Doris.

Gordon Cameron sat still for a long time after Doris had gone. In the end, he made a note of what he had seen on Doris's card.

"You're joking," said Jess when his father showed him what he had written.

"No, I'm not," said Gordon. "Sometime, somewhere, Doris Delaney Palmer gave birth to a child."

"I can't believe it," said Jess. "Adam never said anything about a child."

"I don't think Adam knows," said Gordon. "She's had that scar a good long time. For much longer than she's had Adam."

The next few weeks were hell for Doris. She was sure that Gordon Cameron knew something and that he would go to Adam Palmer with it. But the weeks drifted into months and Gordon treated her as he always had, with a sort of quiet courtesy, and Doris breathed easily again.

He doesn't know anything, thought Doris in relief. He never did. His question was one that he might ask any woman.

No one ever mentioned anything even faintly connected with a child to Doris again until years later, during the Second World

80

War. Doris was serving on the board of the Red Cross chapter in Cooper's Mills when Lisa Pappas came to her one day to complain that her allotment cheques were not arriving on time.

"I've just got to have that money when I'm supposed to, Mrs. Palmer," said Lisa. "I've got the baby to think of."

Afterwards, Doris could not remember if it was because she was tired or whether she had had an exceptionally trying day or if it was because she sometimes mourned the passing of her own youth that she spoke to Lisa as she did.

"If you'd behaved yourself before you were married," she said to Lisa, "you wouldn't have to worry about a child now."

And Lisa Pappas, striking out with fear and hatred, gave out with the purest shot in the dark.

"At least when *I* was in trouble," she cried, "the man responsible married me."

Lisa turned and ran out of Doris's office in the Red Cross building and Doris sat quite still until the trembling stopped.

She knows, thought Doris in horror. Somehow, she knows.

And no matter how often, after that, that Doris told herself it was impossible that a child like Lisa could know anything about her, Doris could never quite believe it. It seemed to her whenever Lisa looked at her that the knowledge stood out on her face.

I know about you, said Lisa's look. You're not so much. If the truth were known, you'd have to leave town in a hurry.

And now Lisa Pappas was going to move right into Cooper Station unless Doris prevented it. She'd be the wife of a schoolteacher and at every school function Doris would have to watch Lisa looking at her with the look of knowledge in her eyes.

Not that she really frightens me, Doris thought. She's probably sleeping with Jim Sheppard. That's probably how she got him to sponsor Chris Pappas.

Doris had hated Jim Sheppard from the day he was elected to the Town Board of Guardians. Her best friend, Callie Webster, had run against Jim and practically everyone in town said that Jim hadn't a prayer against Callie. But Callie was defeated for the same reason that many popular candidates for office are defeated. Over-confidence on the part of the constituents. People were so sure that Callie would be elected anyway that many of

81

them didn't even bother to attend the meeting, and when the ballots were counted, Jim Sheppard had won by two votes.

"It's impossible!" Doris Palmer had raged.

But it had happened and from that day on, Jim Sheppard was Doris's sworn enemy. He would not bow to her wishes and he would not be put under her thumb. On practically every issue he sided with Nathaniel Cooper, and Doris's rage grew.

Doris began to circulate her petition. She spent all her evenings and most of her afternoons calling on people and by the time it was June she had all but fifty names she needed signed up. She also saw to it that no one with a house for rent allowed the Pappases to even view the place and if it hadn't been for Jess Cameron, Lisa and Chris would never have moved into Cooper Station at all.

When Jess became aware of what Doris was doing, he went at once to Nathaniel Cooper.

"That bitch is trying to keep Lisa and Chris from finding a place to live here in town," said Jess angrily. "It's about time that someone fought that woman."

"Well, what do you want me to do?" asked Nathaniel. "I can't very well move them into my house, can I?"

"No, but we can go to Anthony," said Jess. "The gardener's cottage behind his place has been sitting idle for years. The Pappases could live there."

"Good Lord, Jess," said Nate. "You know how Anthony is. He'd never hear of it. He likes being alone too much."

"We could ask him," countered Jess stubbornly.

Nate shrugged. "They're your ear-drums, Remember that when my dear nephew blasts off."

But Anthony did not blast off. "Sure," he said when Jess and Nate spoke to him. "I've always been a sucker for a lost cause. Just tell Mrs. Pappas to keep her kids away from me and we'll get along fine."

Lisa threw her arms around Jess when he told her the news, and the very next day she drove to Cooper Station to begin the job of cleaning the long-empty cottage, Anthony Cooper watched her walk down the gravelled drive that led to the little house.

You can tell by the way she walks that she was made for loving, he thought. Then he smiled cynically. And you can also tell that she's not getting enough of the right kind.

He was still smiling when Lisa had rounded the curve and disappeared from view.

Anthony dropped the curtain he had been holding aside to watch Lisa.

Maybe this afternoon, if he felt up to it, he'd take a walk down that way and see if there was anything he could do.

7

SMITH ROAD, which crossed Benjamin Street at a point three blocks beyond the town's business section, was a winding, tree-shaded road that looked more like a country lane than the best street in Cooper Station's residential district. The two Cooper houses stood at the extreme western end of the road, where the paving ended and gave way to acres of rolling fields and picture-postcard view of forests and mountains. The one occupied by Nathaniel Cooper II was a square, brick Colonial with white painted trim which stood on a slight rise of ground on the northern side of the road. At both ends of its curved, gravelled driveway were wrought-iron gates set into twin stone pillars and into each pillar had been set a polished brass plate about the size of a dollar bill on which the name *Cooper* had been lettered in script. Inside, the brick house was panelled in dark wood, its windows draped with maroon velvet and its floor covered with thick carpeting of the same colour. The furniture was massive mahogany, almost as dark as the walls, and the upholstered pieces were covered in the same dark red as the draperies. This was the home that Nathaniel Cooper I had built for himself in 1861, the year after his factories at Cooper's Mills had begun to make money, and now, almost a hundred years later, with the house occupied by Old Nate's grandson, almost nothing in it had been changed. Twelve years before, when Nathaniel had brought his bride home to Cooper Station, Margery had laughed and said,

84

"Good Lord, Nate, how long do you thing it will take us to turn this enormous velvet-lined coffin into a home?"

Nate had squeezed her hand and said, "It'll take us a year just to clear out the attics and get this furniture moved out. And all the while we're doing that, the noise you'll be hearing will be Grandpa whirling around in his grave. To him, all this was the epitome of plushness."

The first year of her marriage, Margery redecorated the master bedroom. She had the walls covered with a rose-printed white paper and the woodwork painted French grey. She sent to New York for an outsize bed and covered it with a white rose-printed spread and she had a rose chaise-longue.

"Good God," said Nate. "You make me feel like I'm coming in to visit a French whore."

Margery assumed a heavy-lidded look and stretched out one languid arm from her position on the chaise.

"Venez ici," she said huskily.

Nate bent down and scooped her up in his big arms.

"Only French girl I ever met with a southern drawl," he said.

Margery ran the tip of her tongue over his top lip.

"Y'all lay down on the bed, Massa, and Ah'll show y'all a couple of little ole French tricks."

The second year, Margery began on the small south-east bedroom which she turned into a nursery for the baby who would be born in the fall.

"Isn't it perfect, Nate?" she asked when it was finished.

Nate looked at the once dreary room which was now full of sunlight and air and soft baby colours.

"Perfect," he agreed. "Just like everything you are and do."

"Before I get done everything is going to be perfect. This house and the grounds and our first baby and all his brothers and sisters."

Nate kissed the back of her neck and put his arm around her so that his hand rested gently on the barely perceptible swelling of her abdomen.

"How many is 'All of them'?" he whispered.

"Six," said Margery decisively. "I can't stand odd numbers.

85

They make me nervous. Six is an absolutely round, perfect number."

It was not surprising that Margery took perfection for granted, for all her life she had known little else. She had been born Margery Stevenson in Charleston, South Carolina, the only child of a wealthy tobacco-grower and his wife who, to the end of her day, referred to Northerners as carpetbaggers and barbarians. When Margery was little she had a coloured Mammy for a nurse (just as her mother and grandmother before her), and she could remember little of her childhood that had not been covered and surrounded by softness and set solidly in a base of security. There was the gentleness of her mother's Southern voice, the soft croon of her Mammy, the caress of expensive clothing next to her skin and later, the ease of an intelligent child in a private school run by old Southern gentlewomen, the safety of expensive, well-groomed horses and, most of all, the comfort of money that need never be thought of because it was there.

Margery made her début when she was eighteen years old and then she was allowed to go off to Smith College because, as her father put it, "After all, Mother, the North *is* there and Margery might just as well find it out now as later."

Margery whirled around to show off one of the new wool skirts that would go north to school with her. She kissed her mother and laughed.

"Yes, darling," she said, "the North is there, plain as the nose on your pretty face, and I understand that they're quite civilized up there these days. They even smoke cigarettes, which makes it nice for Daddy. My going to Smith will be a sort of public relations job, and if I catch one single girl smoking anything that doesn't have Daddy's tobacco in it, why, I'll just snatch her bald-headed."

"My baby," said Mrs. Stevenson and began to cry. "You'll get up there in the North and those awful girls—why, all those girls have legs like colts and simply horrible voices, and they'll go to putting ideas in your head and introducing you to Northern boys and I don't know what all."

"Don't you worry, darling," said Margery. "If I get tied up with a Northern boy, I'll bring him right back here real quick and

86

you can turn him into a Southerner and Daddy can make him into a tobacco expert."

Mrs. Stevenson sniffed wetly into her white linen handkerchief. "Southerners are like great geniuses," she said. "They are born. Not made. And your Daddy practically cut his baby teeth on a tobacco leaf. There isn't a man living in Massachusetts who can say the same."

Margery was a sophomore at Smith when she met Nathaniel Cooper, who was then a senior at Harvard. They were introduced at a football game and within three weeks of their meeting Nate was cutting classes and spending every cent of his allowance on trips to Northampton while Margery was frightening her mother with letters about a Northerner with whom she declared herself madly in love.

Ferguson Cooper was now deep in his seventies and Nate would be taking over the rule of the vast Cooper empire as soon as he graduated.

Only rarely did Nate think of his old dream of being a botanist. The only person to whom he ever mentioned it was Margery Stevenson who held his hand and sympathized with him and respected him for doing his duty.

"Why, Nate, honey," she said, "lots of people don't get to do what they want to do. I guess it's just the way things happen. Look at me. Just suppose I'd been a boy instead of a girl. Why, I'd have to go and grub in some filthy tobacco place all day, just like Daddy. And that's not what I want to do at all."

Nathaniel ran his fingers softly up and down on the inside of her forearm.

"What do you want to do, Margery?" he asked.

They were sitting on a river bank and a May breeze moved sweetly across the water. Margery lay flat on the ground, her head pillowed on Nathaniel's sweater. She breathed deeply and sighed and stretched.

"I want to get married," she said at last. "I want to live in a big house and send down to Charleston for Virgie to look after me and I want to have a whole bunch of children and a horse for everybody and two cars of my own and the prettiest clothes and a set of silver hair-brushes with my initials on the back."

"Well," said Nathaniel slowly, "we've got a big house up home."

He looked down into the incredible blue of her eyes and felt the quivering that went through him every time, just before he kissed her.

I thought that it was only in books that a girl's eyelashes made shadows on her cheeks," he said against her mouth. And in the same whisper, without moving his lips away, he said, "In fact, we not only have a big house, we've got two whole towns. And a stable that my grandfather used to use that's big enough for a dozen horses. And I'm crazy about kids and silver hair-brushes."

"I know it," said Margery. "What did you think I meant when I said that I wanted to send to Charleston for Virgie?" She traced the outline of his lower lip with her finger. "Oh, Nate, honey. It took you so long to say it that I thought you were never going to speak up at all."

He held her tightly against him. "When?" he asked, over and over again between kisses.

"In the fall," she said. "You'll be through school then and we'll have the whole summer to get ready. I want to buy the prettiest hats and dresses and shoes and nightgowns ever made, and I want Mama to have the house all fixed beautifully so that every single thing about getting married will be perfect. Oh, Nate, honey. Hold me. Kiss me some more."

That summer, in July, Ferguson Cooper died and some said that it was just as if the old man had been waiting for Nathaniel to get through school and get married.

"I don't want you to wait if anything happens to me, Nathaniel," Ferguson had told his son. "Don't you worry none about what folks'll say. You belong here in this house and this house is no place for a man alone."

"Pa, don't talk like that. You're going to be up and on your feet before Labour Day. You wait and see."

"Well, if I'm not I don't want you fiddling around waiting to get married. Margery's a nice girl and a good girl, even if she doesn't come from around here, and girls like that aren't easy to find. Also, she reminds me of your mother, and your mother was never one to wait for anybody."

88

Margery and Nathaniel were married in September in the garden of her parents' home in Charleston. Margery wore her great-grandmother's wedding dress and she had eight brides-maids and a huge three-tiered cake. Margery's father had checked Nathaniel through Dun and Bradstreet and was satisfied with what he had learned, and even Margery's mother allowed that Nathaniel was not bad at all, for a Northerner, and really quite presentable when you came right down to it. But mostly the Stevensons were happy because Margery was happy, and now they could lean back, content with the thought that their only child had never lacked for one single thing that she had ever wanted.

That night, in the living-room of a New York penthouse apartment which Nathaniel had borrowed from a friend, Margery sipped champagne and admired the way her legs looked though the thin silk of her négligé.

"Wasn't it perfect, Nate?" she sighed.

"Yes, darling," replied Nathaniel. "Absolutely two thousand per cent beautiful, wonderful and perfect."

He walked slowly around the room, turning off lights, and when the room was dark he opened the double doors that led on to the terrace. Immediately, the room was filled with the warmth of the September night and the only sound was the distant murmur of traffic on the street twenty floors below.

"Oh, how beautiful!" cried Margery and went to stand at the terrace's parapet.

Nathaniel stood behind her and together they watched the lights of the city until, in both of them, there was an almost simultaneous breath-quickening, and still they stood, not touching one another, waiting. Gently, Nathaniel lifted her heavy hair to one side and put his lips softly on the back of her neck and when his arms finally encircled her, Margery felt a silent gasp within her that hurt her chest and made her want to cry out, but her throat felt locked and no sound came. It was only when he had slipped off her négligé and she felt the palms of his hands against her nipples that she could whisper, "Oh, Nate, Nate, darling."

And then it was as if the words had released her from fear, so that she circled his neck with her arms when he carried her

89

inside, and no matter how or where he touched her she could want more and more.

"I don't want to hurt you, darling. I don't want to hurt you."

And Margery strained towards him, raising herself to him, and said, "I'm not afraid, darling. Here I am, darling. I'm not afraid."

Margery did well in Cooper Station, or, as the townspeople put it, she seemed to fit right into things. That Margery's "fitting in" was part of a careful plan on her part, no one ever suspected, not even her husband. Margery moved slowly. She was friendly without being forward and always she waited for Cooper Station to take the first step in her direction. When she decided to re-decorate Ferguson Cooper's house she realized that it was going to take her at least five years if she were to prevent anyone in town from regarding her as an outlander who had come in and couldn't wait to start ripping down what it had taken Ferguson and his father almost a hundred years to build. The big brick house was understaffed, for Margery allowed herself one cleaning woman and a part-time cook, and it was not until she was three months pregnant that she sent to Charleston for Virgie Perkins, the coloured woman who had been her nurse.

"You can't blame Margery for wanting a familiar face around her now," said Florence Strickland, who was the wife of Cooper Station's leading attorney. "After all, it's her first baby."

"Well, I'm darned if I'd want a big black face around me at a time like that," said Holly Meade, the art supervisor for the Cooper Station schools.

"Holly, you can't possibly know what it feels like to be pregnant, now can you? A pregnant woman gets the strangest feelings sometimes," said Florence sweetly, and Holly, who had never had a child, was properly squelched.

In spite of her mother's worries and Nathaniel's understandable jitters, Margery's pregnancy was a surprisingly easy one.

"You're as healthy as a good Southern horse," said Dr. Jess Cameron. "Just stop eating so much, Margery, or we'll deliver you a baby as big as a six-month-old child."

Nathaniel rubbed cocoa butter on Margery's swollen abdomen. "I can feel him moving," he said.

90

"Nate, honey?"

"Yes?"

"What if he's a girl?"

Nathaniel buried his face in her hair. "I can wait," he said. "Remember you said you wanted six."

She turned slightly and bit his ear. "But just one at a time, selfish," she laughed.

Virgie made two sets of everything, one pink and one blue, just to be on the safe side, she said, and her love went into every tiny stitch.

"There was never no store boughten clothes on you when you was a baby, Miz Marg'ry she said, "and there ain't gonna be none on this little one."

She made sure that Margery walked and napped. She brushed Margery's hair and rubbed her back and looked critically at every mouthful of food that went into Margery's mouth, and all day long she hummed spirituals under her breath until Jess Cameron said:

"This isn't going to be just the birth of another baby. This is going to be the Second Coming. Wait and see.

Margery's mother telephoned almost every day from Charleston, and she wrote lengthy letters in which she explained that it wasn't as if she didn't trust Nathaniel or anything like that, it was simply that a mother couldn't help worrying about her daughter's first baby and thank God that Virgie was there and was Margery sure that she didn't want her baby born in Charleston.

"I'd come up there myself," said Mrs. Stevenson, "but you know how poor Daddy is. He's like a lost little boy if I'm away from home for even an hour."

"I know, darling," said Margery. "And truly, I've never felt better in my life. Jess says I'm healthy as a Southern horse."

"Yes, well," said Mrs. Stevenson, "I'd feel a lot easier in my mind if you were right here at home with Dr. Wolcott to look after things."

"I am at home, dear," said Margery as gently as she could. "I couldn't leave Nate now any more than you could leave Daddy. Please don't worry. Everything is fine."

Mrs. Stevenson began to sniffle. "Yes, dear, I'm sure it is. But please have Nate or that doctor of yours call me the minute anything happens, won't you?"

"Yes, dear. Of course I will. Don't cry, dear. Call me tomorrow."

Margery hung up and leaned back in bed for her afternoon nap and then she felt the first twinge. Quickly, she looked at her watch and noted the time.

If it happens again before fifteen minutes are gone, she thought, I'll call Nate.

She propped another pillow up behind her neck and put both hands on her abdomen and waited. She counted forty-six roses in the wallpaper before she looked at her watch again. Three minutes had passed. It was half an hour before she felt anything resembling a cramp.

"Dammit," she said aloud and tried to relax.

But by the time Nathaniel got home from Cooper's Mills things had progressed to good, solid, sweat-bringing pains that came once every ten minutes, and by six-thirty in the evening Margery was in the Cooper Memorial Hospital, prepped and properly doped up to the eyeballs.

"For God's sake, Nate, go on home," said Jess Cameron. "Fathers are more trouble than mothers. Everything's fine and going according to schedule. Beat it."

"I'll wait," said Nathaniel and hoped that he wouldn't throw up.

The baby came at eight-thirteen the next morning and it was a girl.

"It's a girl," someone said, and Margery smiled crookedly. She felt drunk.

"I knew it all the time," she murmured. "I was saving it for a surprise for Nate. Robin. Her name is Robin," and Margery slept again.

They did not let her see the baby. "But Jess," she said, "I feel wonderful. I want to see my baby."

She was sitting up in bed with her hair brushed and fresh lipstick on her mouth.

"Maybe tomorrow, Margery," said Jess Cameron. "It's only

92

been two days. We want you to get your strength back. You bled a little more than we like, and we want you to get strong again."

The hospital room was full of flowers and for no reason at all Margery remembered the way the living-room of the Cooper house had looked when Ferguson was laid out in his coffin.

"She's dead!" cried Margery. "Robin's dead and you don't want to tell me!"

"No, Margery. No. We just want you to get strong again."

"Nate," she said. "It's been a week now. I want to see the baby. Why don't they bring her to me?"

Nathaniel Cooper was not the expert liar that Jess Cameron could be on occasion.

"The baby is weak, Margery," he said. "Jess said something about oxygen."

"You lie, Nathaniel," she said. "Tell me what's wrong."

He did not tell her and at last the day came when Margery could get up by herself. She waited until the nurse had left the room and then she got up and dressed. She walked to the nursery and looked at the diminutive cribs, in rows, behind the large square of glass, and she watched a white-robed, masked nurse hold up one baby after another to show to the foolishly smiling fathers who stood next to Margery outside the nursery window. She saw the nurse's eyes meet hers; saw the immaculate hand hover for a moment over one of the cribs, and she saw the eyes over the mask fill with tears.

Margery Cooper waited, sitting on one of the chairs in the hospital waiting-room, for Jess Cameron to walk through the front door of the hospital. She did not see, nor hear, the white-capped nurse who picked up a telephone in the office across the hall.

"Doctor Cameron," the nurse said softly into the telephone, "Mrs. Cooper is up and dressed and sitting in the waiting-room. She walked to the nursery. I'm sure I don't know, Doctor. Pickering said that she was taking a nap, so she left her and went about her other duties. The next thing we knew she was standing in front of the nursery window. No, she hasn't seen the baby. Yes, Doctor, we'll be careful."

Jess Cameron turned to his father. "Christ," he said hopelessly. "Christ." He pounded his fist against the desk.

Dr. Gordon Cameron looked unhappily at his son.

"This is one of the disadvantages that I didn't tell you about that time I lectured you on the glories of small-town doctoring," he said. "If this had happened in a city, to someone you knew only as a patient, it wouldn't be so hard on you. You'd feel badly, but you wouldn't have to watch the hearts of two of your friends breaking."

Jess turned and stared out of the window.

I should have done something as soon as I knew, he thought. One little slip, a mistake. It would have been so easy and the child would be dead and I could face Margery and tell her, Your daughter is dead, Margery. But this . . .

Gordon Cameron went to stand next to his son.

"I know, Jess," he said quietly. "But I couldn't have done it either."

"How did you know what I was thinking?" asked Jess.

"We all think of it at one time or another," replied Gordon. "Some of us can and some of us can't and I'll be damned if I always know which of us is the more fortunate."

Jess's whole body ached with tension. Not Margery. Anybody else in the world, but not Margery.

"She has to be told, Jess," said Gordon Cameron.

"Yes," said Jess.

He telephoned to Nathaniel Cooper. "Nate," he said, "she has to be told. I'll meet you outside the hospital."

A few minutes later the two men walked in together to face Margery.

"Margery, dear," said Nathaniel. "How wonderful to see you up and dressed. Here, let me walk you back to your room."

Margery did not smile back nor even look at him. "Jess?" she said.

So here you are, Cameron, thought Jess wretchedly. The time is now. Just don't look into her eyes when you tell her, and don't beat around the bush.

They sat in Margery's room and a student nurse brought steaming cups of coffee. Margery felt a painful fist clench shut in her stomach. She remembered something that Jess had once

94

said, conversationally, as he sat in her living-room.

"There's nothing a human being can't bear more easily if he has a good hot cup of coffee in his hands."

Margery watched Jess now. He took a long gulp of coffee and lit a cigarette. Margery watched and felt faint with terror.

"Robin is a Mongolian idiot," he said bluntly.

The words seemed to echo in the room. They ricocheted against the walls and the floor and bounced against Margery's brain.

Idiot, said the echo. Idiot. Robin is an idiot, idiot, idiot.

Margery laughed and laughed. She laughed because, of course, Jess was playing a joke on her. It was the same kind of joke he made whenever she was at a party and looking especially well and Jess came up to her and smiled and said, "And you, my dear Margery, look just like a hag!" So Margery laughed.

Robin is a Mongolian idiot, she thought, and laughed. That is very funny. Jess, let go of my arm. Goodness, I can hardly stand up from laughing so hard.

She laughed and laughed, which was very bad of her because she thought that from somewhere, very far away now, she could hear Nathaniel sobbing.

Margery and Nathaniel took Robin home against all of Jess Cameron's urgings to the contrary. Even years later, Margery could remember fragments of sentences and phrases.

"What of the future, Jess?"

"Robin has no future."

"You could be wrong, Jess. Everyone makes mistakes."

"Please, Margery, please believe me. Don't torture yourself by going from one doctor to another in search of a miracle. Go to one other doctor, a specialist, and if his opinion is the same as my father's and mine, stop right there."

"He's right, Margery," said Nathaniel.

"Everyone makes mistakes," she said stubbornly.

During Robin's first year, Margery and her mother travelled over most of Europe with her, seeking a way out for the child, while Nathaniel stayed at home and ran the mills and Margery's father wandered around his big house in Charleston, waiting with quiet desperation for his wife to return. To everyone's surprise, it was Mrs. Stevenson who bore the shock of Robin far better than her husband. Margery's mother came to Cooper Station and took careful stock of the situation. She talked frankly with Jess Cameron and although she agreed with what he said, she could also see Margery's point of view.

"She'd never rest easy, Doctor," said Mrs. Stevenson, "if she thought that maybe there was something she could have done and didn't do."

"There is nothing to be done," argued Jess. "Margery is just hurting herself."

"And that is something that Margery is going to have to find out for herself," said Mrs. Stevenson.

She put her arms around Nathaniel and said, "Don't you worry yourself none, Nate, honey. I'll watch over both of them."

Looking at her, small, gentle-voiced and rather fluttery, Jess said he thought he knew now what the women of the South must have been like when they gave their wedding rings to the Confederacy to be made into weapons of war.

Mr. Stevenson, on the other hand, could not accept the fact of Robin. He blamed the climate of northern New England, Jess Cameron, the hospital and the whole of Cooper Station.

"Margery was never cut out to live in the North," he cried. "We never should have let her go. A delicate girl like Margery, surrounded by strangers. That's what did it to her."

"It happens everywhere, John," said his wife. "Look at Elsie Cartwright right here in Charleston. Her little girl is the same as Robin."

"Trash!" cried John Stevenson. "The Cartwrights have always been trash."

He blamed himself for the years that he had not only allowed, but had encouraged, Margery to ride.

"Horses were made for men," he said. "I never should have allowed Margery on a horse."

"I've been riding horses for thirty years, John," said his wife quietly. "Stop blaming yourself."

But worst of all, John Stevenson blamed Nathaniel Cooper. "What do we really know about him and his family," he demanded. "They've probably been inbreeding for years and we never took the trouble to find out."

"That's enough, John," said his wife. "I never want to hear you talk like that again, and if you ever let on to Margery or Nate that you feel like that I'll turn right around and walk out of this house and never come back."

So Margery and her mother and Robin went from one European city to another until Hitler put a stop to their travels. Mrs. Stevenson went home to Charleston and now Margery and Nathaniel began their wandering around the United States in search of the cure that Margery was sure had just barely eluded her in Europe. They travelled thousands of miles and spent thousands of dollars, and they built up hopes, then picked up the broken pieces of these hopes and looked for still another doctor.

"It is a congenital condition, Mrs. Cooper," the doctors said.

"But what can we do?"

"Nothing," they said. "There is nothing to be done. Something goes wrong in the uterus during development——"

"But what?"

"We don't know."

"It's a pity, Mrs. Cooper, that this child did not die at birth," they said. "There are degrees of Mongolism, and in the case of this child the degree is such that she will probably never talk, never walk."

It was Nathaniel who gave up first.

"It's just the way things are," he said. "Why, I don't know. We'll do the best we can for her."

Jess Cameron enlarged on the idea and put it into words for Nathaniel.

"Once you have accepted the fact that Robin is not normal," he said, "you must next accept the idea of placing her in an institution. You can't help Robin by keeping her at home, Nate. All that will do is harm you and harm Margery."

"An institution!"

"Stop thinking of it in terms of a prison, Nate."

"But, Jess——"

"A mentally defective child, an idiot, Nate, is absolutely helpless. It takes the patience of a saint to care for a child like Robin. Do you have that kind of patience? Does Margery?"

"I'll discuss it with her, Jess."

But there was nothing to discuss as far as Margery was concerned. Her first, final, and only answer was an unqualified "No."

"Darling, will you talk to Jess about it?" asked Nate.

"No."

"Margery, listen to me," pleaded Jess. "You cannot give Robin the care that she needs at home. Caring for a defective child has to be done not only lovingly——"

"Are you insinuating that I don't love Robin, Jess?" she interrupted angrily. "Do you think that just because she is as she is I love her less?"

"If you love her, Margery, you'll do what's best for her and best for you. I know you love her, but love isn't the only consideration."

"Leave me alone!" screamed Margery. Leave me alone, both of you! I love her. She didn't ask to be born. I'll give her as much of myself as she can use, and I never want to hear another word about sending her away, locking her up somewhere, pretending that she's dead. Leave me alone, do you hear? Leave me alone!"

The voices of love surrounded her.

"Margery, darling, darling."

"Margery, Margery."

"Miz Marg'ry, honey."

Ten years later, Margery stood behind one of the maroon velvet drapes in the living-room that Nathaniel Cooper I had furnished and watched Anthony Cooper come out of his house and walk down the path to the gardener's cottage. The room was as wrong for her now as it had been when she had first seen it for, except for the fine lines around her eyes and the tightness around her mouth, she looked much the same as she had as a bride. Beneath the expensive tweed skirt she wore, her hips were as trim as they had been when she used to ride horseback every day, and the thrust of her breasts under the pale yellow sweater was still sharp and firm. The hand with which she pushed the drape aside was still white and slim-fingered, and her hair was still a dark, glossy cap, but the eyes with which she watched Anthony, although as blue as ever, were dull and looked as if they would take weeks and months of crying to be washed clear again.

The house at which Margery looked had been built by Ferguson Cooper as a wedding gift for his son, Benjamin. It was made of white clapboard in an exact replica of the brick house in which Ferguson himself had lived.

"If your father was set on twin houses," Margery had said to her husband, "why didn't he go the whole hog and build Benjamin's house out of brick too?"

"Because at the time, this was the only brick building in town," Nathaniel replied, "and Pa kept it that way because he figured that's the way Grandpa would have wanted it."

It used to amuse Margery that to this day, even though there were now municipal buildings made of brick, hers remained the only brick house in Cooper Station.

"We're so effin exclusive in our brick house," she had told Nathaniel in a moment of vulgarity, "that sometimes I feel like a royal-arsed Duchess."

The house across the street from Margery had the same gravelled drive, the same gates and posts and brass nameplates as the brick house, and it had always meant less than nothing to Anthony Cooper. Margery watched him now as he walked down the path. He was tall and too thin, so that his brown sports jacket seemed to be too large for him. His hair, like that of all the Cooper men, was a dark chestnut, but his face was not a Cooper face. His was thin, with a sharply aquiline nose and thick black brows that rose like little pitched roofs over deep-set, grey-green eyes. His lips were full over a deeply cleft chin and his cheekbones had prominent hollows beneath them.

"None of Benjamin to him at all," Ferguson Cooper had said, and except for Anthony's hair, the old man had been right. Anthony took after his mother. He was all Ford.

He doesn't look well, thought Margery. But at least, he's here, thank God. Perhaps now he'll stay home where he belongs and everything will be all right.

She remembered a conversation that she had overheard several years before, when Anthony had come home for Robin's christening.

"Well, Jess," Anthony had said to the doctor, "maybe I'll find a good healthy girl when I get back to New York. One who'll be willing to marry me and give me a son in a hurry. I'd better, or soon there'll be nothing left of the Coopers except our name on a lot of buildings and a lot of gravestones."

Margery clenched her teeth against memory. Goddamn him, she thought. And then, No, I mustn't. If Anthony doesn't stay . . ., she let the thought drift off. He'll stay, she told herself. This time he has to. He'll stay and settle down and find a nice girl and have a son who'll eventually learn to run the mills.

8

LISA PAPPAS and Jim Sheppard's wife, Polly, had met during the war while both women were serving as hostesses at the USO in Cooper's Mills, and despite the ten years difference in their ages they had discovered in each other a mutual fondness for many things, including books and music and people, and they had become fast friends.

When Lisa and Chris had returned to Cooper's Mills after West Farrington, it was Polly who convinced Lisa that Chris's decision to teach at the State School at Marmington was a wise one, and when the Cooper Station high school needed a new teacher, it was Polly who suggested Chris to Jim Sheppard.

Polly was small and dark with the kind of vitality that caused many people to say, "My! Polly Sheppard is so alive, isn't she?" while others, who were younger, said, "Gee, I hope I have her pep and energy when I'm her age." There were however, plenty of people in Cooper Station who were not so kind and they were the ones who said that Polly was a do-gooder, a busybody and a meddler.

"Always got her nose into something, that woman," said some of Cooper Station.

"You'd think with four kids to look after she'd have all she could do right at home."

"Oh, Polly's all right. It's just that she's got to keep up with everybody and everything all the time."

"Reckon there wasn't enough for her to do down there in Boston, so she had to come here and run things."

Polly, herself, was not unaware of what people said about her, but she went along in her own way just the same and regarded herself as a humanitarian and a champion of the underdog. The truth of the matter was that Polly Sheppard was the victim of a frustration so deep-seated that all her energies were dissipated along a hundred different pathways in a futile attempt to escape. In her headlong flight towards unreality, she had first tried drinking, which left her with nothing but enormous hangovers and a weight problem, and then a lover who first lived off her money and then left her for another, younger woman. It was after these two attempts that she had come to Cooper Station, determined to make a place for herself and her children, and the fact that her husband had come with her was incidental for she and Jim despised one another.

"Don't marry him," her mother had warned. "He's not our kind."

"But I love him," Polly had said. "I'll love him for ever and I'll die if I can't have him."

She was nineteen years old at the time and Jim Sheppard was her first beau.

"He's so handsome," Polly had said. "Every girl I know is blind with jealousy because he dates me."

"There's more to marriage than being handsome and having a good-looking head of hair," warned her mother.

In the end, of course, Polly won. She and Jim were married and for the first year everything was just as Polly had said it would be. She and Jim had a small apartment in Boston and Jim was expected to be a great success in his job with the auditing firm of Hitchcock, Pierce and Jamison. Polly learned to cook and Jim bought her a little cocker spaniel. On Sundays, the two of them went to visit Polly's parents and it always felt so good to get back to their own little place.

"I'm alive!" cried Polly over and over again. "Isn't it wonderful?"

And Jim kissed her and laughed at her. "You're a nut," he said.

The only times they ever argued were when they went to parties. Then Jim was apt to pay too much attention to every good-looking woman and Polly always felt as if she were dying a little every time it happened.

"You belong to me!" she said angrily.

"For God's sake, Polly. All I did was bring her a fresh drink. Does that mean I want to take her to bed?"

"Don't even say such a thing!"

"I'll say it if I feel like it."

"Is that what you were thinking? That you'd like to sleep with her?"

"Oh, Christ!"

"Then how come you mentioned it if you weren't thinking it?"

"Please, Polly. Let's just forget the whole thing."

"Forget it! How do you think I felt with you making a fuss over everybody but me?"

"I wasn't making a fuss over anyone."

"You were so!"

They went to bed stiffly and kept their backs turned on each other and invariably it was Polly who relented first.

"Honey?"

"For God's sake, what now?"

"I'm sorry."

"Sure you are."

"Truly, I am."

"That's what you say every Goddamned time."

"Honey?"

"What?"

"Please don't be mad at me."

"I'm not mad."

"How can I tell? You sound mad."

"Well, I'm not. Now for God's sake, let's get some sleep."

"Honey?"

"Now what?"

"Turn over."

"All right. So now I've turned over."

"Put your arms around me."

Then she would begin to stroke him, to try to excite him, and most of the time she succeeded. It was the times when he refused to be aroused that were terrible for Polly.

"You don't love me any more."

"Polly, I'm just tired."

"I don't believe you."

"Well, don't then. Just let me get to sleep."

The only solution that Polly could think of was to keep away from parties but Jim wouldn't hear of it.

"If you don't want to go, all right. But I'm going."

"Jim! You wouldn't!"

"Yes, I would."

Several times he did. Then Polly would sit home alone, torturing herself, wondering what he was doing, and thinking that if he would cheat on her right here in Boston what in the world would he do when his work took him away from her to northern New England where his firm frequently sent him.

In the end, of course, Jim had a trite little love affair with his secretary and Polly found out about it. At once, she went home to her parents.

"I can't stand it!" she wept.

"We told you he wasn't our kind."

"But you should see her! She's not even pretty!"

Jim came to get her to bring her home and Polly knew that she had to go because now she was pregnant.

"Look, Polly," said Jim. "We had it pretty nice together. So I made a mistake. Let's try to patch it up."

Polly's eyes were hard when she looked at him.

"I gave you everything," she said. "All the love I had in the world. And it wasn't enough for you."

"Polly, say you forgive me."

And she did, just as she had known all along that she would.

But within two years it happened again, and it happened while Polly was carrying her second child.

"I hate you," she said to Jim. "I'll hate you all the rest of my life."

She locked him out of her room but she would not lock him out of her life.

"Divorce? Don't be a fool, Jim. Do you think I'm going to admit to the world that I made such an abysmal mistake in marrying you? Never."

But Polly could not stand the pitying glances of her friends and relatives. She began drinking heavily and kept it up until her figure began to go, then she stopped. She met Bill Cadmus at a cocktail party and had a rather half-hearted love affair with him and she could not even weep when he left her for a young fashion model.

I've got to get away from here, thought Polly in desperation.

Then she remembered Cooper Station and a trip she had once taken through northern New England. Within three months she had bought a house and moved in with the two children.

"You can do whatever you want," she told Jim. "But you're going to take care of the children and me and when you're here you're going to make a nice face and act married. If you want to screw around, you can do it during the week in Boston. But you're not going to do it here."

"You're getting pretty damned bossy, aren't you?" said Jim angrily. "I could take off, you know. Then you wouldn't have a damned thing."

"Try it," said Polly coldly. "I'll follow you everywhere you go. I'll walk into every place you ever work and I'll camp on the doorstep of every tramp you ever take up with and I'll bring the kids with me. Go ahead. You'll see how long you keep a job or a whore then."

Twice, during the years they had lived in Cooper Station, the old magic worked for Jim and both times Polly got pregnant.

"I hate you," she told him savagely.

But most of all, she hated herself and the old weakness that came when he tried to touch her.

The Sheppards were a handsome, popular couple in Cooper

Station. Finally, Jim's firm agreed to let him make his head-quarters in Cooper Station since his clients in northern New England required more and more of his time. And soon after that a group of townspeople decided that he should run for the Town Board of Guardians, and Polly felt that she had truly arrived at her place in the world at last. To the eyes of Cooper Station, the Sheppards presented a solid, united front. One of the few who knew the truth of the whole situation was Lisa Pappas, and the only reason she knew was because Polly had told her.

Whenever Polly had needed someone to confide in, she had always gone to Lisa, and whenever Lisa had found herself in need of a helping hand she had turned to Polly. Now Lisa needed help again, and again it was Polly who stood beside her friend.

"She'll never get anywhere with her damned petition for a referendum," said Polly. "Even Doris Delaney Palmer isn't big enough to be able to argue with a signed contract."

"Oh, Polly, do you really think so?" asked Lisa, almost in tears. "I've been so sick over this thing. Surely, just because Chris quit one job we don't deserve to have this happen to us."

"You just cheer up, hear? Everything's going to work out fine."

"Everybody makes mistakes," said Lisa. "We made ours and Chris paid for it with a whole year at that damned State School."

"You're damned right everybody makes mistakes," agreed Polly, and because she was sometimes addicted to gossip she added, "I could tell you things about some people in this town that'd make your hair stand on end. No, very few people in Cooper Station have any business holding and kind of mistake against anyone."

"Like what?" asked Lisa.

"Not this morning, dear," said Polly and stood up. "I've got the kids coming home for lunch, then I've got to go to a meeting up at the Mills. But I'll try to stop in tomorrow. In the meantime, don't you worry about a thing. Everything's going to work out fine. I just have a feeling."

The days of spring began to lengthen and stretch themselves towards summer and they were long, long days for Lisa. The children, little Chris and Midget, were at school until four o'clock every afternoon and Chris seldom got home from Marmington before six in the evening. The gardener's cottage was small and easy to care for so that by ten o'clock in the morning Lisa's work was finished and the whole day loomed emptily before her. There seemed to be nothing to do except wait for the children and wait for Chris because, except for Polly, no one came to call on her and no one but Polly ever invited her anywhere. Lisa took to reading as she had done during the long years that Chris had been at the university, and almost every day now she sat in a lawn chair in front of the cottage and struggled her way through some of the books Chris had used in his literature courses at school. One Thursday morning she was sitting in her chair, reading, when all at once a shadow fell across the page. She looked up, startled, and Anthony Cooper was standing behind her. She had not seen him since the day she had moved in.

"You've got the damnedest hair," said Anthony. "It's really no colour at all and yet it has more life to it than any hair I've ever seen before."

"How did you get here?" demanded Lisa, jumping up from her chair. "I never heard you walk up behind me at all."

"On my little cat feet," said Anthony. "Come on, sit back down and let's see what you're reading today." He sat down on the grass next to her chair and took the book out of her hands. "Dostoevski, eh? That's pretty dry stuff on a day like this. Got any cold beer in your ice-box?"

"Yes, I have," said Lisa, still startled at the fact that the fabulous Anthony Cooper was sitting at her feet.

"Well, then, let's waste no time. Come on."

He took her hand and pulled her up on her feet.

"But it's only eleven o'clock in the morning," protested Lisa.

"Eleven o'clock or any other time," said Anthony, "if I'm going to explain the Russians to you, I'm going to need a cold beer in my hand."

"You don't think much of yourself, do you?" asked Lisa sarcastically.

"On the contrary, my dear," said Anthony as he led her into the cottage, "I think a great deal of myself."

And that was how it began. Every day Anthony Cooper came to Lisa's house and drank beer and talked to her about everything that came into his mind. Sometimes he stayed for only an hour but at other times he stayed until it was time for the children to come home from school and the only times he left abruptly were when Polly Sheppard came to visit Lisa. Then he said good-bye very carefully and walked down the curving pathway to his own house.

"Every time I come here lately," said Polly, "I trip over Anthony Cooper."

"He's wonderful," said Lisa, suddenly defensive for no reason at all. "He knows more about books than anyone I've ever met. Why, just listening to him is like taking a course in literature at the university."

"I'll bet," said Polly.

"What have you got against him anyway?" demanded Lisa.

"Nothing," said Polly, "except that he's getting you talked about. Just because this cottage is hidden from Smith Road, don't think that it's hidden from the eyes of Cooper Station."

"That's ridiculous," cried Lisa. "What's wrong in my having Anthony for a friend?"

"Nothing, except that the whole town is convinced that he's your lover," replied Polly.

"Well, he's not and he never will be," said Lisa, almost shouting with anger. "And as far as getting talked about in Cooper Station, it seems to me that there was plenty of that going on before Anthony ever stepped a foot into this house."

Polly shrugged. "I know how you feel," she said, "but you have to remember how things look, too. Every single morning Anthony troops into Gage's store and comes out with a bag full of beer bottles, then he heads right for this place like a damned homing pigeon. What do you expect people to think?"

"What do you think?" asked Lisa very quietly.

"I don't care if you sleep with every broken-down writer in the world," said Polly angrily. "You're my friend. All I ask is that you take care a little."

"Damn you!" cried Lisa. "I'm not sleeping with Anthony Cooper. I'm in love with my husband and believe me he's got more in bed than I could ever need or use. One man is too much for me, what the hell do you think I'd do with two of them?"

Polly sighed. "I know that," she said. "You know it and I suppose Chris knows it. But I know Cooper Station, too, and all I'm saying is that you're getting yourself talked about."

"Let them all talk," said Lisa. "Let Doris Palmer get up a petition to have me run out of town while she's at it. I don't care any more."

"You're not doing Chris's cause any good, you know," said Polly.

"To hell with Chris's cause," said Lisa. "Ever since I've been old enough I've had to cope with Chris's causes. First the God-damned university, then a job that didn't pay any money, then West Farrington, the Marmington and now Doris Palmer and her lousy petition. It seems to me that I should be allowed some-thing of my own once in a while."

"And Anthony Cooper is it?"

"For as long as he wants to be bothered to come here and talk to me," said Lisa. Then she added, "We don't even have con-versations, Polly. He just sits and talks *at* me."

Polly sighed again as she stood up to leave. "I was just trying to help," she said. "I hope you're not going to be mad at me."

"I'm not mad, Polly," said Lisa. "And I'm glad you stopped by. Come tomorrow if you can."

"Sure," said Polly, "if I can."

The next morning Anthony Cooper sat at Lisa's kitchen table holding his inevitable bottle of beer and talking about Bertrand Russell when all of a sudden Lisa looked down at his hands. They were long, slender-fingered hands, and with something that was almost a blow in her stomach Lisa began to wonder how they would feel against her bare skin. She stood up quickly and went to the refrigerator and took out a bottle of beer. As she uncapped it, Anthony stopped talking.

"What's this?" he asked in exaggerated surprise. "I thought you never drank beer and especially in the morning."

"I just felt like it today," said Lisa curtly.

"Your hands are shaking," observed Anthony.

"Well, so what?" demanded Lisa angrily. "I've seen yours shake plenty of times."

"Yes, you have," agreed Anthony. "But then I never get up without a hangover and I know damned well that you haven't got any such ailment as that."

"Why don't you just shut up and go home?" cried Lisa and slammed her beer bottle down on the table.

Anthony got up slowly and stood looking down at her. Then he circled her body and put his hands under the curve of her buttocks.

"The first thing I ever noticed about you is the way your behind moves when you walk," he said in the same conversational tone he used when he spoke of poets or philosophers. "There's sort of an up and down piston-like action to it that's the most exciting thing in the world."

It was only when Lisa tried to move backward, away from him, that he tightened his hold on her and when he bent to kiss her he was smiling.

"Get out of here!" cried Lisa, breaking away from him. "Get away from me and don't ever come back."

Anthony still smiled. "I'll be back," he said.

"If you come back I won't let you in," cried Lisa, "so just take your lousy beer and go drink it at your own house. Just don't come back here."

But he was back the next morning and he acted as if nothing had happened between them. He opened his bottle of beer and began talking about how he had felt when he finished writing his first novel.

"I imagine it was a little the way a woman must feel when she is finally delivered of a child after a long and painful labour," he said.

Lisa tried to match his matter-of-fact attitude. "How would you be able to imagine such a thing?" she asked. "No man can possibly imagine what it's like."

"Then tell me," said Anthony and leaned back comfortably in his chair.

Lisa began to talk and too late she realized that she was speaking of one of the most intimate experiences a woman ever has and that the thought excited her and frightened her at the same time.

"I don't want to talk about it any more," she said abruptly.

"All right," said Anthony agreeably and went back to talking about his novel.

But Lisa could not stop the trembling inside her and now when Anthony pulled her gently to her feet she leaned against him and let him hold her.

"That bad, huh?" he asked.

"No," said Lisa. "Not really. I don't know what came over me. It wasn't all that bad and Doctor Cameron was wonderful to me."

"Was he very gentle with you, my darling?" asked Anthony against her hair.

"Oh, yes," said Lisa. "He was just wonderful. He kept trying not to hurt me. I could tell."

Anthony began to caress her back. "You like to be gentled, don't you, baby?" he asked softly.

Lisa leaned her whole weight against him with a feeling of such relief that she almost sobbed.

"Oh, yes," she sighed. "I love everything to be gentle and soft and nice."

He undressed her with great care and even when he carried her into the bedroom he was very careful not to jar her or to set her down too quickly. He held her for a long moment against his chest and kissed her with soft, gentle kisses that clung to her mouth. His touch on her body was the lightest she could ever imagine and it awakened every single nerve under her skin until she quivered and almost cried out. Now he was stroking her with a gentle, feathery touch and he breathed softly into her ear.

"Come on, baby," he whispered. "Come on, baby. Give it to me. Give it all to me."

And then it was as if his hand were a magnet and she made of some resistless material that could not help but be drawn up tighter and tighter against his touch.

"I can't stop!" she cried out. "I can't stop."

"Don't, baby," he whispered. "Don't try. Come to me."

She could feel the scream forming in her throat and still he would not stop and then it was too late.

111

He held her while she shivered afterwards and he kissed her cheek and her neck and smoothed back her hair.

"It was becoming too much," he laughed against her mouth. "I mean all those poets and philosophers and ancient Greeks. Now I can teach you about love."

He began to caress one of her breasts. "And I'll teach you, darling, I'll teach you everything."

9

PRACTICALLY everyone in Cooper Station took sides in the question of Christopher Pappas and for those who seemed to be hugging the middle of the road there were plenty of people to help convert them to one opinion or the other. Of course there were a few who started out on one side of the fence and then by strength of persuasion or force of out-and-out threat were soon convinced of the folly of their thinking. One of these was David Strong, who taught music appreciation at the Cooper Station high school and in addition gave private lessons at his home. David held out against the pressure of Doris Delaney Palmer's determination for almost a week and then he squeezed his temples in frustration and said:

"All right, Mrs. Palmer. All right. I'll sign your petition."

"Believe me, Mr. Strong," said Doris Palmer with her small smile, "you're doing the right thing. A man like you has stature in this community and I'm sure you'd never want it said that you approved of someone as undesirable as Christopher Pappas."

David often thought later that he would perhaps have been stronger with Doris if she hadn't put her extra pressure on him on a Friday. Fridays were always bad for David because on that day he gave five piano lessons in a row and when he was finished his nerves screamed and his head pounded with the sound of piano keys being manipulated by inexpert fingers.

Still and all, thought David, Friday or not, I shouldn't have

113

signed that petition. It's not right. I'm not that good a teacher myself that I should sit in judgment of another.

The courses in music appreciation which David taught at the Cooper Station high school were electives and he knew very well what most of the students thought and said.

"Snap course," they told each other. "An easy two credits."

They soon learned differently, though, thought David in satisfaction.

His examinations in music appreciation were no snap.

Then they swore. "Jesus! I took that damned thing for an easy two credits and now I'm flunking that lousy course!"

Clods, thought David. Each and every one of them, clods. They were almost as bad as the nitwits who took piano lessons. Almost, but not quite. Nobody could possibly be as bad as the frizzy-haired girls who looked at him with moist eyes and said, "Oh, Mr. Strong. How long do you think it'll be before I'll be able to play something pretty like *The Maiden's Prayer* or *The Lost Chord*?" Or the greasy-faced boys who had mothers who insisted that their darlings were loaded with talent and who said to David, "Look, Professor, I don't like this any more than you do but it's the only way I can get my allowance every week and you're being paid, so let's get it over with." No, thought David with a small shudder, nobody could be as bad as the ones who took piano lessons.

But perhaps it was because he wasn't much of a teacher that he had so much trouble while Pappas, he had heard, was a very good teacher who not only loved his work but who could instil the desire to learn in young people.

I shouldn't have signed that petition, thought David again. I'm nobody to hold a man's mistakes against him. I've made too many myself.

Then he gave himself a severe mental shake. Stop it, he commanded himself. It's Friday. No more piano lessons until Monday and tonight Mark is coming to visit. I've got to get busy and clean up this place. It looks like a sty. Damn it, right or wrong, I have to think of myself once in a while. Mrs. Palmer is a big influence in education here and if I hadn't signed her petition she might hold up my contract for next year. It isn't as if

114

one name more or less were going to change things.

David began to move about, picking up things and straightening out what he called his Studio.

But still, he thought, it wasn't right.

David Strong lived in a house owned by a woman named Valerie Rutgers on the north-east edge of Cooper Station. He lived there because he had a passion for Victorian architecture and Mrs. Rutger's house, which was painted dark red and trimmed with white gingerbread, was just about as Victorian as a house could be. It had a large, round room leading off the second floor and Val Rutgers called this room the Tower while David, who rented it from her, called it the Studio. Under the streetside windows in his room, David had a wide couch upholstered in dark-green raw silk and decorated with many small satin-covered pillows. He had a large refectory table in the centre of the room on which he kept copies of music and theatre magazines and two small brass ashtrays while the opposite side of the room was completely taken up with his Steinway concert grand piano, a gift from his father on the occasion of David's graduation from the Cincinnati Conservatory. On the wall over the piano were two small water-colours which had been done by a friend of David's in Paris. The Studio also held a glass-topped coffee table, three arm-chairs covered in chintz, a Capehart radio phonograph, a small red leatherette bar with shelves of bottles behind it and a fireplace with two brass candlesticks on the mantel and a pen-and-ink sketch of David on the wall above.

"He's got more junk in that room than a second-hand shop," Val Rutgers often told her friends. "But I'll say one thing for Mr. Strong. He keeps the place up good. Neat as a pin, he is."

And sometimes David himself waved a deprecating hand around the Studio and said, "We're a little cluttered here, but cosy, and that's what really counts."

There were some people in Cooper Station who thought that David Strong was a little peculiar. After all, it wasn't natural for a man to wear Cologne nor to polish his fingernails, even if he did use colourless polish, nor to be so finicky about his food.

"Peculiar, hell!" said others who were not so kind. "That guy's a fairy if I ever saw one."

115

"You're crazy," said David's defenders. "He's been living here in town since right after the war, and nobody ever heard of him doing anything out of the way."

"I'll vouch for that," said someone else in mincing exaggeration. "Heaven only knows, I've given him every chance in the world and he never tried anything fresh with me."

"Maybe you're just not his type, sweetness."

"Oh, stop that, you!"

"Well, I don't care what none of you say. As long as he keeps his hands on the piano and off anyone in Cooper Station, I say he's all right."

"You'll see!"

"And as far as that goes, it seems to me I heard a saying once. 'It takes one to know one'."

David, of course, knew that he was different from other people. His own mother had told him so many times, whenever anyone had laughed at him.

"Whenever people laugh at anyone, David," Mrs. Strong had said, "it's only to cover their own wicked envy of that person. Do not be disturbed, my dear. Just put your faith in God and everything will come your way."

So David knew that the people who ridiculed him were just so many boors and he went right on being careful of what he wore, how he smelled and what he ate. As far as eating went, he had to watch his diet because he had a nervous stomach. Even the Army doctors had admitted that when they classified him for limited service only during the war.

David enjoyed the years he spent stationed at an Air Force base in Brazil. As a second-lieutenant in charge of a special service group, it was his job to plan entertainment for the troops and to stage productions for the officers' club. It was warm in Brazil and David had developed a taste for South American music and had learned a smattering of Spanish and Portuguese. He also met people who understood him and he didn't want to come back to the United States when he was demobilized. But he came back, and, as he often told himself, here he was stuck in Cooper Station, a town with a complete disinterest in culture, and his nervous stomach had turned into a vicious case of ulcers. He knew he had ulcers even though that damned Jess Cameron argued that he hadn't.

"The X-rays show that you don't have a sign of an ulcer," Jess had told him. "But I warn you, if you keep on the way you're going, you soon will have. Is there something bothering you, David? I mean, something other than this constant worry about your stomach?"

"Please, Jess," David laughed and put up a protesting hand. "Don't try your psychosomatic theories on me. If you don't know what to do for me, just say so, and I'll find someone who does know."

His remark hadn't jarred Jess Cameron in the least. The doctor continued his insistent prying until David lost his temper completely and stamped out of Jess's office in an absolute rage. Jess didn't understand him any more than did anyone else in Cooper Station.

But even in a community as drab and rustic as this one, David was sometimes lucky enough to run across someone who was different, someone who did understand him. Someone like Mark Griffin. Mark had known instinctively how to talk to a sensitive soul like David.

"It's so peaceful here in your ivory tower, David," Mark said. "When you play things like that fugue, Davy, all the tenseness in me just flies away."

And David could talk to Mark. He could tell Mark anything and everything. Well, just about anything and everything. There were some things he would never tell anyone in spite of Jess Cameron and his nosiness.

"The smart thing to do, David," Jess had said, "if something is bothering you, is to get it off your chest."

"For heaven's sake, Jess, don't be so damned Freudian. The next thing I know, you'll be asking me about my sex life!"

"What about your sex life, David?" Jess had looked sharply at him. "Is that what's bothering you?"

"Well, *really*!"

"David, let me help you. I can't do anything for you if you won't let me."

"The only things you can do for me, Jess, are to give me

117

something for my stomach and then leave me to hell alone. I don't need anyone to go about prying into my past to find out whether or not I had a wretched childhood and the effect this has on me. When I feel the need, Jess, of a couch and a psychiatrist, I'll go out and find one."

And again David strode out of Jess's office in anger. He had read a little psychology himself, he thought angrily, and he certainly didn't need anyone like Jess Cameron to tell him that his childhood had been completely miserable. David just thanked God that he had been intelligent enough to rise above the influence of his parents. But sometimes, even now, his stomach knotted itself when he remembered how it had been.

David's father, Alan Strong, was a black-haired, black-browed giant of a man who had made a fortune with his acres of virgin pine in the state of Maine. When he started he had dealt in lumber exclusively and had built a small paper plant as a sideline, but as the years went by and lumbering in Maine became an industry of the past, the Strong Paper Products Company grew and spread. Alan Strong closed his sawmills and devoted himself to paper. He manufactured paper towels, cups, napkins, plates and other such small items and he grew enormously wealthy, but his greatest pride always remained the fact that he had started with nothing but a handsaw and the tall pine of Maine. He had always pushed the paper angle, though, and in the old days he used to go out to solicit orders himself and as he prospered he found himself going as far south as Boston to see prospective customers. That was how he met Julia Bancroft. He happened, one day, on to a small printing shop in Stuart Street and in the absence of the owner, Harold Bancroft, Alan spoke to Bancroft's daughter, Julia. As he spoke he watched the colour come and go in her pale cheeks and noticed the softness of her brown hair piled high on her head. He never saw the thinness of her lips nor the almost gaunt look of her cheekbones. He went back home but suddenly all the fun was gone from his life.

Alan Strong had been in the habit of going into town on Saturday nights with his men where he drank with the best of them and spent the hours after the saloons closed with one of the painted women who hung around the hotels during the logging season. It was his boast that he could make any whore alive yell "Uncle" before he was through with her and when this pleasure, too, lost its savour, Alan was surprised, worried and upset. The only time he seemed able to work up any enthusiasm about anything was just before he went to Boston on a selling trip. It took him three months to discover that what he wanted was a good woman to manage his house, bear his children and look after him. And then he began to court Julia Bancroft in earnest. He plied her with candy and flowers and loaned money to her father when the print shop seemed on the verge of bankruptcy. Gentleness settled in him for the first time when he noticed how tiny Julia's waist was. There were times, of course, when he wanted to plunge his hands into the wavy, brown mass of Julia's hair and kiss her until she became aware of the heat in him, but he controlled himself.

They were married in Boston and after a two-week trip to New York and Philadelphia, Alan brought his bride home to Berlinton. Within a month he realized that he had made the one big mistake of his life. At first, he had accepted Julia's reluctance as natural for a virgin, but before the month was gone he knew that he was married to a frigid stick of a woman who resented her marriage to an ignorant brute of a man who had dragged her from civilization to a wilderness of brawling men and loose women.

"If I had know then what I know now," was Julia's favourite prefacing remark.

"I thank God that my poor mother cannot see me now," said Julia damply.

"Filthy drunkard!" shouted Julia.

"Beast!" cried Julia on many a Saturday night.

They had been married for three years when David was born. During Julia's pregnancy she almost went out of her mind and drove Alan out of his, but when her time finally came, she kept him at her side during her entire labour. She clung to his hands with a fantastically strong grip and she screamed in terror when he tried to leave her. Alan saw his son born and he swore that he would never again be compelled to watch such a procedure. He never had sexual relations with Julia after that, and although she was thankful for this at first, there grew in her a terrible anger that she should be so ignored. She devoted the rest of her life to her son, David, and to the task of purging the father's blood from the veins of the boy. Towards her husband she maintained a cold courtesy and she called him Mr. Strong to the end of her days.

David was a timid, pallid boy addicted to chest colds. He was too delicate to attend school regularly so his mother tutored him herself and though his early education consisted almost entirely of Bible study, the child did learn to read. Later, he hid in his room and read books of every description which he borrowed secretly from the public library.

Julia was an ardent member of a sect called Christian Adventists which, unlike the Seventh Day Adventists with which they were confused by the uninitiated, celebrated Sunday on Sunday, a fact which they pointed out with great care. Julia was forever exhorting her son to "Repent, David, repent", and if, at times, the child wondered just what it was that he was to repent, his mother fixed him with such a stern and staring eye that myriad feelings of guilt churned in him until his mind fastened on some little act that he could be sorry for and then both mother and son were satisfied.

"Give your heart to Christ that you may be saved, David," said Julia.

And regularly, twice a week, once at the Wednesday evening prayer meeting and again at the Sunday evening service, David was the first to kneel at the altar rail and give his heart away.

The Christian Adventists would have screamed in outrage had anyone mentioned Freud and his theory of the sublimation of the sex urge to them. Yet, they practised a religion that was almost entirely composed of capitulation, submission and exaltation. In northern New England, the religious orgasms of these Christian Adventists outdid those of the uneducated Negroes from the swamps of Georgia, so much more fiery were their sermons, their hymns, their rolling about on the floor.

By the time he was seven years old, David Strong understood that he must always be on guard against the evil within him and although his father was to blame for this misfortune, he must pray for his father also. Sometimes Alan Strong was so filled with rage at the sight of his velvet-clad son that he would go out and get very drunk and then come home to shout obscenities at his wife and taunt David with vile names. The boy cowered when his father called him "Sissy" and "Pantywaist" and after these times David prayed harder than ever that his father might be saved.

When David was ten, his mother bought an upright piano and sent her son twice a week to a Miss Overstreet for lessons. In no time at all David could play hymns and when he was thirteen years old he was made organist at the Christian Adventist Church. Tears would fill his eyes and his heart beat as if it would burst whenever he heard the congregation rise behind him to sing.

David practised long hours on the upright piano in the Strong living-room and when Alan, fed up with eternal light, suggested a good, rollicking tune, David tried fixing him with the look that the Reverend Charles Parmenter sometimes turned on his congregation, a look full of pity for the sinner left unredeemed.

"And don't look at me with those Goddamned cow eyes!" yelled Alan

If Julia were close by, David dared to remonstrate with his father.

"It is sinful to take the name of the Lord in vain, Father," said David in a tone that matched his pitying look.

"Balls!" roared Alan and stamped out of the house.

Wherever Alan walked, his boots left little clods of mud on the immaculate floors and the sight of these, coupled with the sound of his father's heavy tread, filled David with a little kind of shivery thrill that he could not have explained.

By the time David was fifteen years old, Julia had made up her mind that her son had received a divine call to the ministry. He had the thin physique and the noble brow for it and his voice would no doubt register in a lower key as he grew older. At seventeen David left Berlinton to enter the Christian Adventist College in Illinois where he would begin his theological studies and where the course of his life was set for ever.

His trip to Preston, Illinois, was the first he had ever made without his mother, and he was lost and miserable. Julia had

121

engaged a room for him in a house run by the president of the Ladies' Circle of the Christian Adventist Church in Preston but even this woman, who was so like Julia in many ways, could not take Julia's place. David had never made friends easily and after a few rebuffs his fellow-students left him strictly alone. He cried into his pillow at night and actually became ill with homesickness, but his mother had told him that no matter what, he must stick with his divine calling, so David never complained. He studied hard and went out seldom.

One of the few places that David did frequent, however, was a small restaurant at the edge of town. Coffee was forbidden by his religion on the grounds that it was poisonous and that it was a sin to poison the Temple of the Soul, but David indulged himself in this one defection and comforted himself with the fact that when he drank coffee he could study better and that if he studied better he could become a minister that much faster. The restaurant to which David went was called "Sal's" and it was out of bounds for all Christian Adventist students. The administration at the college considered Sal's a hot-bed of vice, a place whose only customers were truck-drivers who smoked, danced, swore, and committed adultery every night of the week. David's stomach had churned the first few times he had ventured to Sal's, but after a few weeks his fear of discovery passed and he began to look forward to his trips across town.

Sal's daughter, Millie, worked as a waitress in the restaurant, and when Millie had no customers to take care of she often sat down in David's booth to talk with him. She was a big girl, with long yellow hair and very white teeth. She wore skirts that hugged her buttocks and her breasts seemed to be forever struggling against whatever material restrained them.

David coloured the truth a little whenever he talked to Millie. He made his divine call to the ministry sound rather like the vision of St. Paul and he was careful not to mention his mother to her. The fact that he was a divinely chosen minister of God enhanced David in Millie's eyes. He was different and therefore interesting.

Millie was the sort of girl for whom "reader identification" had been invented. No matter which magazine story she read, nor

122

what movie she saw. Millie immediately became the heroine of the piece. One day, when she had been forced to take refuge from the rain in Preston's public library, Millie came across a book that someone had left lying on one of the tables. It was an anthology of short stories and the first story in the book was W. Somerset Maugham's "Sadie Thompson".

Millie saw herself as a much more attractive version of Sadie Thompson than Maugham's plump-legged heroine and she set out to inspire David to convert her to religion.

David, unfortunately, had never read "Sadie Thompson". Here he was, still in his freshman year at school, and already had a potential convert.

He spent hours talking to Millie.

He pointed out to her the error of her ways with truck-drivers and other unsavoury characters. He shuddered when she related episodes from her life, most of them untrue, and he realized what a tremendous job it was going to be to save Millie. But even as she confessed her sins to him, her long hair falling on either side of her face, her breasts heaving with the passionate relief of telling all, David's feelings of horror and pity were mixed with one other emotion. It gave him a wonderful feeling of power to watch this girl whom he considered beautiful prostrate herself before him. He felt a surging thrill whenever he watched the tears form at the corners of her eyes and his finger-tips ached to place themselves on her bowed head.

"You must repent, Millie," he said. "There is no sin so great that the Lord will not forgive you."

Millie wept and David felt that the moment was at hand when Millie would throw herself on her knees and give her heart to Christ.

"I can't talk any more in here, David," Millie said.

And indeed she could not talk any more for she had run out of things to say. According to the story, David should have succumbed long ago to her charm.

The little punk, she thought, angry with disappointment. Who the hell does he think he is? He ain't human. He's dead.

"Come, then," intoned David in what he hoped was a ministerial voice.

He took her by the hand and led her out of the restaurant, but once they were outside it was Millie who took the initiative. She led him away from town and down a dirt road to the bank of a river. They found a place where the ground was flat and soft with pine needles and they sat down. Millie could hear the river flowing and she suddenly had a brilliant idea.

"I want you to baptize me, David," she said.

"Oh, I couldn't do that, Millie. I've not authority to baptize anyone."

"Yes, you can. Anybody can baptize anybody. It says so right in that Bible you gave me."

She was not sure that the Book said anything of the kind, but perhaps David also was not sure.

"Please, David," she said. "I'll do anything you say. I'll be good if you'll do it, David. Truly I will."

"But I can't, Millie. Besides, it wouldn't serve any purpose. You'd only have it to do over again when you join the Church."

"Please, David. I want so much to be good. Even if it doesn't count this time, I'd feel as though I were at least on the right path."

"All right," said David at last.

He walked to the edge of the water and took off his shoes and socks and decided that if he rolled up the legs of his trousers he could still wade in deeply enough to immerse Millie.

"David!" called Millie. "David, it's so dark. I can't see you. Come back!"

When David returned to where he had left her, he saw that she was on the ground.

"Oh, God!" he cried, suddenly frightened. "Millie, did you fall, Millie? Are you hurt?"

He knelt down on the ground next to her and in the next second she had swept both of her arms around his neck and was forcing his mouth down on to hers. At first, David was so dumbfounded that he could do nothing but remain as he was but when her lips opened and he felt her sharp teeth and probing tongue trying to force his mouth open, he tried desperately to break away from her. She was remarkably strong. Without moving her mouth she flung him on to his back and held him pinned to the ground while she pressed her naked body against him and then, to his horror, her powerful hands gripped his wrists and turned his hands palms upward so that they were filled with the soft, hot mass of her breasts. She writhed on him and little moans escaped the hot, wet mouth glued to his. David felt a terrible sickness rise in him. He had a sensation of drowning. He could not breathe and he struggled futilely with the panting creature who held him. He felt her clawing at his trousers and she squirmed as if she were trying to press him into the ground.

"Sonofabitch," she said through her teeth when his belt buckle would not yield.

She had to use both hands and in that moment David pushed for all he was worth and managed to roll her away from him. He staggered to his feet, gulping air in great, sobbing lungsful, and then he hung on to a tree and threw up and threw up and threw up.

David developed a serious chest cold and ran a high fever for days. When his cold was better he had such violent stomach upsets that he could not attend classes and every day he put off going to the head of the school to hand in his resignation. He tried to forget his experience with Millie, but the harder he tried the sharper-edged grew the images. Every time he looked down at his hands he felt the soft mushiness of her again, and his stomach tightened and quivered.

I shall have to leave here, thought David, I'll go right now to tell the dean that I must leave.

He dreaded the ordeal, *the questions that were sure to be asked*, but he forced himself to get up and dress. He was halfway to the school when he met the local telegraph boy.

Julia was dying.

David ran back to his room and packed his belongings, then he raced for the Boston train.

"Mother," he cried silently. "Wait until I get there. Don't go. Don't leave me. What shall I do if you go and leave me alone?"

But Julia was dead when David arrived in Berlinton.

"She had a stroke a week ago," said Alan Strong. "The doctor said it wouldn't do any good to send for you then. He thought she might get well, David, or at least live. He told me yesterday that if she had lived she would have been completely paralysed."

So, thought David, even as I lusted with whores and harlots my mother lay dying.

He could not excuse himself now on the grounds of innocence. The Lord knew well the secrets of his black heart even if David himself had tried to deny their existence. And He had struck him down with swift and just punishment for the wickedness of his soul.

"The Lord giveth," said David, "and the Lord taketh away. Blessed be the name of the Lord."

"Yeah," said Alan Strong.

Alan made the arrangements and everyone in Berlinton said it was the biggest, most impressive funeral the town had ever seen and that even when the mayor had died last year there weren't half as many flowers for him.

Through the years Alan and David had arrived at a sort of truce whereby, though they still detested one another, they could at least speak civilly together.

"Well, David. How's school?" asked Alan.

"I'm not going back," replied David.

"Why the hell not?" demanded Alan. "I thought you were so all fired set on getting to be a preacher."

"I've simply decided that I'm not fit for the ministry, Father."

"Well, that's fine," said Alan, and for the first time in his life he clapped his son on the back. "Now you can come into the office with me. It's a fitting thing that a man should have his son in business with him."

David winced and shrank from his father's touch; the Lord had not finished punishing him.

"What's the matter?" asked Alan. "Don't you want to come in with me?"

Thy will be done, thought David, and aloud he said to his father, "Of course I do."

During David's six weeks with the Strong Paper Products Company, Alan discovered that his son had neither the brain for figures, the tongue for salesmanship nor the back for labour. He gazed in disgust at the tall, thin boy who had always had the

126

look of a calf going to slaughter and his temper grew hot and exploded.

"Look here, you," said Alan, "for years I've watched you sit on your arse and pick your nose while your old lady tit-fed you and I'll be Goddamned if I'm going to have you underfoot any longer. Just what is it that would suit Your Royal Highness? Not the ministry again, I suppose, and you'd run my business into the ground in a year. Just what good *are* you? Just what in hell do you intend to do?"

David felt his stomach contract. He hated this man! Yet, there was always that odd sensation whenever he looked up at his giant of a father.

I know why he is a success, thought David. He has bullied and smashed his way through every obstacle. Nothing has been able to withstand him. Nor anyone. Not even my mother.

"I want to be a musician," whispered David at last. "A pianist."

"Jesus God!" roared his father.

David spent four years at the conservatory in Cincinnati. He met people whose ideas were incomprehensible to him and whose morals appalled him. But he had determined to try to learn from these people. He did not freeze now when a friendly overture was made but forced himself to respond. Now that the Kingdom of Heaven had been closed to him, he intended to become a citizen of the world. He sat in on bull sessions where his new friends conversed on every subject from communism to sex and, while he did not form a single idea of his own, he adopted those that appealed to him.

Roger Merritt, a second-year student who was also a pseudo-psychologist and had a fetish for four-letter words, set himself the task of "straightening out David, psychologically".

"Listen, Dave," said Roger. "These stomach upsets of yours are nothing more than a manifestation of sexual frustration. If you'd just go out and get yourself laid regularly you wouldn't spend so much of your time puking."

David had taken to smoking cigarettes which he inserted in a long, ebony holder. He had also cultivated the habit of looking at people through half-closed eyes since he was convinced that this gave him the aura of a thinker and of a man who considered every thought and attitude with great philosophical care.

"What would you say, Roger, if I were to tell you that I am a virgin?" asked David through a cloud of exhaled smoke.

"I'd say that you're either a liar, a complete damned fool or a fairy. One of the three."

"I am neither, Roger," said David. "I simply regard sex as a mere nothing and I shall always remain celibate."

"Horseshit," said Roger bluntly.

During the years that David spent in Cincinnati, there were a few women who became intrigued by him. In spite of his adopted mannerisms, he had an innocent expression that was apt to bring out the most violent maternal emotions in some female personalities, and besides, David was good company. He could talk about styles of dress and shades of make-up and nail polish. Several girls at the conservatory claimed that they never bought a new dress until after David Strong had seen and approved it.

"But that neckline, darling," David would say. "It's just not you."

Or,

"That colour is magnificent, my sweet. It does something for your skin."

Other women were piqued by what they termed David's oddness. He recoiled from their touch and at the first suggestion of a tender glance he ran like a jack rabbit.

"Maybe he really wants to be a monk instead of a pianist," they told each other.

"Maybe he had an unfortunate love affair and it turned him against women for all time."

"Maybe he's queer."

"No. If he were, we'd have heard it from some of the other boys."

Near the end of his senior year, David wrote Arthur Aronson of New York who prepared pianists for concert work and was granted an appointment. The week after graduation, David left for New York.

David played Franck's *Prelude, Chorale and Fugue for* Arthur

128

Aronson and he was sure that he had never played more brilliantly. When he had finished he sat quietly, his hands folded in his lap, and waited.

Arthur Aronson was small, round-shouldered, shrivelled, with hair the colour of skimmed milk. He stood up and went to the one window in the room. For many minutes he stood and looked down at the traffic below him and then he turned slowly to face David.

"You are a fine technician, Mr. Strong," he said. "But I should advise you to give up the idea of concert work. I do not believe that I can help you."

David swallowed against the sudden nausea that his stomach flung up violently into his throat.

"What do you mean?" he demanded when he could speak. "I've spent years at the piano. Do you mean to imply that I've learned nothing in those years?"

"I said that you are a fine technician, Mr. Strong," said the old man gently. "Never think of the years that you have put into your music as wasted. You are a very talented amateur. Being able to play will always be a source of pleasure to you. Perhaps you could teach."

David's voice went shrill. "Are these the verbal inanities that you are paid to utter?" he cried. "Is this what I came all the way to New York to hear? Tell me what you are thinking, sir! When I am ill, I go to a physician. When I want the answer to a question of fact, I go to a textbook. I came here for an opinion of my playing and you give me half-witted suggestions about teaching."

"I did not want to be cruel, Mr. Strong," said Arthur Aronson, his voice more gentle than ever. "However, if you demand a cruel but honest answer I can give you one. There is something missing in your playing, Mr. Strong. A depth of feeling, of understanding, which should be there but which is lacking and which, furthermore, I do not believe you will ever be able to achieve. Fine playing is a combination of craftsmanship and an extension of the pianist's personality. There is a lack in you, Mr. Strong, a shallowness that shows through your talent. I'm sorry, but I cannot help you."

129

David felt so ill that when he stood up he had to cling to the edge of the piano.

"Thank you, Mr. Aronson," he said quietly. "And please accept my apologies for my rudeness."

"Think no more of that," said the old man. "I'm used to the reactions of disappointment."

David straightened his shoulders. "I'll find it," he said. "I'll find this depth and understanding that you speak about and when I do, I'll come back."

"Please do, Mr. Strong," Arthur Aronson said. "I should be delighted to listen to you at any time."

"I'll go to Paris," said David. "I'll go for a year and I'll work very hard and then I'll be back."

"At any time, Mr. Strong," said Arthur Aronson with a little bow.

As David was leaving the studio it came to him, with just a little jolt way at the back of his mind, that still the Lord had not done with punishing him.

David did go to Paris that year but when he got there he neglected his work, learned to drink and tried very hard to become a Bohemian. He grew a beard and pretended to himself that he was an atheist. Then he met and became friendly with a young artist named Martin Mallory and they decided to share an apartment together.

David noticed Martin's little idiosyncrasies almost at once. The way Martin's hands caressed things, small pieces of pottery, soft materials. The way his eyes seemed to burn into David's in a way that David found disconcerting but rather pleasant. Whenever David undressed in the room, he could feel Martin's eyes on him, caressing, probing, and although this embarrassed David dreadfully and first he grew to love the sensation it gave him. He enjoyed, too, the way Martin made him lie down after hours at the piano and the way Martin rubbed his temples with strong, thin fingers. It excited him to know that he could make Martin miserable just by paying the most casual attention to other people and he loved the way Martin's eyes flashed fire during their frequent quarrels. After an argument, Martin would sulk for hours, a black frown on his face, until David apologized. A simple apology was never enough for either of them. David had to plead and beg.

"Please, Martin. Please. I'm sorry. It won't happen again."

Once, after they had both spent the evening drinking and David had deliberately ignored Martin for hours, Martin struck him. David fell to the floor, frightened at his own anticipation, and Martin whipped him with a leather belt. When it was over Martin stood over him and David, looking up, saw Martin's brutally clenched fists and noticed the way Martin's feet were planted squarely and firmly on the floor in an exact replica of the way David's father used to stand.

"Get up," said Martin and went to the door of the room and locked it. He stood with his back against the door and watched David get to his feet.

"Come here, David," said Martin.

David came back to America just before the war broke out in Europe. He took a job with a small dance band and he never spoke of his year in Paris. He remembered his stay there with self-loathing and disgust and he could make himself physically ill just by thinking of the name Martin Mallory. He had terrible nightmares in which he heard Martin's voice saying, "Come here, David," over and over and he could feel his unwilling legs propelling towards the gigantic, dark-haired figure that stood waiting for him with outstretched arms. And he had even more terrible dreams in which his mother appeared to him and stood with her hands folded, gazing at him in horror.

Then he would cry out, "It's not true, Mother. It's not true. He made me do it. I didn't want to. I hated him. He made me do it!"

But his mother continued to stand and stare at him, shaking her head, and when he tried to reach out to her she shrank back and faded away from him.

Then he had quiet, beautiful dreams in which he seemed to be lying on something warm and soft and he felt so at peace that he dreaded to wake. But when he did awake and remembered his dream, he turned cold and sick and hurried to the bathroom to vomit.

David never went back to play for Arthur Aronson, but when

the war was over and he was home again he decided to take the old man's advice about teaching. There was an opening at the Cooper Station high school for a music appreciation teacher and Arthur Everett approved his application and passed it on to the Town Board of Guardians. A few weeks later, David moved into Val Rutger's tower.

David had just finished his housework when there was a knock at the door of the studio.

"Mark!" said David. "Do come in. It's so good to see you."

"Hello, Davy."

Mark Griffin was tall and slender. He had blond hair and rather slanted eyes and a very red, full-lipped mouth.

"I've had a devastating day, Davy," said Mark who lived with his mother and never did anything more strenuous than bring up the old lady's breakfast tray and give her an occasional back rub. "Do put on some Bach and pour me a drink."

David's tenderness was almost tangible. "Of course, Mark," he said. "Now tell me. What in the world has happened to exhaust you this way?"

Mark began a recitation of his day from the moment of his arising to the last harried movement that had brought him to David's door.

"Well," said David, "I had my usual ghastly Friday, but made even ghastlier today by a little set-to with Doris Palmer. She wanted me to sign that damned petition for a referendum to reverse the Guardians' appointment of Christopher Pappas."

"And did you?"

"Of course. Believe me, after the day I put in I'd have done anything to keep that old harridan off my neck."

"Mother signed it, too," said Mark. "Of course, nobody asked me. Nobody ever does, but I'd have signed in a flash."

"You would?"

"Of course. Isn't this town full enough of wretched people without adding more? Good grief, the Pappases are the worst type of peasants and of course you've heard about her?"

"No, I haven't," said David. "I've never even met her."

132

"Well, I must say you're not missing much .She's just become Anthony Cooper's mistress, that's all."

"Not really?"

"It's all over town."

"Well," said David with a sigh, "that certainly makes me feel better. Here I was, thinking that Doris Palmer was being dreadfully unfair and all the time she had good and sufficient reason for not wanting those people here."

"Exactly," said Mark.

They began to talk of other things and the Bach played softly in the background. They drank whisky and soda and the room was very peaceful and softly lit.

"Did it ever occur to you, Davy, that we have something in common with many of the great of the world, you and I?" asked Mark.

"I don't quite follow you," said David. "What do you mean?"

Mark put his glass down on the coffee table and went to sit next to David on the couch.

"Why should we be ashamed and frustrate ourselves just because the world of so-called normal people is not ready to accept us?" asked Mark.

David sat very still. "I'm afraid that I don't understand you at all," he said.

Mark moved closer to David and put a gentle hand on his thigh.

"Poor Davy," he said, "did you think that I wouldn't find you here in Cooper Station? Our kind always find one another. That's what I meant by our having so much in common with the world's great, Davy. We, too, should be proud of our love and be able to forget the bigoted world outside, even as Wilde and Gide and the countless other great ones."

David jumped to his feet, sweeping Mark's hand away as he did so.

"You filthy pig!" he cried. "You've taken advantage of my hospitality and my friendship with nothing in the back of your mind but your own perverted, rotten desires. Let me tell you, I'm not like Wilde or Gide or you or anyone else like you. Now get out of here. Get out of my studio!"

133

David shook with rage and insult and he took Mark's jacket and flung it at him.

"Get out!" he shouted.

Mark was calm and white-faced. "David," he said, "why fight it? It's all right. I understand. I understand everything. You needn't keep up a front with me. Believe me, Davy, I can sympathize with the bad times you've had and I can understand the squelching of your desires and the frustration that follows. I went through the same ordeal myself before I developed enough honesty to admit what the matter was with me."

"You queer!" David screamed and tears began to pour down his face. "You fairy! You perverted sonofabitch! Get out of here and leave me alone!"

Mark's face had a carved look as he stood and looked at David.

"*You* calling *me* names, David?" he asked at last. "*You* calling *me* those horrible names? Who are you trying to fool, David? You're a homosexual and everyone in town knows it. Even the peasants who don't know the proper word for you realize that you're different. Even Jess Cameron trying to get you to admit it to yourself in the mistaken hope that he could help you. I realized that Jess knew as soon as you began telling me that he wouldn't treat your silly, non-existent ulcers."

"Shut up!" cried David. "Shut up and get out!"

"You should hear the way people talk about you, David," Mark went on in his cool, relentless voice. "Did you know that every parent with a son who studies with you tells him to be careful, to run right home and tell if you ever try to put one hand on one boy? Did you know that, David? And did you know that Nathaniel Cooper and Jim Sheppard know all about you and that the only reason your contract is ever renewed at all is that Doris Palmer is on your side? No wonder you signed her silly petition."

"If you don't get out, I'll throw you out," said David quietly.

"Oh, I'll go, David," said Mark and picked up his jacket. "But when you finally wake up and realize what you are, don't you dare come crawling back to me, begging me to take you. I'll spit in your face."

David stood for a long time in the centre of his studio after

134

Mark had gone, then he went to the piano and began to play softly.

He's mad, of course, thought David. Absolutely stark, raving mad. I'm not like that. I've never been like that. How could any-one possibly think such an evil thing of me?

But every note he struck echoed the same sound. Martin Mallory, said the music. Martin Mallory. Martin Mallory.

David's hands came down on the keys with a discordant crash.

10

"THE long, hot summer," said Anthony and stretched his naked body lazily against the rumpled sheets. "Your belly is damp, my love."

"So is your hand," murmured Lisa and moved languidly under his touch.

"What time is it?" he asked.

"Time for me to get up and go home," she replied.

They had taken to using Anthony's house for their days of talk and love-making not only because Lisa enjoyed the Cooper house more than her own but because now that it was summer there was an element of danger to the gardener's cottage. Chris had taken a job as a supervisor of summer activities at the State School but sometimes, when the weather turned unfavourable, he came home early, or the children, who attended a day camp run by the town, returned at unexpected times. Then Lisa, hearing Chris's car or the day camp bus, would stand up and go to one of the windows in Anthony's bedroom. She would stand behind the curtain and watch her family.

"Why don't I feel rotten and dirty?" she asked Anthony. "I should, you know. I'm being unfaithful to my husband and a bad mother to my children. I should feel like a tramp but I don't. I wonder why."

Anthony came to stand at the back of her and his hands caressed her naked behind.

"Because I've taught you not to," he told her.

Anthony had taught her well. In the beginning, after the first time, he had refused to rush things. He had wooed her slowly, building up a sensuality and a need in her as great as his own. During the first three weeks of their relationship, he did nothing but touch her and caress her, arousing her to unbelievable heights of passion. He taught her, too, to be proud rather than ashamed of her body. He made her stand in front of the full-length mirror in his bedroom and then he stood behind her.

"You're beautiful," he said. "And you should enjoy the fact."

Lisa stood in front of the mirror and watched his hands on her body and later she could not remember whether it had been the sight or the way he touched her but she was overwhelmed with a sudden need for him. She turned and pressed against him.

"Do it to me," she said. "Now."

But even then, Anthony went slowly and carefully, waiting until she hovered at the edge of the chasm of ecstasy before he took her.

When it was over he held her and caressed her gently.

"You have the makings of a fine little animal," he said.

In the weeks that followed, he used and abused her body. He taught her everything that his years and his worldliness had taught him. And Lisa, of course, did the unfortunate thing. She fell in love with him.

"I love you," she said. She said it against his mouth and against his body and she said it when he touched her.

"You're a nut," he told her gently. You're in love with sex and that kind of love isn't the right kind. Come September and I'll be going back to the city and you'll go back to being a dutiful wife who is in love with her husband. This is fun. It's wonderful and exciting but it isn't love."

"You're a beast," said Lisa and felt like crying. "Don't you love me just a little?"

"That is a question that a woman should never ask a man," said Anthony. "Come here."

"Sometimes I absolutely hate you," she said.

"Good," replied Anthony, reaching for her. "That's the way it should be."

"But haven't you ever been in love?" she asked.

"I've been too busy," he said. "Besides, I don't believe in love. It makes slaves of people and I love freedom."

"But aren't you ever going to get married and have a family?"

"Now you sound exactly like my Aunt Margery and my Uncle Nathaniel," he said. "No, I'm not going to marry. I'll go to my grave as the last of the Coopers and a good thing it will be."

"That's a dreadful way to talk about your own family," objected Lisa.

"Maybe, but I mean every word of it. Now will you please shut up and let me kiss you?"

The summer wore on, green and heavy with heat and moisture, and Doris Palmer had the names of twenty-five per cent of the voting population of Cooper Station on her petition.

"A tempest in a teapot," Anthony told Lisa. "And much ado about nothing and every other cliché in the world. This thing is a farce."

"Don't you care about anything?" demanded Lisa.

"Not particularly," replied Anthony.

"What in the world ever made you this way?" she asked.

"I was born this way," he said.

But it wasn't true. Anthony could remember well the jagged edges of too much feeling, of too much caring.

Anthony Cooper had been a bright child but a puzzling one to his family. Certainly neither his father nor his grandfather had ever understood him and if, sometimes, the child thought that he recognised a kinship of feeling with his Uncle Nathaniel, there had never been the time nor the opportunity to turn this feeling into friendship.

When Anthony had been taken to the mills as a child, he had not turned ill and feverish as Nathaniel had done. Anthony had looked and watched and been overcome with rage and pity. It had been hot that day, he remembered, and the windows of the factories were shut tight against the breeze that might snap the precious yarn or blow lint on the finished goods. The machinery thundered and over everything was the smell of oil. The men and women stood in front of their machines, drenched with sweat, and even as Anthony watched a woman staggered on her feet and fell fainting to the floor.

"Get her a drink of water," said Benjamin. "She'll snap right out of it."

Anthony looked up at his father. "Aren't you going to take her home?" he asked.

"Don't be silly," snapped Benjamin. "We can't afford to stop one spinning machine. She'll be all right in a minute."

Someone fetched a drink of water for the woman and in a few minutes someone else stood her on her feet and then she began to work again. She was pale and her hands shook, but she was working.

It's as if she were part of the machine, thought Anthony. As if she had been doing her job for such a long time that she had become part of the machine.

"Good girl, Annie," said Benjamin.

Her eyes had a sunken look and she smiled tiredly.

"You know me, Mr. Cooper," she said. "I'm tougher than I look."

"Tough girls are the only kind we can use here," said Benjamin and led his son on to watch the next operation.

Anthony watched and for no reason at all he thought of his new bicycle and of the big, airy bedroom in his father's house in Cooper Station.

As they were driving away from the factories, Benjamin looked back at the brick building.

"Some day you'll be running things here," he told his son. "The sooner you learn how the better."

"I don't want the mills," replied Anthony.

"What the hell do you mean?" demanded Benjamin. "What kind of way is that to talk?"

"If the mills were mine," said the child, "I'd close them all up and set everybody free."

"And I'd come back from wherever I was and give you a good swift kick in the arse," said Benjamin. "We've worked too hard at building up a business here for you to talk like that."

Anthony kept still but then and there he made up his mind

139

that he would never have anything to do with the factories at Cooper's Mills.

When Anthony was fifteen years old and living with his grandfather, a union organizer had come to Cooper's Mills. Ferguson Cooper yelled and stamped around the house for one whole day, and the next day he went to the factories and called his workers together.

"I hear tell," said the old man, "that there's been talk of making the mills into what's called a union shop. Well, that's up to you. Who am I to say that you can't gather to bargain collectively or whatever the hell it is? But I can tell you one thing. If I hear any more union talk in any of my mills, I'll close everything up and damn quick, too. Anybody who doesn't want to work here on my terms can pick up his pay at the office right now. That's all I've got to say."

The workers went back to their machines and as far as Anthony knew, there had never been any more union talk in his grandfather's factories.

"Grandpa," said Anthony. "They may be mill-hands but they have certain rights as human beings."

"Get the hell out of my sight," roared Ferguson. "Go sit in the woods and look at something. That's all you're good for anyway."

Anthony began to write that year. He wrote stories which he was sure were filled with great social significance and in which the hero was always an under-privileged, overworked mill-hand.

As he grew older, he watched the slow, inexorable pressure that was put on his uncle, Nathaniel, and he knew that Nathaniel hadn't a prayer against the old man. His uncle would go into the mills, like it or not, and because Nathaniel was cast in what Anthony called the true Cooper mould, he would not resist.

Freedom, thought Anthony. They'll never make a slave out of me.

By the time he was twenty, Anthony was selling short stories to the better magazines and by the time he was twenty-five he had written a novel which became an immediate best-seller. He had a penthouse apartment in New York and a different girl to amuse him every evening. Some of them fell in love with him and as soon as this happened Anthony dropped them from his list of friends.

"Freedom," he told them, "is the greatest gift given to man. I never intend to give mine up."

Marriage, to Anthony, meant Nathaniel and Margery Cooper. It meant the mills and, worst of all, it meant a child.

"Not for me," he said, often and decisively. "I'll be the last of the Coopers and I'll go out in a blaze of glory."

Nine years and three novels later, Anthony Cooper was in a private sanatorium in a town ninety miles from New York.

He had felt the breakdown coming but he had refused to give in to what he was sure was only weakness. He had known it first when he could no longer work. The typewriter seemed to be a huge, open-mouthed monster that would gobble up his very soul unless he kept away from it.

Let me alone! screamed Anthony silently. Le go of me!

For the first time in his life he began to drink heavily. He took drugs to make him sleep and others to wake him up. He could not eat and he began to feel as if the world were made of slime and he knew he was ill. But still he fought.

If I give in, he told himself, they'll put me in a hospital somewhere and I won't be able to get out.

He had terrible nightmares in which he dreamed that he was enclosed in a small space and that the people who surrounded him had never heard of the word freedom. He would wake up with the bed-sheets wrapped around his body in soggy imprisonment and it would take every bit of self-control he had to keep from screaming.

He remembered very little of his first weeks in the hospital and, as he said to his agent. Kent Purdom, it was a shame because he imagined that it would have made one hell of a good story.

"Don't try to be wise, Anthony," advised Purdom. "You're sick and you might as well face it.

"Nonsense," replied Anthony. "What I had was one hell of a good, smashing hangover. I'll be out of here by the end of the week."

But Anthony was no better at fooling himself than he was at fooling Kent Purdom or his doctor.

"You need a good rest," said the doctor. "You've spent so much of your life running that you're all worn out."

"Nonsense," said Anthony again, but when a nurse came to give him an injection he admitted to himself how he had been counting the time until she would arrive with the medicine that enabled him to shut off his head for a little while.

Anthony spent almost a whole year in the hospital and when he left it was with a number of ultimatums. No drinking, no late nights, as few women as possible and no work.

"You've got a few years left," said the doctor, "if you behave yourself."

"Why don't you just hand me a knife," said Anthony, "and I could finish myself off properly."

"If you don't do as we say," replied the doctor, "that's probably exactly the way you'll wind up and much sooner than need be. Good luck and don't come back to see us again."

"I won't," said Anthony. "I'm going home. Not that Cooper Station is any great Utopia, but at least it's dull there. No women, no liquor and no material. After a few months at home I'll be so Goddamned tranquil that I'll have to come back to the city to keep from going to the bughouse all over again."

And Cooper Station had been good for Anthony, he reflected. There was no pressure on him here. The days stretched ahead quiet and long and he even began to work on a novel that he had outlined a few years before. There was Lisa to amuse and excite him and as for drinking, a few bottle of beer were good for him. They relaxed his mind and sharpened his appetite. The summer that had seemed to be eternal and never-ending pressed on into August and, as Anthony said later, something had to happen to bitch it up.

Anthony stood very still in the middle of his living-room, and he listened very carefully as Lisa spoke and when she had finished every nerve in his body went towards making his voice cool and casual.

"I'll say this much for you, darling," he said as he opened an-

142

other can of beer. "You may be a headache at times, but you're never a bore."

He was trying very hard to keep from trembling and not doing a very good job of it and he turned his back to her so that she could see nothing of his face.

"Well, I must say, this is what is known as a pretty kettle of fish."

Lisa did not answer but sat still and watched him. It was the middle of August and only a few moments before she had told Anthony what she had been rehearsing in her mind all the previous night.

"You're not going to be the last of the Coopers after all," she had said. "I'm pregnant."

"How do you know it's mine?" demanded Anthony brutally.

"Because Chris hasn't touched me since it started with you."

"Don't give me that happy horseshit. He's sleeping in the same bed with you, for Christ's sake."

"It's your baby, Anthony. I wouldn't lie to you about this."

"Well, what are we going to do?" he asked a little hysterically.

"I don't know," replied Lisa.

"I have a friend in New York who knows a doctor. I'll call her tonight."

"You go to hell, Anthony," said Lisa. "If you think I'm going to have an abortion, you're crazy."

"Well, what else?"

"We could get married."

"Are you out of your mind?"

"No, I'm not. Of course there'd be a stink, but then, you always told me that you didn't mind shocking Cooper Station. anyway."

"I've got to think," said Anthony.

When she had gone, he sat for a long time and then he knew what he was going to do. He would go to see Doris Delaney Palmer. Perhaps he could be of some use in getting Chris and Lisa Pappas out of Cooper Station.

And in the gardener's cottage Lisa, too, was thinking. She had not been entirely truthful with Anthony. Chris had had intercourse with her twice during the weeks of her affair with Anthony

Cooper, and then she had pleaded pain and had said that she must go to see Jess Cameron.

Chris Pappas was not an unkind man.

"Maybe it's nerves," he offered. "All this foolishness about that damned petition and everything. You go see Jess anyway, but I'll bet it's just that you're all upset about Doris Palmer. Don't you worry, honey. She'll never get anywhere with her campaign. I've got that signed contract and there's nothing she can do about that."

Lisa sat at her kitchen table and her fingers drummed soundlessly against the Formica top.

It was just twice with Chris, she thought. It can't possibly be his baby. I know it belongs to Anthony.

But she knew that she did not know for sure and that if she went ahead and had the baby she would wonder for the rest of her life.

11

It was raining.

Margery Cooper sat in Robin's room rocking the cradle that
was the bed of the ten-year-old child. It was a large cradle, a bed
actually, with rockers where the legs should have been.

"Hush-a-bye, my baby, slumber time is coming soon," sang
Margery softly. "Lay your head upon my breast while Mammy
croons a tune. The darkies are humming, their banjoes are strum-
ming, soft and low."

The pretty room was very still. Its pale-blue walls soft in the
dim light.

"Hush-a-bye, my baby, slumber time is coming soon . . ."

Margery let her voice drift off.

The pale-blue walls had a dado of brightly coloured circus
animals. There was a light-blue rug on the floor and crisp white
curtains at the windows and all along one wall there were white-
painted shelves stacked with dolls and stuffed toys.

Perfect, remembered Margery. Everything was going to be
perfect for her baby.

In the cradle the child who slept there fitfully was truly ugly
to look upon. She had a short, broad skull, coarse black hair,
yellowish skin and slanted eyes. But the most terrible thing of all
was to see the child awake and to gaze into the emptiness of
those slanted eyes.

Margery Cooper looked away from her daughter and stared

out of the windows of the room. The summer rain fell heavily, as if they were going about a job they had been sent to do and meant to do it well. Water washed at every window-pane so that Margery could barely discern the shapes of the trees outside. Once Margery had loved the rains of summer falling in fruitful torrents to the waiting earth. But today she merely stared, unseeingly, at the blurred windows.

There were times when she felt that if she ever once let go of the tears that she kept dammed behind the wall of her self-control, they too, would fall like the summer rains, hard and unabatingly, to cover the earth. But her tears would not be fruitful drops to fall and enrich the soil. They would be salty and bitter and they would leave barrenness in their wake.

Margery turned and looked again at her daughter. Automatically her hand began its rocking and her voice picked up the lullaby.

"Hush-a-bye, my baby, slumber time is coming soon . . ."

"Why?" She asked silently as she had so often.

And the answer was always the same. Nobody knows.

But what shall I do?

There is nothing to be done.

"Hush-a-bye, my baby . . ."

Margery Cooper no longer asked her questions aloud. She went about the business of breathing, moving, living, as if there were really something in the world that mattered besides Robin.

Now her hand stopped its gentle pushing against the cradle, for the child slept soundly. She tucked a soft blanket around her and kissed her daughter's forehead.

"Sleep well, my darling," she said softly. "Sweet dreams."

Margery went quietly down the maroon-carpeted stairs of her house. It was going to be a long, long day and a longer evening. At seven o'clock there was going to be an emergency meeting of the Town Board of Guardians at which Doris Palmer, everyone knew, would present her petition for a referendum and ask that a date be set for a town meeting.

How ridiculous, thought Margery and sat down in one of the huge arm-chairs in her living-room. Who could possibly care about one school-teacher more or less? Nate seemed to care,

146

though. In fact, he had managed to work himself into quite a state about the whole thing. What in the world is the matter with me today? wondered Margery.

She could not seem to sit still and asked herself worriedly if she could possibly be coming down with something. In ten years Margery had never allowed herself to become ill even once. If she fell sick, who would look after Robin? Certainly Virgie was a help but she couldn't do everything alone and Nathaniel was worse than helpless around his own daughter. Jess Cameron? Margery shook her head. Jess was good and he meant well, but every time he was around Robin he began to nag Margery about putting the child into an institution.

"What will you do if you have another child? he had asked.

And Margery remembered her own words to the doctor.

"Are you crazy?" she had demanded. "Another child after Robin?"

"Lightning doesn't usually strike twice in the same place," Jess had said. "You can't save Robin, but another child might save you."

"Save me! What are you trying to say?"

"I'm trying to say that if you had another baby you might save your sanity and Nate's and your marriage."

"My mental state is in fine condition, Jess, and as for my marriage, it's fine, too."

"Margery, you might try it my way, you know. I wouldn't do anything to hurt you."

Margery sighed. "I know you wouldn't, Jess.

"There's a doctor I know," continued Jess. "He is a very good man, fine and kind and gentle, and his only child is like Robin. He's given his whole life to caring for children like yours and his. He has a home, a sort of school, where he cares for them. Margery, for your own sake as well as Robin's and Nate's, go to see him."

"All right," she said wearily. "If it'll make you and Nate happy, I'll go."

Margery had gone alone to see Jess's friend, Dr. Nathan Alter. The doctor showed her around the house and the school and explained everything to her in his soft, gentle voice.

It's true, Margery admitted to herself. Jess was right. Dr. Alter is a kind man.

The children, all so like Robin, came running to him, smiling as he walked across the lawns. They nuzzled against him, loving him. Margery saw a girl who seemed to be about twelve years old, playing on one of the walks. The child had a miniature broom and she was making awkward, hesitant sweeping motions at the ground.

"You see," said Dr. Alter. "Some of them *can* be taught!"

"Oh, yes, I know," said Margery. "One doctor told me that Robin would never walk, but I've taught her to walk. How long did it take you to teach that little girl how to play with the broom?"

"Five years," said the doctor proudly. "Notice, please."

He walked up to the girl.

"Hello, Marya?" he said gently.

The child dropped the broom and reached for the doctor. Patiently, so patiently, smilingly, he picked up the broom and held it out. Marya fixed her eyes on the broom, reached for it hesitatingly and then, with an air of heart-breaking concentration, she gripped the broom, held it in the correct position and began to make the sweeping motion.

"You see?" asked the doctor jubilantly. "You see how well she remembers?"

Five years, thought Margery and burst into tears. At once Marya dropped the broom and gazed at her. Slowly the child's eyes filled with great tears that spilled on to her cheeks.

"Please, please," begged the doctor. "Please, Mrs. Cooper. It upsets the children."

He went to Marya and turned the child away so that she could not see Margery. Instantly, Marya stopped crying and the doctor handed her the broom.

"Come, please," said Dr. Alter and led Margery rapidly down the walk towards the house.

When they were seated in his office again, he said, "Mrs. Cooper, Mongoloids, such as the ones we have here, are very sensitive to affection and they respond just as quickly to tears. You must learn this first, before anything else. We do not weep."

148

His voice softened. "It is not easy, Mrs. Cooper, to look at them and keep from weeping. But we must all learn. And you must also learn, in fact, you must come to believe that an institutionalized child is happier than one who remains with the parents. We love the children here, Mrs. Cooper, but we are also impersonal. We have taught ourselves to take our days off and our vacations, and we have learned to forget the children while we are away. But most of all, Mrs. Cooper, we have learned not to weep."

Margery stood up quickly. She was afraid that if she sat still any longer, listening to the doctor's calm, quiet voice, she would begin screaming.

"I'm sorry, Dr. Alter," she said rapidly. "But I could never bring myself to leave Robin here. You have a lovely place and I know you treat the children well, but I simply could not leave Robin here."

"What if you ever became pregnant again, Mrs. Cooper? What would you do with the second child?"

"In the first place," said Margery, "Mr. Cooper and I do not plan to have a second child. However, if it happened we would all manage together as best we could."

"I strongly advise you to abandon that latter idea, Mrs. Cooper," said the doctor. "Do you actually suppose that a normal child could grow up happily in a home with a child like Robin? Don't you understand that your tension and nervousness and concern with your first child would communicate itself to the second one and make him miserable? No, Mrs. Cooper, with Robin at home you would never be able to give a second child the love and attention that is his right."

Margery kept her eyes on her gloved hands.

"Then there won't be a second child," she said.

"And your husband?" asked the doctor.

"Robin comes first," said Margery.

"My dear," said Dr. Alter, "you are making a very grave mistake."

All the way back to Cooper Station, Margery remembered all too vividly the sights she had seen at Dr. Alter's school and she shuddered.

149

I'll teach her myself, she thought. I'll never send her away to a place like that. I'll teach her everything she needs to know and I'll do it alone.

And Margery tried. She tried with every grain of determination that was in her. She talked to Robin, sang to her, held her in her arms and rocked her. She spent long, long hours repeating one word, over and over again.

"Ma-ma."

She pressed the child's fingers to her lips so that Robin could feel the sound of the word.

"Ma-ma."

Robin looked at her mother with slanted, empty eyes and smiled. She rubbed against her mother's shoulder like a kitten seeking attention.

"Oh, please, darling," Margery begged. "Please try. Please listen. Ma-ma."

And Robin smiled.

Margery began to cry and immediately, the child, too, was weeping.

Margery grabbed her up and held her against her shoulder.

"I'm sorry, darling. I'm sorry. Please don't cry." She rocked back and forth in the chair and smoothed back the child's coarse hair. "Hush-a-bye, my baby, slumber time is coming soon. Hush, darling. I love you, darling. Hush. Hush."

The rain was letting up, Margery noticed vaguely. Then she stood and started back up the stairs to see if Robin still slept. From the window in the upstairs hall she saw Lisa Pappas run across the gravelled pathway and into Anthony Cooper's house.

I suppose it's true, thought Margery. What everybody is saying about her and Anthony. No wonder the town doesn't want her husband teaching here.

Even as Margery watched, the lights went on in Anthony's living-room and in the moment before he drew the drapes Margery saw Lisa standing in the middle of the room in sharp outline.

I wonder what they say to each other, thought Margery. Do they talk about everything, or do they just talk about love.

As if she could pierce the darkness and the curtains in the house across the street, Margery stared at the windows of Anthony's living-room.

Maybe he has his arms around her, thought Margery. Maybe now he's kissing her and whispering that he loves her. Nate used to do that.

Margery turned away and went into Robin's room.

A mistake, she was thinking. A very grave mistake.

And what of Nathaniel? How does he feel? It's been a long time since I wondered what Nate was feeling. I wonder if Lisa Pappas knows how Anthony feels about everything. Odd, the way I noticed Nate's eyes today. It's been a long time since I looked into his eyes at all. But when I left him earlier today to come upstairs to Robin, he had such a bleak look about him.

Margery walked to the cradle and looked at Robin, who still slept, and suddenly she was tired, achingly, painfully, bone tired. Her throat felt thick and her eyes burned.

The first thing you must learn, Mrs. Cooper she remembered, we do not weep.

She heard Nathaniel's car drive into the garage and a moment later the front door opened and closed softly.

Nate's always careful like that, she thought. He never makes a sharp noise that might wake Robin because he knows that it will hurt me.

And suddenly, with no warning, Margery Cooper's dam of self-control broke into a million pieces. Her tears came in a flood, pouring unbeautifully down her face. Her whole body ached with the pain of loosening and she ran out of Robin's room and down the stairs.

"Nate!" she screamed. "Nate! Where are you?"

Nate dropped his hat and brief-case and rushed with his arms outstretched to catch her while her voice, shrill and insane, filled the whole house. He could see Virgie, her wide, black face grey with fright, standing in the doorway, her hands twisting her white apron, her eyes watery.

"For God's sake, Virgie," roared Nate. "Don't just stand there. Get Jess, quickly!"

151

He saw Virgie turn and run to the telephone and he watched helplessly as she fumbled with the receiver.

"Come quick," said Virgie at last. "Mist' Cooper, he say come quick!"

Nate stood still in the hallway, holding Margery. He saw the pattern of the black and white parquet floor and he realized that he had never really seen it before. In the centre of the floor, surrounded by black and white squares, the parquet was arranged to depict a gigantic snowflake. How odd, he thought foolishly. A black and white snowflake.

Jess Cameron came rushing through the front door.

"Robin?" he asked quickly.

Nate was unable to speak but just stared dumbly at Jess while his big arms cradled Margery.

Jess dropped his black bag on the floor and took Margery away from Nate almost roughly.

"Go pour yourself a drink, Nate," he ordered. "A big one."

"Nate!" Margery screamed. "Nate, where are you?"

"It's all right, Margery," said Jess gently. "You're going to be all right."

Her eyes searched wildly and her hands pushed at Jess.

"Nate, where are you?" she screamed, and it was the cry of a child caught in a nightmare.

Jess carried her upstairs and put her down on her bed. His fingers found the vein in her arm and he injected the quick, merciful needle.

"Nate," she moaned. "Nate, I'm so tired. Where are you Nate? Where are you when I need you so?"

Nathaniel knelt beside his wife's bed.

"I'm right here, darling," he said. "I'm right here. Don't be frightened, darling. I'm right here."

Jess Cameron and Virgie, standing in the open doorway twisting her apron, heard him and realized that Nathaniel was speaking to his wife in the same soft croon with which Margery habitually spoke to Robin. There was something horrible about Nate's voice, something frightening, and at last Nate heard it himself and stopped.

Margery slept and Jess put his hands under Nate's armpits and raised him to his feet.

"Virgie," said Jess, "I want you to sit right here with Mrs. Cooper. If she wakes up, call me. I'll be downstairs with Mr. Cooper."

In the dark, chill library, Jess struck a match to the waiting paper and wood in the fireplace.

"Here, Nate," he said. "Sit down."

He poured brandy into two glasses and handed one to Nathaniel. "Drink it up, Nate," he said.

"What is it, Jess!" asked Nate. "What's happened to Margery?"

"She's tired," said Jess as calmly as he could. "She's tired in a way that you and I can't even begin to imagine. It's the kind of tired that is called a nervous breakdown and the only miracle I can think of is that it hasn't happened long before now." Jess sipped at his brandy and lit a cigarette. "I think that today all the strain that's been building up since Robin's birth is finally beginning to splinter in Margery. The time's come when you're going to have to make a choice, Nate. Robin or Margery. You're going to have to choose one because now it's going to be impossible for you to keep them both."

"But what shall I do?" asked Nate, and in spite of the fire and the brandy he could barely keep his teeth from chattering. "If I pack Robin off to some place or other, I'm afraid that it would finish Margery completely."

"If Robin stays, she will kill Margery," said Jess. "She's close to a complete breakdown now."

"What are we going to do?"

"I don't know," replied Jess. "Perhaps in a few days we'll be able to talk to Margery and when we do we are going to have to convince her that Robin must go."

Nate stared out of the window at the grey lines of rain.

"Is Margery going to get well, Jess?" he asked at last.

"I don't know," replied the doctor. "I hope so. I think she will, but I'm not sure."

"When will you be sure?"

"Maybe tonight, when she wakes up. Maybe not for several

153

days." Jess finished his drink. "I'll be back tonight and I'll send a nurse over from the hospital to look after Robin. You and Virgie will have to take turns with Margery. I don't want anyone strange around her right now."

That night, for the first time in years, Margery Cooper slept in her own bed instead of on a cot in Robin's room. Nate and Virgie undressed Margery and slipped a nightgown over her head, then Nate sat in a chair and held her while Virgie smoothed the sheets on the bed.

"I'll stay with her, Virgie," said Nate. "You go to bed now."

"I dunno, Mist' Cooper," said Virgie worriedly. "I dunno if that white gal gonna do all right with Robin and if she don't that jes' fret Miz' Marg'ry."

"She'll do all right, Virgie," said Nate. "You go to bed."

Nate put his wife to bed and then he undressed and lay next to her and Margery slept. Nate lay on his back and cradled her head on his shoulder and listened to her breathe.

Please, he prayed. Not Margery. Let Margery be all right and I'll never ask another favour as long as I live. Haven't You done enough? Can You hear me? Does even one word break through to You? Make Margery well.

He knew that she was awake when he felt her tears against his shoulder. He brushed her hair away from her face and tightened his arms around her and Margery began to sob. Nate had never heard a woman weep like this. It seemed to him that Margery was lost in a sea of tears and heaving sobs. She twisted against him and beat her clenched fists against the blankets and her cries were hoarse and jagged, and Nate could do nothing but hold her and try to soothe her.

For the first time in ten years the Cooper household did not function around Robin alone. Jess Cameron came every four hours to give Margery an injection and if the nurse who looked after Robin and could just as easily have given Margery her shots thought this peculiar, she said nothing. Her name was Iris Boulton and she had worked for Gordon long before Jess was out of medical school. She saw the extra gentleness in the way Jess touched Margery, the way his fingers smoothed her hair away from her forehead and the way he held her wrist so that it was

154

almost a caress when he took her pulse. Iris Boulton was sorry and she turned away when Jess looked at Margery for surely if there were anyone who deserved more than this, it was Jess Cameron. Margery turned her face away from Jess and wept.

"Do you think he hates me?" she sobbed. "Does he hate me, Jess?"

"Of course he doesn't hate you," replied Jess. "Nate loves you. Always has and always will."

"He's always been so kind, Jess, and I never took the time to be kind in return. I only had time for Robin."

"I know, Margery."

"But I love him, Jess. I've always loved him and I didn't stop after Robin. I just didn't have time any more, that's all."

Jess turned away from her and stood up. "I know," he said.

"I just lost my way," she said. "And for a while I forgot all about him, but I never stopped loving him."

"Why don't you tell him, Margery?" said Jess gently.

"I used to watch Lisa Pappas," Margery told Nate. "I was like a spy the way I watched her and Anthony, but I couldn't help it. I'd see her going into Anthony's house, or I'd watch him walking towards the cottage and I'd picture them together."

Nate laughed and held his wife close to him.

"I guess everybody in town has been watching Lisa and Anthony."

"Yes," said Margery, "except, you see, I couldn't make myself think that they were doing wrong. At first I told myself that it was terrible, the way she was carrying on her cheap little love affair right under the eyes of her husband and children, to say nothing of the whole town, but then I started thinking about love, and the whole thing didn't seem bad at all any more."

"You mean you think that Lisa and Anthony really loved each other and should have counted the world well lost if they'd been caught out?"

"Don't laugh at me, Nate," said Margery.

"I'm not laughing, darling," he said. "I was just thinking that you must be the only person in town to put a nice connotation on the Pappas mess."

"Whenever I watched them," Margery said wistfully, "I got to thinking how a lot of people just shove love away from them. Lisa and Anthony didn't push it away when it came to them. They hung on for all they were worth and said to hell with everything. It's more than I did, Nate, when things got bad for us."

Nate stroked her hair and kissed her temple. "That's not important now, dear," he said. "The only thing that's important is that you are well."

The tears began to run down Margery's cheeks as they did so easily these days.

"Sometimes I can't bear to think of it," she said. "All the years I wasted. I left you alone and you were so kind and gentle and patient."

"Don't cry, darling," said Nate. "And don't think about it any more. As you can see, I survived very nicely. I guess I knew all the time that you'd come back to me."

"Oh, Nate, honey, I've got so much to make up to you."

He put his fingertips to her lips. "Not a bit of it," he said softly. "All I want is for you to be well again and strong and happy."

"I'll be well, honey," she said, and her eyes began to grow heavy as the sedative began to work in her.

"Sleep now, darling," said Nate. "I'll be right here next to you all night long."

Margery sighed and drew closer to him and at last she slept.

12

"OH, the sonsofbitches!" cried Lisa Pappas. She threw her rain-coat on the floor and put her fists up to her temples. "Oh, the lousy, miserable sonsofbitches!"

Anthony leaned against the mantelpiece over the fireplace in his living-room and smoked with long, slow inhalations.

"So they sacked Chris, did they?" he asked.

"You're Goddamned right they did," said Lisa. "Sacked him and paid him off as if he were some stupid mill-hand."

"Well, I hate to say it," said Anthony. "But it's true. You can't win them all, Lisa."

"Oh, shut up," she yelled. "You sound just like some God-damned sanctimonious native."

"Where's Chris?" asked Anthony.

"He stayed behind to talk to Arthur Everett and some other men about a job," replied Lisa.

"Well, cheer up, darling," said Anthony. "People are always screaming for teachers. Chris shouldn't have any trouble."

"Oh, Anthony," wailed Lisa and threw herself against him. "It was dreadful."

Anthony circled her with one arm and carefully dropped his cigarette into the fireplace before he put his other arm around her.

"There there," he said. "It's all over now. Sit down and tell me about it. It couldn't have been as dreadful as all that.

But it had been. The auditorium at the high school had been jammed. Chris and Lisa came in late and sat together in the back row of the hall. Lisa felt as if every eye in the place were fixed on her but Chris sat back comfortably and merely waited. That afternoon he had had a talk with a man named Donald James who worked for the State Teachers' Association.

"Listen, Pappas," James had said. "How badly do you want to stay in Cooper Station?"

"Not badly at all," answered Chris. "As long as I can teach I don't care where I go."

"Well, there isn't a school superintendent in northern New England who hasn't heard about what this town is trying to pull on you. Since this thing started, we've had thirty-five inquiries about you, and there is one that's great. One town down in Massachusetts wants you for three levels of English at forty-five hundred a year."

"How come?" asked Chris suspiciously.

Donald James smiled. "There's nothing like a martyr, Pappas," he said. "Here's a town about to crucify you on the cross of public opinion and here's another town who says, 'No, wait. We are good, broad-minded people. We'll take him.' Makes them look damned good in the eyes of the rest of the world."

And now Christopher Pappas smiled.

"For forty-five hundred a year, I'll be any kind of martyr they want," he said.

"O.K.," said James. "Just take it easy tonight. Let the whole damned town do the talking. You just sit there and take it."

So Christopher Pappas leaned back in his seat and watched Doris Delaney Palmer mount the steps that led to the stage and he listened while a hush fell over the crowd.

"We are here this evening," said Doris Palmer in clear, hard tones, "to discuss whether or not a recent action by the majority of the Cooper Station Board of Guardians was or was not ill-advised."

The crowd moved a little, and murmured, and Lisa felt her face getting hot.

"As I am sure you are all aware," continued Doris, "one of the principal functions of the Board of Guardians is to protect the welfare of our children, their health, morals and education. If they fail in this duty, the townspeople may vote to reverse their action which they feel threatens the children's welfare."

In the front row of the auditorium, Polly Sheppard sat with her hands clenched tightly together.

Goddamn you, she thought savagely, Goddamn you to hell.

But it was another thought, one which she did not like to admit she had at all, that tortured Polly.

You may ruin Christopher Pappas, thought Polly, but you're not going to ruin Jim. I've worked too long and too hard at becoming someone in Cooper Station to have it all shot to hell for the sake of one school-teacher.

No, no, she told herself. I don't mean that at all. Lisa is my friend. I don't mean it at all.

But she did and she knew she did.

After all, Polly rationalized, it wasn't as if Lisa hadn't brought a good deal of this on herself what with her carrying on with Anthony Cooper right under everybody's nose.

Then Polly almost laughed out loud at herself. If everyone at Cooper Station who had ever "carried on" were to be run out of town, it wouldn't take long for Cooper Station to revert back to the forests from which it had sprung.

She glanced over at Jim, who sat next to Nathaniel Cooper, and the first thing she noticed about him, as she always had, was his head of thick, red-gold hair. But where once the sight had fascinated and intrigued her, it now angered and disgusted her. Jim and his damned attention-getting hair. It was the thing that had trapped her from the very beginning.

And now this! thought Polly angrily. I wish to hell I'd never heard of Chris and Lisa Pappas. If I hadn't mentioned him to Jim, he would never have suggested him to Arthur Everett and none of us would be in this mess now.

"However," Doris Delaney Palmer was saying, "we are prepared to deal with Mr. Pappas in all fairness. Not one of us is about to do an injustice to anyone else."

You sanctimonious old bitch, thought Jim Sheppard.

But he knew by now that he was not going to stand up and fight her in front of the whole town. If there was one thing Jim was not, as he put it, it was anyone's fool. He knew when he was licked. A few minutes before the town meeting in the anteroom, Doris had come to him.

"If you fight to keep Pappas," Doris had told Jim, "the town will reverse the board's decision and you know what chances you'll have at the next election."

"That still won't get you out of the fact that Chris Pappas has a signed contract."

"No. it won't," agreed Doris. "But it will get you off the Board of Guardians."

"What about Nate Cooper? I don't think he gives a damn one way or the other."

"Neither do I," said Doris. "But if you're as smart as you're supposed to be, there would be two of us with the town and there won't have to be a vote."

"Even if I agreed with you," said Jim, "I still don't see how we can get rid of Pappas now."

"We are going to offer him the three thousand dollars we would pay him to teach and we are going to offer it to him in public and in a lump sum."

"What if he won't take it?"

"He'll take it," said Doris with her little smile. "I know his kind."

"But are the townspeople going to stand for it?" asked Jim. "After all, it's three thousand dollars down the drain and the whole thing to do over again with a new teacher."

"The money isn't coming out of the town's funds," said Doris. "It's been donated by a private citizen."

"Who?"

"One, as they say, who prefers to remain nameless. Let's just say a Good Samaritan."

"Does Nate Cooper know?"

"No."

And it's probably a good thing that he doesn't, thought Doris. Old Honest Nate wouldn't like it a bit if he knew.

"So in all fairness to Mr. Pappas," Doris went on, "we are

160

prepared to buy his contract from him for the full three thousand dollars."

The crowd shuffled noisily and the murmuring grew louder and into distinct words and phrases.

"What are we paying him for?"

"But he hasn't worked for it."

"Jesus, that's a lot of money."

"Doesn't he know when he's not wanted?"

"Just let him get out of town."

Lisa's face flamed all over again as she related these scraps of overheard conversation to Anthony.

"Can you imagine it?" she demanded angrily. "Just paying him off like a stupid mill-hand."

Anthony opened a can of beer.

"And Chris accepted the money?"

"Of course," said Lisa. "What else could he do?"

"He could have demanded his rights," replied Anthony. "He could have insisted on his right to teach. He had a contract."

"I suppose that's what you would have done," flared Lisa.

"No," he said. "I don't think I would. I've never been the type for the noble gesture any more than Chris has."

Lisa was suddenly very angry.

"Leave Chris out of this," she said. "Who are you to talk about anyone else?"

"No one, my love," said Anthony. "No one at all."

"And don't call me your love," said Lisa. "You don't care about me and you never did. I was just somebody to spend the summer with. You don't even care about the baby."

"Oh, yes," said Anthony calmly. "The baby. Are you going to tell Chris about the baby?"

"He already knows," said Lisa.

A little prickle whispered across the back of Anthony's neck.

"He knows that you think it's mine?" he asked carefully.

Lisa looked at him with an expression that was almost a sneer.

"Don't worry, Anthony," she said. "Your secret is safe with me. It's only in books like the ones you write that people are so honest that they tell each other everything."

And my other secret is safe, too, thought Anthony and lit a cigarette so that part of his face was shielded from Lisa's gaze.

Anthony blew out smoke in a cloud and thanked God that he'd been smart enough to give Doris Delaney Palmer the three thousand dollars in cash.

"How do you know you can trust me with all this money?" Doris had asked coyly.

"Because you want Chris and Lisa Pappas out of Cooper Station almost as badly as I do," Anthony had replied.

But, of course, Doris Delaney Palmer was not the kind to let him off as easily as that.

"Why?" she had asked. "I thought you were rather fond of the Pappases. Well, Lisa Pappas anyway."

Anthony wanted to strike her. "Do you want the money or not?" he demanded.

"Well, of course we do," said Doris.

"Then take it and let there be an end to all this," said Anthony. "You have your reasons and I have mine."

Thank God it's over with, thought Anthony as he turned to face Lisa. They'll go away and I'll go back to New York and we'll all have escaped a mucky mess.

13

"WELL, thank God that's over with," Richard Strickland said to Jess Cameron the morning after the town meeting. "Now we can all go back to being what we were before. A nice, quiet community where nothing ever happens."

"Richard," said the doctor impatiently, "sometimes you are a complete fool."

Richard Strickland was shocked. "What's the matter with you, Jess?" he asked.

"Nothing," said Jess and walked off towards his house.

But later, that afternoon, after the last patient had left his office, Jess sat quietly, his chair tilted back into a patch of sunlight. He was nervous and restless and he not only knew why but also knew what he was going to do about it. He was going to go down to New York where he would get quickly and thoroughly drunk and sleep with a different whore every night. Then he would sober up and come home and perhaps then he could put up with himself and Cooper Station for another six months.

Jess Cameron was one of the few people he knew who could say that he had a completely happy, normal childhood. "If Jess Cameron ever turns into a Freudian mess," said Florence Strickland, who prided herself on the fact that she kept abreast of things, "he'll never be able to blame it on his parents. Amy

Cameron was a saint and although Gordon had his moments, he wasn't far behind her."

When Jess was small, his mother used to sing in the kitchen and she had always had time to answer questions and play games and draw pictures. She played Chopin waltzes on the piano and she laughed a lot. Jess could never remember having seen her angry and he had never heard her raise her voice.

"Gordon, dear," she would say to the husband who idolized her, "don't shout so. Tell me quietly. Tell me what happened."

Gordon Cameron was a big, heavy man with a moustache and a large head covered with grey hair. Jess could not remember the time when his father's hair had not been grey. Gordon Cameron could be any kind of man, depending on the patient he happened to be treating at the time. He could be gruff, gay, pleasant, mean, smiling, sneering or sympathetic as the situation demanded.

"You could have been an actor, Dad," said Jess. "How come you chose doctoring?"

Gordon looked sharply at his son.

He can really make his eyebrows beetle, thought the boy, delighted with this trick of his father's.

Gordon Cameron lit his pipe and sat down heavily, emitting his usual groan.

"God, it's enough to put a man in his grave, all this running around after babies and kids who swallow pins and men who get their arms caught in haying machines," said Gordon. He looked silently at his son for a long moment, then he said, "I guess I'm a doctor because there didn't seem to be anything else I wanted to be. A man's got to do something, and by that I don't mean just anything. He has to do something with his life that brings him a feeling of peace and happiness not only while he is doing it, but also when it is done. There was a philosopher once, French fellow if I remember right, who said something about every man having to cultivate his own garden. Get what I'm driving at?"

"I think so," said Jess, who did not really understand at all but who enjoyed the words his father used.

"The way I figure it," said Gordon, "I was put here on earth

164

for a bigger purpose than just taking up space. One day, when I was just a bit older than you are now, it came to me that the best reason for anyone being here at all is to help out the fellow who's here along with him, and the way that seemed best to me was doctoring. So here I am, cultivating my garden in my own way, the way that suits me best. Dragging babies into the world and chasing after damned fools who get careless."

Jess spoke with the impulse of the very young which is to please a beloved elder.

"I think I'll be a doctor, too," he said, and was surprised when his own words filled him with decision and a kind of peace.

"You just wait a while, boy, before you go deciding anything like that," said his father. "You've plenty of time."

But, excellent actor though he was, Gordon Cameron could not keep the look of happiness from flooding his eyes when his son spoke.

Jess finished his premedical course at the state university. In August, of the same year, his mother died.

Amy Cameron had been spending the summer at the family cottage on one of the northern lakes and one day she had taken her husband's sailboat and had gone out on the water, alone. She was caught in one of the heavy storms that come so quickly and furiously to northern New England in August, but she managed to pull up to one of the small islands in the lake to wait out the storm. She reached home finally, safely and soaked to the skin. A few days later she confessed to Gordon over the telephone that she had managed to catch a rather heavy cold, but when he arrived at the lake the following week-end she had pneumonia and within three days she was dead.

In September, Jess left his suddenly old father in the very old Cameron house and went to Cambridge to enter the medical school at Harvard, and he wondered if it were really true, as he had heard Gordon tell so many patients, that time and work would eventually heal all pain.

Gordon Cameron was the first person Jess had ever seen who was the victim of a thorough, overwhelming loneliness, and he wondered what people who were younger, less strong and more

165

frightened than his father did in defence against the dictatorship of loneliness.

Jess's first year at Harvard brought him in contact for the first time with people who came from places in the world other than Cooper Station and northern New England, and at first he yearned for home with a yearning that was almost a sickness. Then he took up pipe-smoking and learned that the drink for a man to order was Scotch with plain water on the side and he went into Boston with a gang of his class-mates and was introduced to the Old Howard. He began to think that at twenty-one years of age it was about time some of what he termed his hickish rough edges began to smooth themselves out and he would not admit even to himself that pipe tobacco burned his tongue nor that he preferred mixing drinks nor that the strippers at the Old Howard were a bore with their flabby bellies and their dirty net bras. Finally, he met a girl.

"Lorraine," he repeated to himself when he was introduced to her. He rolled the name round on his tongue and liked the feel of it.

"Lorraine," he said to her. "It's a lovely name."

She was small, with masses of red hair and an upturned nose which Jess found fascinating. She had small pointed breasts and a tiny waist and her hips flared smoothly. She giggled. She *adored* things: Clark Gable, fried shrimp, musky perfumes, high-heeled shoes. She was a salesgirl at Jordan-Marsh and she lived in a three-room apartment which she shared with two other girls on Beacon Street.

"Beacon Street," said Lorraine. "Sounds elegant, doesn't it, Jess? You should see the place. A real dump."

"I'd like very much to see it," said Jess.

Lorraine giggled. "Not tonight," she said. "Kit and Eloise are double-dating with a couple of guys from B.U. and they're using the living-room."

In the weeks that followed Jess spent every moment he could spare away from classes with Lorraine. They went to the movies and ate at the Union Oyster House and walked in the Common. Jess took her to all the Harvard football games and his friends began to plague him with questions.

"Have you got to her yet, Jess?"

"Listen, Harkinson," replied Jess angrily, "I think you have a mind like a sewer. She's not that kind of girl."

"The hell, she isn't," said Harkinson. "A tart if I ever saw one."

"You go to hell."

"A pleasure, dear boy. A pleasure." Harkinson lifted his drink. "Here's to hell. May the stay there be as pleasant as the way there. Seriously, Jess, have you *tried* getting to her?"

"Seriously and for the last time, Harkinson, shut your Goddamned mouth. I'm in love with her."

Harkinson nodded. "That's good," he said. "A good, hot love affair will round out your first year at Harvard very nicely."

"I'm going to ask her to marry me," cried Jess who, until that moment, had never had any such intention.

Harkinson had been sitting in a tilted-back chair with his feet up on the table in front of him. The chair and Harkinson's feet hit the floor at the same moment.

"Oh, God," he said. "Oh, Jess! Listen here, old man, a little affair is one thing, but marriage——"

Jess stamped out of the room and the last thing he would have admitted to anyone was that there were times when Lorraine bored him to death. She chattered on and on about things that did not interest him, but he found that when he was away from her he missed her constant talk. Boston seemed an enormous place to him and he was lonely when he walked the streets by himself. All his friends had girls and being with Lorraine was far better than being alone.

It was winter. Jess and Lorraine sat in movie theatres and held hands, then they sat in restaurants where they drank hot chocolate and held hands. They walked in the snowy, deserted Common, shivering, and held hands.

"Of all the Goddamned foolishness!" said Harkinson. "Look, I'll fix you up with a hotel room. Then at least you'll be off the Goddamned streets."

As for Lorraine, Jess was a novelty to her. As she told her room-mates he was the first man she had ever gone out with who hadn't tried to get his hand down the front of her blouse on the very first date, but as the weeks passed and still Jess kept his distance from her Lorraine began to wonder if she left him cold, and in the end her curiosity became almost an obsession.

"Listen," she told Jess. "It's too cold to keep walking. I've got something at home that would keep us both warm. Brandy. Let's go to my place for a while. We could have a drink and sit where it's warm. Would you like to?"

"I'd like to very much," said Jess. "But won't your room-mates mind?"

"Kit and Eloise have gone skiing up to New Hampshire with their boy friends from B.U."

At the apartment, she took his coat and hung it up in the closet with her own and for some reason this gave Jess a warm feeling of belonging there, alone with Lorraine. They sat on her studio couch and drank brandy out of jelly glasses. The apartment was warm and quiet and suddenly there was nothing to talk about.

Jess could imagine Harkinson saying, "First of all, children, you must have the proper setting. Any deserted nook or cranny will do: parked car, graveyard, et cetera, but the most desirable is a quiet room, preferably one furnished with a comfortable bed or couch. Floors are hell on a bare behind." He was suddenly afraid for Lorraine. Suppose she were in a situation like this with a man like Harkinson.

"Lorraine, don't you have any parents to look after you?" he asked.

"They're dead," she said. "I've been on my own since I was sixteen."

"Oh. I'm sorry."

"Why?" she demanded. "They both drank and fought like cats and dogs. I'm better off this way."

Jess had never felt so sorry for anyone in his life. He put his empty glass down on the cluttered end table and Lorraine set hers down on the floor. Then she sat still, gazing into his eyes until finally he took her in his arms. A throat-closing desire to protect her overcame him so that he tightened his arms around her and felt hot tears behind his eyelids.

"I don't like the idea of you living alone like this," he said. "It could be dangerous, a young girl like you——"

"Crazy," she whispered against his lips. "My crazy, crazy Jess."

Her mouth was warm and very soft and her body was small and pliant against him. She let him press her down on the couch and her mouth opened under his insistent lips. Suddenly he wanted to crush her, cover her, smother her, and he made himself draw away, afraid of this strange desire to hurt and destroy.

"Don't pull away from me," she whispered. "Please, Jess, don't pull away from me."

And then it was everything, he thought. *Everything.*

The feel of her rigid nipple against his palm, the whisper of her clothes as she let them slide to the floor, the slim whiteness of her thighs and the way she moaned.

"Darling, darling, darling." Everything.

"Are you sure?" he whispered.

Instead of words she answered him by pressing her mouth against his shoulder and moving her legs against his and when she twisted her head from side to side and cried, "No. No, no, no," Jess clenched his teeth and hated himself for not sparing her this pain and then he thought of nothing and felt only the majestic thrill of taking this woman for his own.

Afterwards, she lay in his arms, shivering and weeping.

"Darling, I'm so sorry," he said. "Darling, don't cry. Please, darling I love you. We'll be married."

Lorraine stopped crying at once and lit a cigarette.

"All right, Jess," she said calmly.

She got up to pour more brandy and as she walked across the room, still naked, to Jess she was the most beautiful thing he had ever seen. She came back to him and they leaned back side by side on the couch and shared one lumpy pillow.

"Of course," said Jess, "it'll be a long time before I can support a wife. After I finish at Harvard I'll have to interne for two years."

"Then that makes five years in all, doesn't it?" asked Lorraine. "After this year, I mean."

"Yes," said Jess, frightened at the thought of so much time. He turned and put his lips against her throat. "But we can wait, can't we, darling?" he asked.

169

"But Jess," she said. "Suppose after tonight I found that I was going to have a baby?"

A baby. He could almost hear the sound of his hopes for the future shattering against a cold wall of fact. A baby!

He studied the pattern of white roses against the green background of the studio couch slip-cover. He reached out a finger and traced the outline of one fat, full-blown flower.

"Then I should have to give up the idea of finishing school," he said at last. "I'd have to get a job."

"But what about your father?" asked Lorraine. Wouldn't he take care of us?"

He turned and looked at her, astonished.

"I'd never ask him to do that," he said.

"Darling!" Her laughter rang out in the small room. "I *adore* you when you look so tragic." She stretched slowly, until her body formed an arc of whiteness. "You big silly. I won't have a baby. I was only teasing you."

"How do you know you won't?" asked Jess.

She stopped stretching and let herself relax with a sigh.

"Jess, darling, for a medical student you're awfully dumb," she said. "It's the wrong time of the month for me to get that way."

"Oh," said Jess stupidly.

He left her just as daylight began to show over the housetops and for some reason he felt rather like a character in a novel as he watched the roofs of Boston turn pink.

"Good-bye, darling," he said. "I love you. Sleep now, and I'll call you this afternoon."

He felt strong and powerful enough to walk all the way to Cambridge. He strode down Beacon Street, smiling, thinking of how wonderful it was to have a girl like Lorraine who adored him, who had given herself to him and who would marry him in five years.

Spring came too quickly. Jess was with Lorraine every day now, but he hated the thought of the approaching summer that would take him away from her. His grades began to suffer and he grew thin from lack of sleep.

"I never thought I'd actually live through a cliché," Harkinson said. "But here I am, watching you, Jess, dig yourself into a sweet little mess. And with a girl like Lorraine Jennings. Why, she's laid half of Harvard and all of B.U. and M.I.T."

Jess struck him on the mouth but Harkinson only shook his head sorrowfully.

"You poor bastard," he said.

Jess and Lorraine still sat in movie theatres and restaurants and held hands and once Jess took her to hear the Boston Symphony but she was bored before the programme was half over so they left and she took him to a place on Scollay Square where a stripper did tricks with tassels. Occasionally they went to her apartment.

"I *adore* you," said Lorraine.

"And I love you, darling," said Jess. "I love you enough to wait until after we're married. The first time was a mistake."

"Are you crazy?" she demanded, and then her voice softened when she saw his shocked expression. "Darling," she said, "I love you and I want you. I have to have you touch me, I love you so much. Listen, we'll be careful. It'll be all right."

Jess held her and kissed her until they were both breathless and he was sure that no one had ever felt as he did when he carried her to the couch and undressed her, when he made her pant and moan and cry out. He never realized how like clockwork were these exciting little tricks of Lorraine's, and he never tired of the things she said, time after time after time.

"I *adore* you," she said.

And, "Take me, darling. I belong to you."

And, "Darling, darling, darling."

"Won't it be wonderful when you're a doctor?" asked Lorraine. "Then you can set up an office in New York and we'll find a gorgeous apartment and go to night-clubs every night."

Jess laughed and rubbed her neck. "Doctors don't go to night-clubs every night," he said. "They go to bed early and sleep with one eye and both ears on the telephone. And I'd be out of place in New York. No, no big cities for me. I'm going in with my father."

"But, darling," she protested. "What would we *do* in that tiny little town of yours?"

She pouted in a fashion that Jess found adorable and he reached out a finger and touched her bottom lip.

"Do I have to tell you?" he grinned.

Suddenly it was June, and without warning Jess first, Lorraine quit her job at Jordan's and decided to go to Cape Cod to work at a summer hotel.

"I'll never get through the summer without you," said Jess.

"Well, you told me yourself that there was always plenty to do in that little old town of yours."

"Nothing is going to be any good without you," he said. "Will you write to me? Every single day?"

"Well, as often as I can," said Lorraine. "Waiting on tables is no picnic, you know."

"I know, darling," said Jess. "But it won't be much longer. After we're married you'll never have to work again."

"Five years," said Lorraine crossly. "By that time I'll be old and have wrinkles."

Sick with the prospect of loneliness and with a sense of foreboding, Jess boarded the train at North Station and went home. He looked around Cooper Station and thought, Damn, damn, damn.

The town seemed to have shrunk and everyone he saw seemed narrow and provincial and uninteresting and, worst of all, his father seemed very old and very tired.

Gordon Cameron grunted in earnest now when he sat down and Jess remembered sadly how he had used to be just a short while ago, when Amy Cameron had been alive.

Amy had laughed at Gordon's groaning. "I swear," she used to say, "you sound like an elephant every time you sit down."

"It'll be good to have you back when you finish your schooling," said Gordon to his son. "Not only to take the load off me, but this is one big house for a man alone."

"I've been meaning to talk to you about that, Dad," said Jess. "What would you think of my setting up an office of my own when I get through? I mean, an office away from here."

Gordon Cameron kept his voice carefully casual.

"Got any special place in mind, Jess?" he asked.

"Oh, I don't really know. I thought Boston, maybe. Or New York."

"Well, son, that's up to you," said Gordon. "You have a few more years to go before you have to decide. Personally, I can't see you practising in the city. Patients are just sick bodies to a big-city doctor. Up here, they're people. People I know by name and background. People whose fathers I've known and whose kids I know."

"Besides," said Jess, arguing with himself. "There's no money in being a general practitioner up around here."

"Jess," said Gordon, "this is going to sound hickish as hell to you, but believe me, boy, there's a lot more to doctoring than the money you get."

"The money you more often don't get," said Jess. "Why, if everybody who owed you money paid up tomorrow you'd be richer than the Coopers."

Gordon smiled. "Well, we never starved, you and your mother and I," he said.

"Oh, it's not just the money," said Jess. "A man is so limited here. I'll bet there isn't a bigger group of narrow-minded people anywhere in the world than the one we have right here in Cooper Station."

"What do you mean, 'narrow-minded'?" asked Gordon.

It was a question that always induced a long-winded tirade and now Gordon Cameron only half listened to his son. The boy would not say anything that the doctor had not heard many times before from every townsman who had lived away from Cooper Station for a little while. Gordon worked hard to keep the worry from showing in his face, for he had been watching his son. He had seen him mooning around the house, kicking at the furniture for no reason at all and haunting the area around the mailbox twice a day. Gordon Cameron was afraid.

". . . and another thing," Jess was saying. "Of course this is just an example, but just supposing I got friendly with a girl here in Cooper Station——"

Gordon Cameron sat up a little straighter.

"Here in Cooper Station," said Jess, "if a man dates a girl

more than three times it follows that he's sleeping with her and people talk about him over every supper table in town. And when you come right down to it, it's only natural, isn't it? I mean, the natural step after falling in love is for a man to want the girl physically."

Jess had been speaking very rapidly and now he paused for breath. Gordon made a superhuman effort to keep his face empty of amazement, amusement and pity.

"I think you've got things a little twisted there, Jess," said Gordon. "Most often what a man feels for a woman is physical first and then later, sometimes, it turns to love."

"If that's true," said Jess angrily, "then men are no better than animals."

"What's the matter, son?" Gordon Cameron asked gently. "You suffering from an attack of conscience?"

"Oh, Dad," said Jess miserably and began to tell his father.

Gordon listened intently to his son's low voice.

So we failed after all, Amy and I, thought Gordon. We kept him sheltered and happy and close to us and this is the result. We told ourselves that he was the only child we had so it wasn't wrong to keep him so close and to enjoy his growing up. Now Jess is paying for all our years of enjoyment, because I forgot what it was like to be young and away from home and lonely. Oh, Christ.

"She said she'd wait until I was through school and that we'd be married," Jess was saying.

Gordon Cameron wanted to weep for his son.

I used to be amused, he thought, when Jess listened so intently to our man-to-man talks. With me doing all the talking, I guess. I taught him all about love and consideration and honour, and Jess got the idea that every woman in the world was going to be just like Amy.

"She hates small towns," said Jess. "She wants to live in the city. She said she'd write as often as she could, but it's been more than two weeks now."

My son, my son, thought Gordon.

"Perhaps she's ill," he offered. "Why don't you drive down there and find out?"

174

But the next day there was a letter for Jess at last and his fingers were numb as he fumbled with the envelope.

"Dear Jess," he read, "I guess this will come as kind of a surprise to you seeing as how we were so friendly and all while I lived in Boston. Well, Jess, I'm married. I guess it's best to tell you right out straight like that. I met him the very first day I came up here to the Cape. He's a salesman and sells restaurant equipment and he makes very good money at it. Honest, Jess, he just swept me off my feet and I guess I did the same to him. Anyhow, we got married last week and I have quit my job. We are going to live in Boston and have already found an adorable apartment. Well, Jess, I guess that's all I've got to say except that I'm sorry about the way things turned out between us. I guess we were both lonely before and mistook friendship for love. Anyhow, I hope we'll always stay good friends. My married name is Mrs. Walter Paquette and I'm enclosing my new address in case you should want to write to me or stop by the apartment the next time you're in Boston. As always, Lorraine."

Hopelessly, Jess read the letter over three times, but the words remained the same. *Friendly*. Friendship for love. Friends. He and Lorraine just *friends*.

Jess sat in a wing chair in the living-room and waited for the pain to start. It came. It came in great black waves when he thought of his Lorraine in another man's arms, when he thought of her mouth against another man's mouth, saying, "Darling, darling, darling." He was sure that he would die, and he jumped from his chair and began to pace the floor. Then he went to his father's liquor cabinet and poured himself a large drink of bourbon and he pounded his fist against the door-frame.

How *could* she? Had she forgotten the nights that the two of them had spent in her apartment? Had she forgotten the plans they had made? Had she forgotten how much he loved her?

The answers came to him. Clear, precise and final. She had forgotten, or worse, she had never really cared in the first place. She had never loved him in the first place.

Jess stamped out of the house and began to walk. He walked for miles and came at last to a small hill that looked down on

Cooper Station and was isolated and protected all around by a circle of tall pines.

Never again, he vowed silently. I'll never let myself in for anything like this again.

"I'll never touch another woman as long as I live," Jess shouted to the cloudless sky. And his voice echoed back to him and he sat down and wept.

In the years that followed, Jess laughed at himself many times and to parents who complained to him about the behaviour of teen-age children he often said, "Don't worry. It passes. I was still an adolescent in my twenties, but I got over it."

It was almost true. As the years passed he became friendly and slept with and almost loved a great number of women, but something always stopped him at the brink of serious courtship. In the end he always found it easier to leave a woman than to face the possibility of spending a lifetime with her.

"You oughta get married," said Marie Fennell. "Ain't fittin' a man in your position and all. I remember your sainted mother. This house needs a woman."

Jess had known Marie all his life. Ever since he could remember she had come to help his mother with the house, and after Amy's death she came every day.

"Why don't you get married yourself, Marie?" he joked. "Fine-looking woman like you shouldn't have any trouble and maybe that'd put an end to your match-making tendencies."

Marie's eyes filled with tears.

"Marie, for God's sake, I was only kidding. What did I say to make you feel like this?"

Marie brushed her hand angrily across her eyes.

"Nothin', Doc," she said. "You didn't say nothin'. I'm just an old fool."

Marie was almost fifty now, with a tendency towards stoutness, but once she had been almost beautiful. She had been born Marie Johnson, the daughter of a dairy farmer who owned a farm three miles out of Cooper Station. Sometimes, Marie drank. Not enough to make her drunk. Just enough to blunt the edges of things and make life a little softer and pinker than it really was.

"I dunno when I begun wonderin' about other places, Doc,"

176

she once said to Jess. "Places outside of Cooper Station and the Mills, I mean. But I did. Didn't do me no good, though. I was the only one and I had to help Pa with the cows and Ma with the house. They was never much for galivantin'. Pa, he was happy to stay home after supper. He'd set there after he was done eatin' and read the paper and Ma, she set and read her Bible all the time after her first sick spell. But I used to go out on the porch at night. The stars was so big out there you felt like you could just reach up and grab yourself a whole bagful if you felt like it. I used to think I'd write poems about them stars some day. I went to school right up through the fourth grade but then Ma, she got took bad and after that I had to stay home with her. Your Pa looked after Ma. He was always good with her, makin' her laugh a little and easin' her pain and all. I guess I was sixteen before I started goin' out some. Yep. Sixteen. The year after Ma passed away. A whole bunch of us farm kids used to go around in Hap Elkin's old Model-A Ford, and I'm tellin' you, Doc, we had more fun in that old car than kids have today for all their shiny new convertibles. Pa, though, he'd have fits when I went off with Hap and the gang, but I didn't care none and as long as I stayed on helpin' him with the farm, he couldn't say much. Anyway, that was the year I met Conrad Fennell. I wasn't all fat the way I am now, Doc. I was slender like, with all my weight where it counted. My hair was long and black then, and Hap Elkins always used to say I had skin like cream. Anyway, we all went to a barn dance one night and that's where I met Conrad. He was playin' the cornet and right away he noticed me.

" 'What's you name, beautiful?' he says to me."

"And I says, 'Marie Johnson. What's your name?' "

" 'Conrad Fennell,' he says. Then he kinda bowed a little like and says, 'Miss Marie, your servant!' "

"Well, I'm tellin' you, Doc, I went for him right off. He was from Manchester and I only knew him two weeks when he asked me to get married. I thought Pa was gonna blow a fuse."

" 'Where's he come from and what's he do?'

" 'He's a cornet-playin' man from the city,' I said, thinkin' I might as well get that over with.

"Well, Pa, he was never much of a one for cussin' but he

cussed that night until I thought the air'd turn blue. Didn't do him no good, though. I married Conrad anyway, and we stayed right there on the farm so's I could keep on helpin' Pa. Conrad, he was supposed to help Pa, too, but he never did get the hang of anythin' like milkin' or the plantin' or nothin' like that. He used to set around the house, writin'. Writin' all the time. Stories, poems, music. Conrad, he could write all kindsa things. Well, Pa, he was about crazy. He said as how no self-respectin' man with a wife would set around the house all day and not work.

" ' Well, Pa,' I told him, 'Conrad is workin'. He's writin'.' "

"But Pa, he couldn't see how anybody could call settin' around writin' work and he and Conrad was always at it, arguin' and cussin' each other out. At night, though, it was different. After supper, me and Conrad'd go for walks. We'd walk up the hill behind the farm and set up there and Conrad, he'd tell me these poems he made up. And afterward we'd go into our room and lay there in the dark and he'd tell me stories. Oh, Doc, you can't begin to think of the stories he'd tell me. He'd tell me about places I'd never been and he'd tell me so plain I could see them right there in front of my eyes. Well, anyway, I guess we was three or four months married when I found out I was in the family way. Pa, he said that was the last straw and that Conrad was gonna have to start helpin' around the farm. And Conrad, he tried, Doc. Don't you think he didn't. His beautiful hands got all calloused and he was always sunburned. He tried and he tried hard but it was too much for him. Between Pa naggin' him all the time and the way I'd started gettin' heavy with the baby and all, it was just too much for him. He ran off one night. One night he told me a story and rubbed my back for me and after I was asleep he just ran off and I never saw him again. Well, Pa, he was good to me, I gotta give him that. He wouldn't let me do any work and he saw to it that I took care of myself and all. It was your Pa delivered little Ira. Named him Ira after Pa. I wanted to name him Conrad but if I had, Pa'd just have been more tore up than he was already and I didn't see no sense to that. I thought I was gonna die sure, for a while back there. It seemed like I was just hell bent on killin' myself with all the runnin' around I had done. Pa, he hired a woman to look after

178

little Ira and I went off to Cooper's Mills and got me a job. I had a room and a job and didn't lack none for attention, I can tell you. It's true I ran around and drank like a fish for a while. But it ain't true what some folks say about my whorin' around when I lived in Cooper's Mills. I ain't never whored around, Doc. I never took no money from nobody. Sometimes fellers'd give me presents and buy me a few drinks but that don't make a woman a whore. But you wanna know somethin', Doc? All that drinkin' and runnin' around didn't do no good. I still used to wonder about Conrad and sometimes, even now, I still do. I wonder where he went and if he's happy and if maybe sometimes he's sorry he went. I look at little Ira, and he ain't so little no more. He's graduatin' from high school next June and he looks just like his Pa. And I catch myself wonderin' if maybe things shouldn't've been different. Anyway, Doc, that's how come I don't look to get married again now and why I never did, even when I was still young. Once somebody's had the best there is, it's mighty hard to be satisfied with second best. Somehow I never got the hankerin' to try."

All the rest of his life, whenever Jess thought of loneliness, he thought first of his father whom loneliness had made old before his time, and of Marie, the butt of every unkind joke in Cooper Station.

Once, Jess had asked Marie, "What if you had it to do over again, Marie? Would you still marry Conrad Fennell?"

Marie had smiled sadly, the way she always did when she had had a few drinks.

"Sometimes I ain't quite sure, Doc," she said. "But most of the time I know I would."

"You mean you'd let yourself in for all that pain again? And for the loneliness and wondering?"

Marie shrugged and picked up a dustcloth. "It wa'nt all loneliness," she said. "I got plenty to remember and that's more than lots of folks've got."

The third person that Jess Cameron thought of when he thought of loneliness was a man named Philip Hastings whom he had known during the Second World War. But even when the war was long over, he still did not like to remember Philip Hastings.

Hastings is going to be the voice of my conscience for the rest of my life, thought Jess ruefully. Goddamn him.

Jess finished his interneship at the Mary Hitchcock Hospital in Hanover just in time to be drafted into the Army. He served four years with the Medical Corps, and spent almost three of those years on the islands of the Pacific. From the moment he received his commission and put on his uniform, Jess hated every single thing about the war. Even years later, he could not bear to talk of the waste, the terror, the helplessness of war and he could not understand the way old service men clung together when it was over, the way they sat around in bars and remembered the war, the way their eyes misted over as they remembered what the tones of their voices seemed to recall as the good old days. Jess never spoke of the broken and mutilated bodies and minds of men at war. He had patched, sewn, cut and bandaged and he knew he had done his job well. Except with Philip Hastings.

Philip Hastings had been a captain in the Infantry. He came from Detroit, Michigan, where he had a wife and two sons. He carried pictures of his family with him at all times and he showed them constantly to anyone who would take the time to look.

"The wife," he would say. "Her name's Gwenyth, but everyone calls her Gwen. That's my son Tommy there on the left. He's six, and believe me there are no flies on Tommy. Smart as a whip. Everybody says so. And that's my son Mike on the right. Three years old and a hellion. Believe me, if Mike doesn't grow up to be a fighter, I miss my guess."

Everybody got a charge out of Captain Hastings. He was the perfect picture of the typical American husband and father who had been doing well at his job, had minded his own business and had voted for Roosevelt. And here he was now. In the Infantry.

He was brought into the hospital with a broken arm.

"I don't know how the hell it could have happened," he said.

180

"I guess I landed wrong or something when I dived for my hole."

"Christ, what a mess," said Major Jess Cameron.

Jess fixed Philip Hastings's arm and then he arranged for the captain to spend several days at a rest area.

"You'll be out of it for a while," said Jess. "But you'll be back. See you around."

Exactly one week later, the captain was waiting for Jess in the hospital's small waiting-room.

"Well, Hastings," said Jess. "Welcome back. You're my first customer this morning. Come on in. How's the arm?"

"Listen, Major, I'm not here because of my arm," said Hastings.

"Oh?"

"No. Listen, Major," Hastings leaned forward and almost whispered. "I've got it."

"Got what, Hastings?" asked Jess a little impatiently. He was very tired.

"V.D.," replied the captain.

"Oh, for Christ's sake," said Jess. "A week out of the hospital, a cast on your arm and you manage to get into that kind of trouble. Are you sure?"

Captain Hastings put his head in his hands and burst into tears.

"Yes," he sobbed. "I'm sure. There was a girl back there, a Red Cross girl. Honest to God, Major, I never meant it to happen, I just wanted to talk to someone. I just wanted to talk to a woman."

"Hastings, pull yourself together," said Jess. "Red Cross girls don't usually have V.D. Come on in. We'll have a look."

"What am I going to do?" Hastings wept. "How will I ever face Gwen and the children, tainted the way I am now?"

"For God's sake, Hastings, shut up and hold out your arm."

The Wassermann was negative.

"Hastings, sometimes it takes a while before we can be sure of these things," said Jess. "I'm going to keep you here in the hospital for a few days and we'll see what develops."

"I'll never be able to go home again," cried Hastings. "Gwen will leave me and take the boys——"

"Will you stop blubbering," Jess snapped impatiently. "You

181

don't even know whether you have it or not. Come on, now. Go with the orderly and get into bed. You're just tired."

"Oh, God," moaned Hastings. "Oh, God, forgive me."

"What's with him, Major?" the orderly asked later. "A nut?"

"How the hell do I know?" said Jess. "Guilty conscience more likely."

Every morning Captain Hastings was waiting for Major Cameron.

"Major," he begged. "Help me. Listen, I've got it. You've got to do something."

A week later, Philip Hastings's Wassermann again proved negative and Jess's careful examination showed him to be free of anything below the belt save for a rather puckered appendectomy scar.

"Well, Hastings," said Jess. "Good news today. You're O.K. Clean as a whistle."

Captain Hastings stood with his shoulders bent and kept his eyes fixed on the floor.

"You don't have to worry about telling me the truth, Major," he said. "I can take it. I know I've got it."

Jess was tired. When he stopped to think of it, he could not remember a time when he had been as tired as he was now.

"Listen to me, Hastings," he said and stood directly in front of the captain. "You haven't got V.D. There's not a damned thing wrong with you. Except for that arm you could get the hell out of here this morning and go back to your outfit. Now stop bucking for a section eight and get the hell out of here. I've got work to do."

Philip Hastings just stood there with tears running down his cheeks and Jess supposed that there was something amusing about the conscience-stricken captain but he was too tired to laugh.

He'll get over it, thought Jess. He hates himself for sneaking a little bit of tail on the side, but he'll get over it. He'll go back to Detroit one day and start selling cars again and every time he has a fight with his wife he'll remember his little Red Cross girl with nothing but sweet memories.

But Captain Hastings did not get over it.

"Sir," an orderly complained. "Captain Hastings keeps on my arse all the time. Keeps begging me for penicillin. Pulls his rank on me and everything else. Tells me he's going to the Colonel, the General and to President Roosevelt if he had to because we won't help him."

Jess sighed with annoyance. "Put Hastings on the list of men going back to the general hospital," he said. "Maybe they'll have a psychiatrist there. In the meantime, give him shots of sterile water whenever he asks for penicillin and just keep him the hell out of my way."

The tiny hospital buzzed with talk about Captain Hastings. He was not sick nor really hurt and was, therefore, a welcome change from men with dirt-encrusted wounds and men who screamed for their mothers.

"Hear about Hastings?" the orderlies asked one another. "Shacked up with some broad back at the rest area and now he thinks he's got syph."

He's a riot to watch. Keeps swivelling his head around to look over his shoulder. Like his wife and kids were following him."

"A real nut, that one."

"Jungle jolly."

"Poor bastard."

"Just keep him the hell off my neck," said Jess Cameron. "I haven't time to wet-nurse him."

The night before Captain Hastings was scheduled to go back to the general hospital, he went into the latrine and put his revolver against his temple and blew his head off.

Jess Cameron met with his Colonel and together they decided what had to be done. Eventually, they sent Captain Hastings's things to his wife with a letter saying that while in the performance of his duty, the captain had been killed by a fall from a truck and all the reports ever filled out tallied exactly with the words read by Gwenyth Hastings.

"It's your arse and mine if we ever get caught," said the Colonel.

"I know," replied Jess.

"Can't have men knocking themselves off right under our noses, though," said the Colonel. "Looks bad. Besides, his family'll feel a lot better if they think he was killed in action."

"Yes," said Jess.

But afterwards, he couldn't get Philip Hastings out of his mind.

Your fault, Cameron, he thought. You could have saved him. A little time, a little kindness, that's all it would have taken. But I had no time, he argued silently with himself. And kindness? During a war kindness it time-consuming and I had no time. You killed him, Cameron. You might just as well have held the gun up to his head yourself. But I didn't know. I didn't realize that he was as sick as he was. O.K. O.K. Forget it. Forget it.

In July, 1945, Gordon Cameron dropped dead of a heart attack only minutes after he had finished delivering a baby in the Cooper Station hospital. By the time Jess heard of it on an island in the Pacific, his father had been buried for nearly a month. Richard Strickland's father, Joshua, had taken care of everything and when Jess finally returned home it was to a clean, well-ordered, empty house. There were fresh flowers in all the vases and milk in the refrigerator, but the first thing Jess noticed about the house was the single brass plate on the front door. He discovered later that after Gordon Cameron had died, the townspeople had formed a committee to remove the brass plate that had had two names lettered on it and to replace it with the one that now read, *Jess M. Cameron, M.D.* In the fashion of northern New England in general and Cooper Station in particular, neither Jess nor anyone else ever mentioned what had been done. But Jess knew that even without his father, the town still wanted him for its doctor, and the town knew that Jess would stay.

He started right in on his father's old schedule the day after he was discharged from the Army. He spent his mornings at the Cooper Station hospital and he had office hours between two and four every afternoon and from seven to nine o'clock every evening. By the time Jess had been home less than six months, it was as if he had never been away at all and the thought that he might ever leave Cooper Station was as ridiculous as the idea that someone might try to transplant the giant oaks that had been on his front lawn for over a hundred years. Jess worked hard and well and as the years passed he re-read many times the letter

184

that his father had written and left for him only a few weeks before he died.

"This is my town and they are my people," Gordon Cameron had written. "Please be good to them, Jess. Everything that has been said of them, is true, in part. They are sometimes narrow, vicious, cruel and very small-town indeed, but they are also loyal and once in a great while they will surprise you with their nobility. No matter how you find them, remember that most of them have belonged to me and I to them and that from birth your life has been interwoven with their lives. I know that you won't come back to us the same as you were when you left. War changes ideals and values but if I'm sure of anything, I'm sure that you will be able to find peace here and I know that you'll do a good job. The house is yours, of course. Jess, fill it for me with the laughter of my grandchildren."

Dr. Jess Cameron looked through the patch of sunlight that came through his window. He looked out across the wide, elm-shaded lawn that was his to the street beyond. The street, too, was his.

My town, my people, my arse, he said angrily silent. Then aloud he called, "Marie!"

She opened his office door quietly. "Yes, Doc?"

"Pack a couple of bags, will you, please? I'm going down to the city for a few days."

He got into his car and headed for the highway that would take him eventually, to the city of New York. As he passed the town line he glanced at the sign there that read, YOU ARE NOW LEAVING COOPER STATION. PLEASE COME AGAIN, and he almost snorted aloud.

The sign was another Cooper Station enigma. There might be no words of welcome at the entrances of the town but there were cordial words of farewell.

It's as if they were implying that it's all right to say good-bye nicely as long as you've managed to wangle your way into town in the first place, thought Jess sourly.

He wondered what his father would have said about Chris and Lisa Pappas and whether or not Gordon would still have claimed

185

to find the qualities of greatness and nobility which he had seen in his town. Would Gordon, like the great majority of Cooper Station, have been glad to be rid of the Pappases so that neither anyone nor anything any longer marred the calm surface of the town? Jess was not sure, for while Gordon had been a champion of right over wrong, he had also been a pacifist and he had loved Cooper Station second only to his wife and his son. And what would Gordon Cameron have thought of Lisa Pappas and Anthony Cooper?

"Infidelity," Jess remembered his father saying, "makes for nothing but guilt and unhappiness and anyone who goes in for it is a fool."

But what of loneliness? wondered Jess as he drove towards New York. Lisa thought she was in love with Chris because she was lonely. She got pregnant by him because she was lonely. And she was unfaithful to him because she was lonely. Jess remembered his father and his house the way they had been after Amy Cameron died, and he was sure that Gordon would have understood. Just as he had always understood about Marie Fennell and the way he would have understood about Philip Hastings. He would, perhaps, even have understood his son who rushed through the night towards the anonymous city, running from the fact that all his years of caution had failed to protect him from loneliness, because Jess had been in love with Margery Cooper from the first day that Nathaniel had brought her home. And, Cooper Station being what it was, there was nothing for a man like Jess Cameron to do but to run away and try to forget for a little while that he had not built his defences strong enough and that he was as vulnerable as anyone else after all.

186

14

THEN it was autumn. Not obviously, colourfully autumn, but autumn with just a little edge to the air in the morning and a sudden relief from humidity so that if you had been born in northern New England you knew, without actually seeing a change, the summer had passed. Autumn had come and Lisa and Chris were gone from Cooper Station and practically everybody said that it was just as if they had never come to town in the first place. There had been a little trouble and a few arguments over the Pappases but now they were gone and everything was just as it had always been. If people who had been friends for years had turned on each other over the question of Christopher Pappas, they mended their differences and there was nothing in the fabric of friendship to show that there had ever been a tear in it in the first place.

There was a new teacher at the high school by the name of Thomas Porterfield. Mr. Porterfield was married to a slightly buck-toothed woman who had been a teacher herself before her marriage and who, as Doris Delaney Palmer put it, certainly understood all the problems connected with teaching and living in a town like Cooper Station. The Porterfields were the parents of two children ages twelve and fifteen who had inherited their father's quiet ways and their mother's teeth.

"A nice family," said most of Cooper Station.

"There's nothing wild and irresponsible about Mr. Porterfield," said Doris Palmer. "He taught at the same school sixteen years before coming here and the only reason he wanted this job was to get his family out of the city."

"They're a nice, quiet family," said Callie Webster and rented a small house she owned down by the river to the Porterfields.

It was hard to imagine that Chris and Lisa had ever lived in Cooper Station at all. For a little while Christopher Pappas had been like a pebble tossed into the quiet waters of Cooper Station but eventually the pebble ripples had reached the outer edges of town and had disappeared from sight.

In the first days after Chris and Lisa had left Cooper Station, a little smile had hovered on Doris Delaney Palmer's face whenever she passed Anthony on the street and there had been a wise, all-knowing look in her eyes, and she had stopped him several times to impart news of the activities of the Board of Guardians to him.

"What the hell do I care whom you've hired to replace Pappas?" he had demanded.

And Doris Delaney Palmer smiled her little smile and said, "Do forgive me, Anthony, but I did think it mattered to you about who was teaching at our schools."

That was something else that annoyed Anthony. The way she had started calling him Anthony right after the Pappases had left town. It had always been Mr. Cooper before but suddenly he had become Anthony, her dear friend.

F—— you, dear Mrs. Palmer, thought Anthony whenever she spoke to him. But he was invariably courteous to her out loud, and what puzzled him was that he did not want to be. He wanted to tell her to go straight to hell and cut her dead on the street, but after the first time she had called him Anthony and said that she thought the teaching staff at the high school did matter to him, he had found himself tolerating her, even being nice to her, and every time he was more and more annoyed with himself.

Goddamned old bitch, he thought viciously whenever he had to speak to her.

"Tell me, Anthony," she had asked him chummily, "what do you think of David Strong?"

"I don't know as I've ever given David Strong any thought at all," Anthony had replied.

"Well, what I mean is, don't you think there's something a little queer about him?"

"Dear Mrs. Palmer," said Anthony, "I've never had the time to concern myself with other people's sex lives."

Doris's little smile was already on her mouth.

"No," she said, "I don't imagine you have."

Anthony made himself chuckle. "You are the discerning one, aren't you?" he asked, sickened with his own coy words.

"Not really," said Doris Palmer. "Adam says that I'm hopelessly naïve."

About as naïve as a two-bit whore on a fifty-dollar day, thought Anthony savagely, and smiled at Doris.

In his moments of honesty, Anthony admitted to himself that the only reason he tolerated Doris Delaney Palmer at all was to keep her from talking. He knew women of her type. All it would take would be a few innocent-sounding dropped hints and all of Cooper Station would be gossiping about Anthony. He could hear her now.

"We were lucky to get the money to pay off Christopher Pappas," she would say. "Thank heavens for the few generous public-spirited citizens we have left in Cooper Station."

"Oh, I'm sorry," she would say with that infuriating little smile of hers, "but I can't tell you who it was. I gave my word."

"Well, as you can imagine, it was someone with means," she would say. "Three thousand dollars isn't pin money to most people, you know."

Then Cooper Station would begin to wonder. It hadn't been Nathaniel Cooper, certainly, for he had fought to keep Pappas. Jim Sheppard didn't have that kind of money and if Doris

Delaney Palmer did, she wasn't about to part with a nickel of it. It was common knowledge in town that Doris Palmer would argue over the price of a pound of hamburger. Well, who *did* have three thousand dollars to throw away. Anthony Cooper? But why would Anthony Cooper want to get rid of the Pappases? He'd been having himself a time all summer with Lisa Pappas. Everybody knew it. Why pay to get rid of a good thing? Unless there was trouble. And if there was trouble, who was to make it? Christopher Pappas? Never. He was the prototype of all cuckolded husbands. The last to find out, if he ever found out at all. Then what kind of trouble? Trouble with a woman in Cooper Station meant one of three things: the husband had discovered his wife's infidelity, the wife had run off with her lover and abandoned her children or the woman was pregnant by the lover. And since it was obvious that neither of the first two was the truth, then it would follow that Lisa Pappas was pregnant with Anthony's child.

No, thought Anthony wearily, he'd keep on being polite to that bitch Doris Palmer. Just supposing the doctor was wrong and he wasn't going to die, he might want to settle down permanently in Cooper Station, and if and when he did, he wanted to do it in comfort and dignity, as the last of the Coopers, the heir to a decent name and a respectable fortune. He definitely did not want to become a legend.

"Anthony Cooper? Huh. Respectable enough now in his old age, but I remember when he was younger."

Anthony could hear the voices of the town and he kept right on putting up with Doris Palmer even while he laughed at himself and called himself the most improbable victim of blackmail on earth.

The thing that Anthony would never have admitted out loud, either in Cooper Station or with his circle of New York friends, was that he enjoyed being a Cooper of Cooper Station. Out loud, he scoffed often and openly.

"The Coopers?" he would say to whatever pretty woman he happened to be with. "Don't be impressed, my dear. A decadent lot, we are. My Uncle Nathaniel and my Aunt Margery stay up there in that big house of theirs, locked away from the world

190

and each other by their idiot child, and here I sit, drinking my life away and writing only to keep myself in liquor. Oh yes, I have to work for a living, you know. Textiles are dead in northern New England. Everything's moved down South except the Cooper Mills and they're losing money hand over fist."

He never mentioned that although the Cooper Mills were not what they had once been, the money that had been accumulated by his father and grandfather and wisely invested was more than enough to keep any future Coopers for all time and keep them very well.

"No," Anthony often said, "I'm the last of them and it's a good thing, too."

But Anthony enjoyed being a Cooper. He enjoyed being the young heir, the one Cooper who had gone away and made something of himself apart from the mills, and he enjoyed it when interviewers and book reviewers mentioned that he was of an old New England family, a respected, old, wealthy family, a family with roots and traditions and a name to be upheld.

Anthony didn't want Cooper Station saying, "The last of the Coopers? Don't be funny. Down country somewhere there's a Greek school-teacher's wife with a child by Anthony Cooper. That's where the last of the Coopers is. Not here."

Then a week after Lisa had gone, Anthony met Polly Sheppard on Benjamin Street.

"Hello, Anthony," she called from across the street in that high, carrying voice of hers. She crossed over to meet him, the same Polly who had been so cool towards him when Lisa had still been around.

"How are you, Anthony?" she asked, all smiles.

"I'm fine, Polly," he replied suspiciously. Ever since his first encounter with Doris Delaney Palmer after the Pappas incident, he had been suspicious of nearly everyone he met.

"Jim and I were talking about you just last night," said Polly.

I'll bet you were, thought Anthony bitterly.

"We were wondering if you'd like to come to dinner one evening next week," said Polly. "We're both terribly interested in writing, you know."

191

"Is that so?" said Anthony. God, how he hated people like her.

"Yes. When I was in college, I wrote a novel," said Polly and laughed out loud at herself. "I never did anything with it, though.

Oh, Christ, thought Anthony. The next thing I know she'll ask me to look it over for her and tell her what I really think. And to forestall her he asked her the question he'd really wanted to ask in the first place.

"Have you heard from Lisa?"

"As a matter of fact, I had a letter from her just the other day," said Polly.

Anthony waited, but she did not offer to tell him what Lisa had said.

"Poor little thing," said Polly. "It couldn't have been easy for her."

"What does that mean?" asked Anthony, annoyed almost beyond endurance with Polly's phony expression of sympathy.

"Well, the moving and all. Getting settled in a new place and Chris starting a new job and putting the children in school and everything. And, of course, feeling the way she does must have made it all the harder."

"What do you mean, feeling the way she does?" asked Anthony, and for the first time in his adult life he felt a twinge of concern for someone else.

"Why, she's sick for hours every single morning," said Polly. "It's been like that with every single baby she's carried. She gets morning sickness and there isn't a thing Jess could do."

"Why not?" demanded Anthony and felt a quick rage towards the doctor. "They've got cures for practically everything else."

"I know," said Polly. "And they've got some kind of drug for that, too, but it just doesn't take on Lisa."

And then, very slyly Anthony thought, Polly let him have it.

"You didn't seem surprised when I mentioned Lisa being pregnant," she said. "I didn't think she'd told anyone but me. Even Chris doesn't know, or at least he didn't when they left here."

Anthony could think of nothing to say, and Polly went on: "Will you come for dinner next Tuesday?" she asked. "I'd love to have you look at my novel. For kicks, I mean. You'll probably get a big laugh out of my scribbling."

"Yes," said Anthony, helplessly, "I'll come."

It was deadly. Jim Sheppard was a typical suburbanite.

"Have one of these!" he said, extending a glass towards Anthony. "Man, this'll put hair on your chest."

Anthony sipped his Martini.

"Ten to one," said Jim proudly.

They had roast beef for dinner and Anthony wondered if anyone in Cooper Station ever served anything to guests except roast beef, potatoes and green peas. The wine was a rosé that almost made him gag and when it was over Polly dragged out her bulky novel as if serving him up some rare dessert.

"I'll take it along home with me," said Anthony. "I'm too full of food to start in on it now."

Polly giggled. "I suppose you'll laugh your head off," she said. "I never showed it to anyone but Lisa, and Jim, of course, before we were married. Lisa liked it and said I ought to get it published, but I never bothered to try."

Again, Anthony felt the unfamiliar twinge.

What the hell is this? he thought.

But he didn't have a ready answer. He only knew that when he had thought of Lisa reading Polly's novel and trying to make deep remarks about it, he had felt a stab of pain. In a quick second he had seen her bent over the manuscript, her long hair falling across her face the way it did when she was preoccupied. And he remembered the way she nibbled at her thumbnail when she was reading.

I'll have to read this in a hurry, he thought, and then we'll have a good laugh over it.

And then the ache hurt him again and he thought, What am I thinking? Lisa and I are never going to laugh together about anything again.

"Of course, it isn't as if I took Lisa's comments seriously," Polly was saying, as if nothing could possibly have passed through Anthony's mind since she had last spoken. "Lisa was a sweet enough girl, but she was always reading beyond her depth."

193

Anthony felt his jaw clench as if the simple action would lock out memory and pain. He could remember Lisa with her forehead wrinkled a little, her fingers twisting a bit of her long hair.

"I don't know, Anthony," confessed Lisa. "Dostoevski is supposed to be a great writer and all that, so I guess there must be something wrong with me. He just doesn't reach me."

Anthony laughed. "What do you mean, he doesn't reach you?"

"Well, I just can't believe that life is all that sad and full of his kind of people. All grubby and futile and all that. Maybe all those Russians were like that. I tried to read Tolstoi once, and he was all sad and futile, too."

"I have to be going," said Anthony, and Jim Sheppard came to the door with him.

"Listen, Anthony," he said, "if you have to let Polly down about her book, do it as gently as you can, will you?"

"Sure, Jim," said Anthony and thought later that he would have said anything at that moment just to get away.

He went home and started to drink in earnest and after about an hour he began Polly Sheppard's novel. He finished it at two o'clock the next morning and was, as he put it, ready to commit suicide over the thought that anyone could string words together that badly. The novel was called *Pagan's Way* and it was full of bold, handsome men, and women with big breasts that were continually being handled by the flashing-eyed men who took a quick roll in bed and then were off to more feats of derring-do. Except that Polly Sheppard never came right out and said that. She was an asterisk writer and Anthony reflected that all that was missing was for Polly to have written the line about drawing a curtain of gentleness over the ensuing scene. But Lisa had liked it, just as she liked all novels full of sex and action and brave deeds.

My poor baby, thought Anthony and before he could stop himself he was weeping.

But the next morning he had his excuses ready. He'd become drunk, a lot drunker than he had thought, and he'd gotten maudlin over a dumb little broad whom he'd taught to be good

194

in bed. That was all there was to it and he'd make damned sure it didn't happen again.

Maybe I was a little in love with her for a while, he told himself. If you can call sex love. But that's long over and done with. So I had a little summer fun. There's no need to make a federal case out of it. It's over and she's gone and I'm damned lucky to have escaped as easily as I did.

He returned Polly's novel and told her exactly what he thought of it.

"It sounds like something an overly romantic college girl would write," he said unkindly. "For Christ's sake, Polly, burn this before anyone gets hold of it by mistake. It'd be terribly embarrassing."

Polly's face flushed angrily and Anthony laughed.

"What're you mad at me for?" he asked. "You said yourself you were giving it to me just for laughs. Well, I laughed all right. It was a riot."

"Lisa didn't laugh," said Polly and tried to laugh now herself. "She thought it was great."

"What does Lisa have to do with it?" demanded Anthony, angrier than he had been in a long, long time.

"Why, nothing," said Polly. "It's just that she's the only person I ever showed it to, except Jim, and he'd be prejudiced, of course. All I meant was that Lisa's was the only outside opinion I ever had about it. Uutil you. And of course, Lisa wouldn't count, really. She was never very bright. I mean, she was a sweet girl and all that, but she's never been anywhere of done anything."

The crafty, sly look came into Polly's eyes again, the look Anthony had seen there before, and the look he had seen in Doris Delaney Palmer's eyes.

"And now there she is, poor thing, pregnant again," said Polly with her false sympathy. "Now I don't imagine she'll ever get to go anywhere or do anything. She'll be more tied down than ever with a new baby coming."

Anthony longed to slap her face but he merely smiled.

"Oh yes," he said. "Lisa was dumb all right."

"I'll say," say Polly in a tone that seemed to imply that now that she and Anthony were in agreement about something, they were close friends. "If she hadn't been rather stupid she'd never have let herself be caught the way she did. Certainly she and Chris can't afford another baby."

"If Lisa hadn't been so dumb," Anthony went on as if Polly hadn't spoken, "she would have advised you to write about something you know."

They were alone in Polly's big, countrified kitchen, with its fireplace with a false Dutch oven and its wide-board floor. Anthony looked around and sipped at the beer Polly had given him when he had come in. He looked at Polly in her slacks and open-necked shirt, one leg flung casually over the arm of her chair. Phony, he thought. Phony Colonial house, phony country wife and phony friend.

"Why don't you write about some of the more interesting relationships between husbands and wives?" said Anthony.

Polly laughed. "I'm afraid I don't know much about things like that," she said. "I've always lived a rather insulated life as far as the grimier things are concerned."

"Oh, I don't know," said Anthony suavely. "Take infidelity, for instance. That would make interesting reading properly written up, of course."

He saw fear in her eyes and knew what she was thinking.

How much had Lisa Pappas told him?

"I don't know what you mean," protested Polly.

Anthony laughed out loud. "Polly Sheppard," he said, "you're a complete phony. You know Goddamned well what I'm talking about."

So Lisa had told him everything. Polly slammed her beer glass down on the kitchen table.

"I'm no phonier than you are," she said coldly. "You knew Lisa was gullible and you led her on, making her believe that you were in love with her, sleeping with her, even getting her pregnant. Oh, yes," said Polly viciously. "Don't bother to deny it. She told me herself that the baby was yours."

Anthony put down his glass next to hers, then he stood up and bowed slightly.

"My dear Polly," he said. "Before you go about looking for

skeletons in other people's closets, wouldn't it be wiser to clean out your own?"

"You bastard," said Polly softly.

"My dear," replied Anthony, "you know the old cliché about how it takes one to know one."

"That goes for phonies, too," said Polly, wanting and getting the last word.

15

MARK GRIFFIN sat in David Strong's studio sipping a tall drink while David played a Chopin étude on the piano. The room was filled with the heavy perfume of a dozen red roses that Mark had brought with him and which stood now, long-stemmed and beautiful, in a crystal vase that David had bought in Paris. From the green-covered couch where he half reclined, his head against three of David's small satin pillows, Mark watched the gleam of the evening star through one of the studio's tall, undraped windows, then he turned away and narrowed his eyes a little and watched the smoke from his cigarette. Every time he exhaled the smoke stood motionless in the air for a moment and then drifted in blue trails towards the room's high ceiling. The smoke was gauzy and ethereal-looking and reminded him vaguely of the filmy costumes of the dancers in *Les Sylphides*. Slowly, Mark moved his head and looked at David.

David's face was partly in shadow but the dim light in the room struck sharp streaks of gold in his hair. He held his head tipped backward slightly and his eyes were closed.

David is extraordinarily beautiful, thought Mark. He has such a pure, youthful look about him that it seems impossible to believe he's over thirty. He looks so innocent. So sweetly virginal. I wonder if he is.

Mark thought of his last evening in David's studio and smiled indulgently to himself. How ridiculous, he thought. The things they had said to each other, like children in a quarrel! How ridiculous it had been for him to say that he would never come back and how foolish David had been to think that he would not call him back. It was fate that had brought them together and it was fate that held them together now. They were like twin roots, he and David, meeting, entwining and growing together. Mark Griffin smiled and sat up as David's fingers struck the last note of the étude.

"Would you like another drink, Mark?" asked David.

"Please," replied Mark.

The conversation had been constrained at the beginning of the evening, but now David relaxed and tried to speak more expansively.

"Mark," he said, "I sent for you because I need someone to talk to before I go completely out of my mind."

"Yes, David," answered Mark with a little smile.

"Mark, what was it that first made you suspect that I was——" The hated word formed itself in his mind but he could not speak it aloud. "That I was different?" he concluded.

Mark raised one eyebrow and made his favourite *je ne sais quoi* gesture with his shoulders.

"I don't know, really," he said. "I just knew, David. It was something I felt."

"Mark, I've spent a lot of sleepless nights since you were last here," said David intensely. "I've been trying to figure myself out and I think I've come to some sort of conclusion. Well, perhaps not really a conclusion but at least an admission about myself."

Mark sipped from his glass. "Yes, David?" he encouraged.

"Perhaps I'm really the way you and Jess Cameron seem to think I am, but even if what both of you think is true, I'm still capable of distinguishing right from wrong." David stopped and reached out a long, white hand towards his drink. "And if I know anything at all I know that it's wrong for anyone to be the way you say we are."

Mark's eyebrows went up again. "Wrong, David?" he asked.

David put up a restraining hand. "Let me finish," he said. "Mark, I need some advice from you."

"It goes without saying that I'm only too happy to be of any service at all to you, David."

"Then tell me how you live with yourself, Mark," said David. "Tell me how you've rationalized being what you are until you've managed to make it not only acceptable but even desirable."

Mark leaned back against the sofa pillows and lit a fresh cigarette.

"David, I don't have to tell you how happy I am that you've finally admitted the truth to yourself," he said. "But accepting the truth, well, that's quite a different matter." He looked at David for a long, quiet moment and then his voice took on a low, musical, persuasive quality. "Listen, David, the first thing you must do is to rid your mind of all the dreadful labels you've picked up along the way. There's no such thing as right and wrong in our case. What's 'wrong' for most people is 'right' for us, so you see how little sense there is to putting name tags on anything, don't you?"

David looked at him helplessly. "I don't know," he said.

"David," said Mark, "please listen to me carefully. There's nothing wrong in my loving you. Even that Bible of yours that you seem to set such a store by teaches you all about love. Love is good, kind, sweet and merciful, so how can you think for a minute that there's something 'wrong' about it?"

His voice was firm with deep undertones of assurance and, listening to him, David felt rather like a child whose hand is being held in the dark. Mark was nearly ten years younger than David, but still he made David feel like a boy.

"Listen to me," said Mark. "Don't ever let yourself be influenced by others. By the so-called 'normal' people. I mean. Don't be impressed with their actions and especially not by their words. If you listen to them, your very soul will be lost because they'll try to make your thoughts, your passions and your hopes fit their tiresome little pattern and you'll wind up as nothing but a carbon copy of them. Oh, David, listen to me with your heart as well as with your mind," said Mark imploringly, and it occurred to David that perhaps his friend was getting a little drunk. But still, his words did not slur and his eyes remained as clear as ever. "You are you, David," said Mark. "Nothing can change that. You must allow yourself to develop or you'll die acting out a part for which you should never have been cast. Believe me, David, there's no such thing as sin in this world of ours. There's only fear. Fear of the law, fear of what people will think and say and fear of God."

David fixed fresh drinks for himself and Mark and hope had begun to flare in him. Just suppose for a moment that Mark was right? David shut off his mind. Mark was a mere child and of course he had an immature set of values. Still, just suppose . . .

"Just think, David," Mark was saying. "Think of what it would be like to live your life without fear! To live fully, completely and to be rid of this imaginary bogy man that you call Sin. Imagine it, David! Imagine yourself giving expression to every thought and passion, resisting nothing. You've never done that before, David, and this very denial of yourself shows in your face and in your music and it even makes you physically ill. If you'd only let go, David, and accept yourself as you are, you'd be well again."

David noticed with surprise that his glass was empty again and now the hope that had only made itself known to him before began to burn with new vigour. Mark was right, thought David. He had to be.

"You know the old saying about the only way to be rid of a temptation is to yield to it, don't you, David?" asked Mark. "Well, it's true." He raised his glass as if in salute. "Give in to your desires again and again, until your appetite is satisfied and the temptation is gone," he cried, then he lowered his glass and his voice simultaneously. "Resist and your soul is lost," he said dramatically. "Your soul is lost, consumed with longing for the things it has forbidden itself. You must know this, David. In the very core of your being you must know that I speak the truth. You've had desires that have frightened you, dreams that have terrorized you and memories that have tormented you and made you writhe with shame. And all the time, you needn't have suffered at all. You needn't suffer ever again if you'll only reject the thought of sin and admit the golden presence of pleasure."

201

"Stop it, Mark," said David. "I have to think."

"You *have* thought, David," said Mark quickly. "And it's done you nothing but harm. Don't think any more. Just accept what I tell you. Believe me, if anyone in the world understands how you feel, I do. I've walked through the same valley of fire more than once. But now I *know*, David, and it's only to spare you future suffering that I speak to you as I do now."

Mark leaned forward and David stared into the eyes of his friend. He felt his whole being strain forward to grasp an edge of Mark's shining, sin-free world. But there was one harsh chord in David that would not be still. It struck the same monotonous note over and over.

Evil. The word would not dislodge itself from his consciousness. Evil. Evil, said David's mind. This person is not a boy at all. He is a man, and he is evil.

The candles on the coffee table reflected their flames in Mark's eyes so that David could see tiny, flickering lights in the blackness that stared at him.

There must be something that I can say to him, thought David. There must be an answer of some kind that will prove him wrong. He must be wrong.

Mark Griffin knew the value of words but he knew also the greater value of silence. He could see the conflict in David and he smiled and gazed into David's tortured eyes.

But what if he's right, thought David, and felt a curious new excitement flow through him. He felt as if part of him were on fire and his face grew flushed and his hands were moist. Music did this to him sometimes. Really great music played in a great auditorium. Music that contained a great many crashing crescendos. But music often left his mind in chaos while now, suddenly, his thoughts seemed to be articulate.

He could be free! He could be unafraid. He could do anything without fear of the consequences. If he chose, he could lead an utterly bacchanalian life without a single fear of punishment.

What have I missed? David asked himself. How could I have missed knowing that life could be happy and carefree and fearless?

202

David drank from the fresh glass that Mark put in his hand and wondered if he might be getting a little tight.

Well, what if I am? he asked himself angrily. What difference does it make? I guess I've got a right to get slightly plastered if I feel like it.

"You can't afford to waste time, David," said Mark. "You're young and beautiful now, but youth and beauty are soon gone. If you hesitate now to take all the joys and pleasure that are rightfully yours, you'll wake up one day and find that it's too late. You'll be old and bent and you'll sit and weep for all your wasted golden years. Don't waste time, David. Don't torture yourself in trying to become what you can never be." Mark gave a short, sharp laugh. "Just think how tiresome it would be to be a dreary so-called normal man with a fat wife and a slew of runny-nosed children and a house in Cooper's Mills. No, David. Live the wonderful life that is yours. Enjoy it."

"Perhaps it's too late already," said David and felt like crying. "Too, too late."

Mark Griffin walked slowly through David's studio, extinguishing lights.

"Don't be silly, Davy," he said. "Of course it's not too late."

The room grew darker and darker and it seemed to David that Mark's words still sounded eloquently in the room.

"Not too late?" asked David.

"Of course not," replied Mark, and as he walked towards David, it seemed to him that all the words he had spoken to David had had a special beauty. A beauty that they had never possessed when Oscar Wilde had put them into the mouth of Lord Henry Wotton that they might fall on the ear of Dorian Gray.

Hours later, in the darkness of his room, David Strong woke suddenly. His cheeks were wet with tears but it was the heaving sensation of sickness that had awakened him and he stumbled awkwardly through the dark towards his bathroom. He vomited until there was nothing left in him but bitter, green bile and still his stomach heaved and he retched weakly. When it was over he stood, shivering, against the cold tile of the walls while sweat broke out all over his body and his teeth began to chatter. At last, he felt strong enough to find a face-cloth and dab at his face, then he brushed his teeth and gargled very cautiously.

"Oh, God," he moaned as he fumbled his way back to bed. "Oh, dear God, help me."

He covered himself with bedclothes that still smelled of Mark Griffin's lavender cologne and although the odour nauseated him all over again. he knew that he hadn't the strength to strip the bed and make it up fresh. So he huddled himself and tried to keep from shivering. He had been dreaming, he remembered, and now he groped vainly for the warm golden feeling of comfort that had enfolded him earlier. He searched his mind for the belief that he had taken for his own, but he could not find it even when he repeated Mark's words over and over.

Sin is nothing and pleasure is all, he told himself. But the feeling of comfort would not come and he knew that his new philosophy was an empty one made up of words that held neither conviction nor truth.

Suddenly, David could stand his bed no longer and he kicked impatiently at the sheets and blankets that seemed to hold him pinned and helpless. At last he was free of their hatefulness and he stood up, shivering in the cold room. He wrapped himself in a heavy robe and felt his way across the darkness to the coffee table where he found a cigarette. As he smoked he walked carefully around his studio and his hands seemed to encounter only the things that were most dear to him. His fingers stroked the satiny finish of his piano and then he caressed a small statuette on the mantelpiece. He walked to a window and stood staring down at the snow-clean, sleeping street and suddenly he was strangely calm. He could see clearly now, as if each of his thoughts were a painstakingly perfect pen-and-ink drawing and he would not allow the blunt, wish-filled edges of his mind to rub across his thoughts, to smudge their clarity with the forgetfulness. He thought first of Jess Cameron and of the doctor's words, quiet and casual almost, so David had thought at the time, to the point of indifference. It had been the day after David's first experience with Mark.

"That's something you'll have to answer for yourself, David," the doctor had replied to David's awkward, embarrassed question. "But if that's what it is, for God's sake don't try to turn it into something else. Face it, admit it, and then perhaps we can begin to do something about it. A good psychiatrist could help you."

It was really comical, David thought later, the way he had always pictured psychiatrists as being short and rather plump with beards like Sigmund Freud's and interesting foreign accents. The one to whom he had gone had been nothing like his mental image. He had the rather improbable name of Henry Smith and he was large and jovial to a degree that seemed almost farcical to David. It seemed to David that Dr. Smith was bent on establishing a buddy-buddy relationship right from the start.

"Strong, I don't believe that your—er—idiosyncrasies have a physical causation which makes you one of the lucky ones. If they had, I wouldn't be able to help you. No. It's my opinion that you were forced into the paths of homosexuality as a child and that means we're going to have to dig, dig, dig. So come on now, start at the beginning if you can and let's have it all."

A few weeks later, Dr. Smith said, "That mother of yours must have been a pip! There are some women, Strong, who should be sterilized before puberty. It seems to me that your mother was one of them. How you must have hated her!"

"But I never hated my mother," objected David. "She was the soul of goodness. She was saintly, I tell you. I can never ever begin to tell you what she had to put up with from my father."

"Saintly or not," said Dr. Smith, "she certainly managed to do a fine job of turning you against women for all time whether you'll admit that or not."

"For all time?" asked David.

"Unfortunately, it usually works out that way," said the doctor. "But don't worry. There are many ways in which we can help you to adjust to your problem."

That night, David decided that he would not go back to Dr. Henry Smith and with the decision he felt almost peaceful. He went to sleep almost at once and he dreamed of Millie.

"What's your last name?" he asked her in his dream. "I don't believe I've ever heard it."

But Millie would not answer his question. She turned and ran a few steps away from him and when she finally spoke her voice was high and shrill with outrage.

"What are you anyway?" screamed Millie, and even the next morning it seemed to David that she had been much too substantial and her voice far too real for her to have been nothing but a dream and he had the eerie feeling that she had somehow actually been in the same room with him. "Just what are you anyway?" screamed Millie. "A Goddamned fairy? I don't make a pass at a guy only to have him puke all over the Goddamn place. That's what you are, a stinkin', Goddamn fairy. I oughta call a cop!"

David woke. He sat up, frightened, trembling and covered with sweat with the sickness hard-fisted in his stomach. He turned on all the lights but of course his studio was empty, and his eyes fell on the water-colour that Martin Mallory had done for him many years ago in Paris.

Martin hadn't called him vile names, remembered David with something like gratitude. In his way, Martin had been kind.

"It's nothing to be ashamed of, David," Martin had said. "What we have is exactly the same kind of love a man has for a woman except unfortunately for us we both happen to be men."

"You're crazy!" David had cried. "And you're dirty and perverted and evil."

Looking down at the quiet Cooper Station street, David remembered his flight from Paris and the months in New York that followed. He had played the piano at a great number of small badly-lit bars and he remembered the high-voiced men who had peopled those places. He remembered the languid glances, the pancake make-up and the soft-tipped fingers that had reached out on many occasions to stroke his arm or his cheek, and for a time he had almost managed to acquire a feeling of belonging, of having found his place in the world at last. But one evening, a couple of tourists had come in to the bar where he was working. The man had a paunch and wore a

206

blue striped suit and the woman had a new permanent wave and wore a violently pink hat.

The man had ordered drinks, after insisting on seeing the bottle, and then he turned to his companion.

"Well, Elsie," he said, loud enough for David to hear, "you always wanted to see one of these pansy beds and here you are."

"Gee, Al," said Pink Hat, "I never really believed there was guys like this, not really I didn't. I thought they was just guys that people told jokes about, you know? My God."

The two of them sat there for a long time, getting even drunker than they had been when they came in and staring around and nudging each other with a great deal of giggling. Pink Hat's hat was tilted slightly and a few wisps of hair had begun to trail across one cheek when she finally pinched Blue Suit playfully and indicated David with a nod of her head.

"Say, mister," she called to David. "What're you doin' in here?"

David ignored her but his fingers trembled as he tried to find the keys to his next numbers.

"Say, mister," called Pink Hat and her words slurred a little. "You don't really look like one."

Every head in the place was turned towards her and David felt his stomach begin to quiver.

"Say, mister. Are you really one of them fairies?" asked Pink Hat and her companion was convulsed with laughter at the look on David's face.

"Come on, Elsie," he roared, "he ain't gonna answer you. Let's go some place else. The perfume in here is beginnin' to make me feel sick."

The room was quiet for a long, stretched-out moment after the two had gone, but at last the bartender came up to David. He put one arm around his shoulders and said, "Don't you care, Davy. They were just stupid, drunken boors and I never should have served them in the first place."

"No, you shouldn't," mumbled David and ran quickly towards the men's room.

But even while he was throwing up, David thought of Blue Suit and Pink Hat. Drunken, stupid boors they might be, but no

207

one outside was ever going to look at them with curiosity, amazement and disgust. Because Blue Suit and Pink Hat had the great gift of normalcy. Perhaps they sneaked around and fornicated in the back seat of Blue Suit's car, but still the world would look upon them as normal, as infinitely to be preferred to people like David Strong. There was no safety, no security, even in the tight, closed little world of the bar outside because at any time its walls could be invaded by outsiders who felt no pity but only contempt.

David Strong turned away slowly from his window and the beautiful still scene outside. He walked directly into his bathroom and reached carefully into the medicine cabinet. Even in the dark, his fingers found the small bottle of sleeping capsules. He filled a glass with water and he did not trip nor spill a single drop as he went back to bed. He swallowed every capsule in the bottle carefully and slowly and washed each one down his throat with a mouthful of water.

Even now, at the end, I've chosen the woman's way, he thought. Pity I don't own a gun. I could have done a real bang-up masculine job of this.

He lay flat on the bed and pulled the sheets up to his chin.

Thou shalt not kill, Mother? he asked silently. Not even one-self, does that mean? Does it, Mother?

He turned his head and looked towards the windows where the wide-open draperies moved gently in the winter cold.

But, Mother, he argued silently, wouldn't you rather have me dead than living the kind of life I'd have to live? Wouldn't you? You wouldn't want me to go through life with people pointing fingers at me, would you? You wouldn't want them pointing stubby, dirty-knuckled fingers at me and laughing and whispering and making vulgar little jokes, would you, Mother? And what if I got caught? Why, it'd be worse for me than it was for Chris and Lisa Pappas and you wouldn't want that, would you? And I'd get caught, don't worry about that. Everyone knows already. Doris Palmer'd call a special meeting and every-one in town would denounce me, just like they did Pappas. There's no place to hide in Cooper Station, Mother. No place at all. Lisa Pappas found that out. Everyone knew about her and

Anthony Cooper and they talked and laughed and denounced her. You wouldn't want that to happen to me, would you, Mother? I'd have to leave town, run away, and it wouldn't do any good. It would happen all over again somewhere else. Mother? Are you listening to me?

The room was filled with a pale, golden light which grew dimmer and softer even as David watched. He smiled sleepily and watched the room turn from gold to a soft rose colour and all around the edges of the rose he could see a border of deep, velvety blue-black that was softer-looking than anything he had ever imagined.

I used to wonder what it would be like to be dead, he thought, and soon, now, I'll know. I wonder if God will look as stern and forbidding as he does in the pictures that men have made of him.

No, Lord, said David and thought he was speaking aloud, I haven't sinned in killing myself. In Your Prayer, You gave me the words Yourself. Lead us not into temptation, You said, but deliver us from evil. Martin was evil. So was Mark. And I allowed myself to be led into temptation. So now I've delivered myself from evil. Please be kind to me now and make Mother be kind. Don't let her scold me. Even if no one else is kind, You should be able to be kind. Be kind. Be kind . . .

At nine o'clock the next morning, Valerie Rutgers walked out of her front door and stood on the walk that led to the street. She looked up and down and all around with an interested kind of curiosity. Not, she told herself, that she expected to see anything different from what she saw every morning but still, you could never tell. She shivered in the cold and looked at the snow-covered landscape, but it seemed to her that there was a trace of softening in the sky this morning. About time, too, she said to herself. Almost March and that meant spring should be right around the corner. Not that March was spring-like by any matter or means, but it did mean that warmer days were on the way. Well, she supposed, the good Lord must have had His reasons for sticking March in the calendar. Probably to get folks to look after their gardens and start the spring cleaning and all. Goodness! There went the quarter-past bell up at the high school. What was she thinking of, dilly-dallying around in the front yard when she should be getting the wash started. Ought to be a good drying day today. Good day for doing sheets. They might freeze right up to the line at first, but it was going to warm up later in the day and they'd thaw out in good shape. She'd best get right upstairs and get the sheets off Mr. Strong's bed. She'd do his first.

Valerie Rutgers went up to the tower room and unlocked David's room with her own key. She saw, at once, that he was still in bed.

"Mr. Strong!" she called, shocked. In all the time David had lived in her house, she had never known him to be late for school once. "My word," said Valerie. "Wake up, Mr. Strong. It's way after nine and you're late as it is."

She reached out a tentative hand to shake his shoulder and her fingertips had no more than grazed his skin before she knew that he was dead and started screaming.

Within minutes the deserted street in front of Valerie's house was filled with people. Some of them burst into the house and followed Valerie's screams to the tower.

"Get the doctor!" shouted someone.

"Call the hospital!"

"Get the sheriff!"

Jess Cameron was called and in a few minutes he was running up the stairs to David's studio.

Please, God, prayed Jess. Don't let me be too late.

"I just touched him, Jess," said Valerie, "and I knew right off he was dead. Cold as a mackerel and stiff as a board." She sat down on one of David's chairs and burst into tears. "He was a good man," she sobbed. "Never bothered anybody in his whole life."

"Val, you get downstairs and have one of the women make a pot of coffee," said Jess. "Quickly, now."

But Jess knew that it was useless and he gave instructions to Valerie Rutgers only to get her out of the room. He, too, had barely touched David and had known, but he went through all the motions of making sure. He saw the empty bottle with its neatly typed label on the table next to David's bed.

"One capsule at bedtime," read the label. "Dr. Cameron. Not to be refilled. The Cooper Station Pharmacy."

"I put the coffee on, Jess," said Valerie Rutgers, coming back into the room.

"Good," said Jess. "I need it now, for myself. It's too late for David. He's dead. Took an overdose of sleeping pills."

Downstairs, in her kitchen, Valerie poured coffee.

"But what did he want to go and do a think like that for?" she asked, already her horror replaced by her incurable curiosity. "He was such a nice fellow. Neat as a pin. Never left a mess around the way some do. And he had a good job at the school and all. What'd he want to go and kill himself for?"

Jess lowered his head and stirred sugar into his coffee. Half-forgotten words flowed into his mind, words which, at one time, he had been sure that he'd never forget, so impressed had he been with their beauty.

And whatsoever I shall see or hear in the course of my profession in my intercourse with men, if it be what should not be published abroad . . .

His mind stopped and he could not remember the next phrase.

"He had ulcers, Val," he said. "A bad case of ulcers. I guess he knew he was never going to get better."

16

MARGERY and Nathaniel Cooper were quiet as their big car carried them almost silently along the highway leading south away from Cooper Station. It was winter. A cold, heavy, northern New England winter, and the shoulders of the road were piled high with snow. On top, the drifts were like diamonds on ermine, shining against soft, white depth, but where the sides dipped down towards the road there were shadows, pale blue and insubstantial-looking so that even when you looked at them in broad daylight you thought of evening. It was cold with the special coldness of February that cuts through the warmest fur like a sharp razor-blade going through flesh and the sun shed no warmth at all. It only blinded you when you looked too long at the whiteness all around you.

Nathaniel Cooper's car was a long, black Buick sedan. The Coopers had driven long, black Buick sedans ever since Nate could remember, for Ferguson Cooper had been of the opinion that Cadillacs were only for gangsters and rich people from New York who came north for the summer. Until recently, Nate had never considered changing the pattern but now he thought longingly of himself and Margery in a pale blue convertible driving somewhere with the top down along a tree-shaded road where it was warm.

Soon, perhaps, he thought. Perhaps very soon.

Margery's left hand rested lightly against Nate's thigh as he drove and her head was thrown back against the seat cushions. It was the way she had used to sit in a car with him before they were married. Nate covered her hand with his and pressed it gently against his thigh.

"Are you sure you feel up to going down there today, darling?" he asked. "We could always turn around and go home if you want."

"I have to go, Nate," she said. "Somehow I have to keep assuring myself that she's all right and that she's happy."

"Are you happy, Margery?" he asked gently.

"Almost, dear," she replied and smiled at him. "Almost. Just give me a little longer."

His big hand ruffled her short hair as he pulled her head down on to his shoulder.

"All the time in the world," he said.

But Nate was frightened at the day ahead of them for he remembered the desperate cry that had come from Margery on the night after they had left Robin, for the first time, at St. Jude's home.

"I can't stand it!" Margery had cried. "We were wrong to do this thing. Take me to her, Nate. Take me now."

"Please, dear," Nate had said. "Try. Try it this way for only a month and if you're still so unhappy then we'll go down and bring her home."

"I can't do it, Nate. Please don't ask me. I can't stand it."

His voice had mingled with those of Jess Cameron and Virgie as they tried to console her.

"Margery, dear."

"Margery, Margery."

"Miz Marg'ry, honey."

Jess had warned Nate of the way it would be right from the beginning.

"The feelings of guilt attendant on placing a child in an institution are staggering, Nate," Jess had said. "And it's going to be harder for Margery than it'll be for you because this has been her decision. You're going to need all the patience in the world, Nate. More than all the patience in the world."

Nate glanced down at his wife as she leaned against him now.

The window on her side of the car was open an inch or two and her hair blew in little wisps across her cheek. She lifted her hand lazily to brush them away.

She's getting well, thought Nate hopefully. It's going to take time, but I know she's going to be well soon. Then we'll go away together. Somewhere warm and quiet. Haiti? he wondered and then smiled at himself. He knew nothing whatever about Haiti except that the name of its capital had always fascinated him. Port-au-Prince. It was a name that he could feel on his tongue. A place he could almost touch and feel and smell just by saying the name to himself. When Nate said Port-au-Prince to himself he thought of heavy, red blossoms trailing lazily down over an old stone wall while somewhere in the background someone played a guitar as he and Margery dozed in the hot sun. He was weary of the cold and tired of fighting the implacable winters of northern New England, and never again would he be able to live through the chill, rainy days of autumn without feeling fear.

He thought of that chill, rainy day of autumn when he had been paralysed with terror at the thought that Margery was never going to be well again. He would never forget that day, though she seemed to be all right now, thanks to Jess.

Nor the time, several days later, when Jess Cameron had spoken to him.

"We're not going to waste time," said the doctor. "Margery's going to get well but first she's going to have to make the decision about Robin."

"Do we have to talk to her about it now?" asked Nate. "She seems to be doing so well that I'm afraid of the least little thing that might upset her."

"It has to be done," said Jess. "And I don't like it any better than you do. But she can't live the rest of her life in this state of suspended animation. I've got her shot full of tranquillizers now, but I can't keep her on them for ever."

"No," said Nate and sighed. "I know you can't. But, Jess, I'm afraid to even mention Robin to her."

"We'll have to tread carefully," said Jess. "We've got to make her believe that the decision to send Robin away is her own and

214

not some trick that we're trying to put over on her."

Nate poured himself a drink. "I admit it," he said. "I'm a coward. You talk to her, Jess. Later, when I'm alone with her, I'll back you up. But I can't face her with it now."

Margery was sitting up in bed. Her face was thin and white, but there was a softness to her eyes now that had not been there before. Jess sat down on the rose-coloured chair next to the bed and Virgie brought him his inevitable cup of coffee.

"Margery," he said at last, "do you have any idea what's happened to you?"

Margery tried to laugh. "I guess I just get lazy, Jess," she said. "I wanted a few weeks off just lying around and getting fat."

"You were all tired out," Jess said. "And you're still tired. I don't mean just plain, ordinary tired, either. I mean totally exhausted, physically, mentally and emotionally. You need to rest. To sleep late every morning, to stop thinking and feeling, to lie in the sun and to stop running up and down stairs."

"And what about Robin?" asked Margery. "What's going to become of her if I allow myself to become a bedridden invalid?"

"What happens to Robin is entirely up to you, Margery," said Jess. "I can't make up your mind for you on that score. But I can give you the facts."

"But Jess, I'm better now. Why, in a few days I'll be up and around as good as new."

"No, you won't, Margery," said Jess. "Some people are equipped to cope with a situation like yours, but you aren't."

"What are you talking about, Jess?" demanded Margery. "Don't talk in riddles with me."

Jess finished his coffee and lit a fresh cigarette. He looked at her for a long time.

"Margery," he said at last, "unless you separate yourself from Robin, you will risk everything of value in your life, and in the end you'll risk your sanity and your life itself. You'll endanger any future children that you might be lucky enough to have, and you'll endanger Nate more than you have already. And you'll give Robin an increasingly neurotic mother until you reach the point of where you'll not only be unable to care for her but for yourself as well."

215

When he finished speaking there was no sound in the room at all, and then Margery pulled a Kleenex from a box and sponged at her wet face.

"I understand you, Jess," she said. "What you're saying is what you've said all along for years. You want me to put Robin away in an institution."

"For everybody's sake, Margery, including Robin's, yes. If you get sick again you may not be as lucky the next time."

Margery thought for a long time while she brushed futilely at her tears with the back of her hand.

"Jess, I could never send Robin to that place that your friend runs."

"Dr. Alter is a good man," objected Jess. "He has a fine reputation."

"I know it, Jess," she said. "But he tries too hard. He just doesn't give up. I saw him and his school and I know. He spends years and years trying to teach one thing to one child as if he were in some horrible contest. I couldn't stand to think of Robin with her little face all covered with sweat and tears of effort in her eyes, trying, trying, trying to learn something that's never going to be of any use to her."

Margery put her face into her hands and wept and Jess went to the windows and stood looking down at the sodden garden.

"There's a place I know of," he said when Margery quieted a little, "where you could leave Robin with absolute confidence that she'd receive all the loving care she could use."

"She gets that here," cried Margery. "Who else could give her what she gets from me?"

"This place is a home for retarded children and for children like Robin, called St. Jude's," said Jess. "It's a Catholic institution."

"Catholic!" cried Margery.

Jess turned to her and smiled. "Yes, Catholic," he said. "Not everybody in the world is a Congregationalist, you know."

Margery smiled back and took the cigarette Jess extended towards her.

"I know," she said. "I guess I was just thinking of all the

216

Coopers who'd take a shotgun to you at the idea of Robin being cared for by Papists."

"And you're right about Dr. Alter," continued Jess. "He's a determined man all right. He's sure, he *knows* that children like Robin can be taught, and he bends all his will and energy towards teaching them. At St. Jude's, though, the Sisters don't know whether the children can be taught or not but they have one belief that's even more firmly rooted in them than Dr. Alter's is in him. They know that the spirit of God is in every child and they treat every child accordingly."

Margery leaned back against her pillows and the time of her thinking now was long and painful. When she sighed and straightened up at last, the sigh came from deep within her and left her feeling heavy and Jess wondered if perhaps this wasn't the first real sigh that Margery had allowed herself in years.

"I tried, didn't I, Jess, to look after Robin the best I knew how?" she asked, but she did not wait for him to answer. "I know I did and yet she remained the same. You warned me, Jess, way back when we brought her home from the hospital that it'd be like this, but I had to try it my way."

"I know, Margery," said Jess. "I don't think you'd ever have been satisfied if you hadn't tried."

"But it didn't do any good," she said. "No good at all. Perhaps it's time now to try it your way. If Nate doesn't mind, I'm willing."

"Will you give it a fair try, Margery?" asked Jess. "Even if you're miserable at first, will you wait and give it a real try?"

"Yes," said Margery. "I'll give it a real try."

Jess had arranged things swiftly and skilfully. Three days after his talk with Margery, Nathaniel took his daughter to St. Jude's Home for Children. He watched the Sisters, dressed in their heavy black robes with starched ruffs of white around their throats and stiff white fans of linen framing their faces. The robes of the Sisters were belted with thick, silk cord and from each cord there dangled a black rosary and a heavy silver cross. Nathaniel had never heard women move so noiselessly. Robin went to one of the Sisters without a backward glance at her father. She took the nun's hand and rubbed her cheek against

217

the dark robe and smiled. Within an hour Nathaniel was on his way home alone.

He felt almost foolishly light-hearted as he drove into the garage and he thought, guiltily, that even the old house looked different. Lighter, somehow, and not quite like the heavy old brick pile that it was. Margery was waiting for him, her eyes gazing anxiously from the living-room window.

"Darling, it's going to be all right," said Nate as he came in and took her in his arms. "It's a wonderful place."

"Really?" she asked, wanting to believe. "Really and truly, Nate?"

"Yes, darling, really and truly. I saw a lot of children today and every single one looked happy and well cared for and loved."

Later, Jess telephoned Nate. "How did it go?" he asked.

"Fine," replied Nate. "And Margery's fine, too. Come on over and have dinner with us."

"Thanks," said Jess. "I'll do that and I'll come armed with several topics of conversation, none of them to do with children."

"Good," said Nate. "We'll have a good evening together."

But it was not a good evening. When dinner was over and the three of them were having coffee, Margery began to cry.

"It's no good, Nate," she wept. "I feel as if someone had cut a piece right out of me. You'll have to go to get her and bring her home. Right now."

"Darling," said Nate. "You promised to give it a fair try. We can't leave Robin somewhere for a few hours and then go yank her home again. She'll be happy, dear. I promise you."

"But I'll never be happy again, Nate," cried Margery. "We were wrong to do this thing. I can't stand it."

Virgie came and led Margery upstairs. She crooned softly and patted her.

"Don't you worry yourself none, honey," said Virgie. "Things gonna be fine. Everythin' gonna work out jes' jim-dandy in a little while."

Nathaniel Cooper sighed.

"It's not going to work, Jess," he said. "She'll kill herself worrying about Robin."

218

"Time, Nate," said Jess. "Give her time. You can't take a child out of a mother's life without leaving a space soon filled with tears of guilt and regret. All we can do is hope that time will take care of the space and fill it with something else."

"She's got to get well, Jess," said Nate desperately. "She's *got* to."

"She will," said Jess. "Margery has strength. If she didn't, she could never have carried the burden of Robin for ten years. I only wish that she'd never picked up the burden in the first place, but she had to. She's been all tangled up with a mess of things she's tried to prove."

"What do you mean by that?" asked Nate.

"It's a great tragedy to produce a child like Robin," said Jess. "And in Margery's case it wasn't only a matter of tragic misfortune but a point of pride as well. She had produced an imperfect child so she felt that she had to prove to herself, to you and the world that she could be a perfect mother. Nate, Margery is a healthy, normal woman. Do you think for a minute that she enjoyed caring for a sick, abnormal child?"

"But it was what she wanted, Jess," objected Nate. "The only time she seemed happy was when she was with Robin."

"It wasn't what she wanted," said Jess. "I've often wondered how she coped with what must have been an almost overwhelming feeling of resentment towards Robin and how she managed to squash her feelings so that they didn't show. And I've wondered how bitterly she must have hated herself for feeling like that and how many times she held Robin to herself, screaming silent denials."

"Good God, Jess. You're trying to tell me that all this time she's hated Robin."

"Yes, I am," said Jess.

"But you haven't seen her as I have. Day after day and night after night there was no one for Margery but Robin, and even after all this time, it's still Robin. How long do you think she can go on without her? You saw the way she was tonight."

"Tonight Margery was deliberately making herself unhappy," said Jess. "She's punishing herself for what she thinks of as abandoning her child. You're comparatively lucky, Nate. You made a good adjustment to Robin. You got used to taking a back seat and waiting. Now you're all that Margery has left and you're going to have to make her feel as needed as Robin did or else she won't feel as if she has any purpose in going on. But most important of all, Margery shouldn't think of herself as a failure as far as being a woman goes and there's only one way to solve that. Another child."

"Another child?"

"Yes, Nate. Another child. A perfect, normal child."

Nate smiled. He was thinking of what Margery had told him, about the way she had watched Lisa Pappas and Anthony Cooper and had thought of love.

"It's queer the way things turn out, isn't it?" asked Nate.

"Like what?" asked Jess.

"Like the way big things are often triggered by little insignificant things."

"Whatever that means," smiled Jess. "I suppose I agree."

Nate shrugged and laughed at himself. "I was just thinking that the Pappas mess wasn't such a total loss after all because there was one little facet of it that triggered Margery into thinking of feeling again."

"And what was that?" asked Jess.

"Lisa Pappas's love affair with my nephew," said Nate. "I imagine that this is probably the only time in history that some good has come out of such a situation. Not that I respect Anthony any for it. I don't approve of a man poaching on another man's land."

Jess looked at the tip of his cigarette.

"No," he said. "I never imagined that you did."

Slowly, the weeks had passed and little by little Nathaniel had begun to notice an improvement in Margery. She no longer wept for hours on end and she did not wake quite so often in the night, imagining the cry of a child. She no longer hurried constantly, as she had previously done, but seemed content now to let things slide a little.

And finally, one day in February, she asked Jess, "When may I go to see Robin?"

He gave her a quick, sharp look. "Do you think you're ready to see her?" he asked.

"I have to, Jess," she said. "I'll have to face it sooner or later and it might as well be now."

"Go any time," said Jess.

The big, black Buick turned into the gravelled drive in front of St. Jude's.

"Here we are," said Nathaniel. He was apprehensive and depressed. It'll never work, he thought. The minute she sees Robin it'll be all over and we'll be right back where we started.

"Please, honey," said Margery softly. "Don't be unhappy and frightened on my account. I'll be fine."

Nate tried to smile, then he took her arm and they went up the steps and through the front door of St. Jude's.

A black-robed Sister came forward and extended her hand. "Mrs. Cooper," she smiled. "How very nice to meet you. I'll fetch Robin. She is playing in the yard with the others."

Margery put a restraining hand on her arm. "Please Sister," she said. "Couldn't we go out with you?"

"Yes, of course," said the nun and led the way.

Margery and Nathaniel followed her down a long hallway and out into the yard. Margery's eyes searched for only a moment before she saw Robin. The child was standing in the snow, bending to gather up a huge handful of the soft whiteness and then tossing it up in the air with giggles of delight. When the Sister walked up to her, Robin stopped immediately and went to the black-clad figure. She nuzzled against the dark robe and smiled into the face that smiled at her.

"Robin, your mother and father have come to see you," said the Sister and she spoke in the same tone she would have used with a normal child.

She led Robin to Margery and Nathaniel, and Margery immediately put her arms around her child. Robin rubbed her cheek against Margery's sleeve and smiled up at her just as she had always done.

But she doesn't know me, thought Margery. It's exactly the

same smile as she gave to the Sister. She'd smile like this for anyone who seemed kind to her.

For a sharp, hurtful moment, Margery felt the quick sting of loss and then she took Robin's hand and the three Coopers walked through the yard of St. Jude's.

It was a short visit and it terminated itself when Robin again took notice of the snow that covered the ground. She dropped Margery's hand and stood still, then slowly she bent forward and picked up two handfuls of snow and raised them to her face. Her tongue came out slowly, to taste, and she laughed gleefully at the feel of the soft cold.

She's forgotten that I exist, thought Margery.

They stood for a long time, watching Robin play, and at last Nathaniel touched Margery's arm.

"Come, dear," he said. "It's time to go."

They walked slowly out of the yard and through the long hallway and out of the front door. Neither of them spoke as the car sped along the highway. Nathaniel was silent because he was afraid and Margery was still because she was busy with her thoughts. They were almost to the town line at Cooper Station before Margery put her hand on Nathaniel's thigh.

"You were right, Nate," she said. "It *is* a wonderful place. Even if I hadn't one single other reason for happiness, I'd be happy just knowing that Robin is happy and loved and well cared for." She paused and smiled up at her husband. "But I do have other reasons, Nate. So many, many more."

She reached up and kissed his cheek gently as Nathaniel turned the car into Benjamin Street and headed for home.

222

ANTHONY COOPER finished his fourth Martini and looked gloomily at his Aunt Margery when she stood up and announced that it was time to eat.

"Roast beef, Anthony," she said, "and spring peas. The first of the season and right out of your Uncle Nate's garden, fresh this afternoon."

God, but she's turned into a pain in the arse, thought Anthony sourly. When they had the kid around there was a certain fine-drawn look about Margery, an aura of tragedy that suited her. But now she's turned into a regular bucolic *hausfrau,* roast beef, new peas, ruffled apron and all. Christ.

"Must we?" asked Anthony rudely. "Personally, I could stand another of Nate's Martinis even if he does eff them up with all that lousy vermouth."

"You've had enough, Anthony," said Nathaniel and stood up next to Margery. "You'll ruin your stomach with all that crap. Come on, you've got to eat."

"My dear Uncle," said Anthony, who was not tight from a mere four Martinis but from several quarts of beer he had sipped on all afternoon, "the only thing I *have* to do in this life is die." He almost managed to swallow a rather large belch. "And I have no intention of doing that right at the moment. I shall take a long time about it. A long, long time. And the path will be paved with nothing but Martinis, beer and good Scotch.

223

Oh yes. And girls. Beautiful, blonde, busty girls who dance in night-clubs and never go to bed before daylight."

"Well, sit there and get plastered if that's what you want," said Nate impatiently. "We're going in to eat."

"Go with God," replied Anthony with a magnanimous wave of his hand.

"Anthony," said Margery, "you shouldn't drink any more to-night. You have that long drive facing you tomorrow and you don't want to start out with a hangover."

"Anthony, you shouldn't," mimicked Anthony. "Anthony, you don't want. My dear Aunt, the things I want and the things I should do are far beyond your ken. In fact, I might go so far as to say you'd be shocked by the things I should do and the things I want."

Margery smiled. "I may be a contented hick well on my way to getting fat to your way of thinking," she said. "But don't count on shocking me, Anthony."

"Then go eat your spring peas and leave me to my silly notions," said Anthony.

"We shall," said Nate. "And when we finish, we're going over to the Stricklands to play bridge, which should also hand you a laugh."

"It should and it does," replied Anthony. "As for me, I shall go home and put my feet up and drink a lot of Scotch."

"I'm afraid you'll have to put your feet up here," said Margery. "Marie and I finished closing up your house this afternoon. Everything is covered with dust sheets and your refrigerator is empty. So make yourself comfortable right here."

"Thank you, ma'am," said Anthony. "That's what I call real Southern hospitality."

"You know which room is yours if you want to lie down," said Margery.

"Indeed, I do," said Anthony and bowed a little. "But I've no intention of lying down. I shall sit here and get drunk and ponder on my sins."

Margery and Nathaniel walked into the dining-room and as they went Anthony studied Margery's figure.

She's got it, he thought as he opened a bottle of Scotch. The walk. All women who are good in bed have it. Towards the end, Lisa had it.

Anthony poured whisky over a couple of ice-cubes and sat down with his drink.

In the beginning, she didn't have it. Lord, no. In the beginning Lisa walked like a frustrated small-town librarian, but not in the end. Not by any means. In the end, she rolled when she walked. She swayed. Her hips were alive. They had promise and meaning. Like Margery's now. Guess there's more to old Nate than a nephew would suspect. But I wonder if Margery's like Lisa. Like metal under his hands and his body, Lisa said. And I was the magnet.

Anthony glared down into his drink before he took a heavy swallow.

God, she was a dumb little thing, he thought. A magnet indeed! But dumb in an interesting way. She could learn fast when she wanted to, and she was fun to teach. Well, that's all over with and tomorrow I'll go back to civilization. No dumb girls in New York. Nobody to teach there. Might even learn a few things myself.

When Anthony Cooper drank Scotch, he did so without any appearance of speed, but he drank continually and methodically so that by the time he heard the front door slam shut behind Margery and Nathaniel, more than a third of the bottle he had opened was gone. He went to the window and watched them drive away in the spring evening. It was twilight and there was a smell of new grass on the air.

Summer's coming, thought Anthony and sat down, rubbing his glass between his palms. The long, hot summer, thought Anthony and the smell of Scotch was very heavy in his nostrils. Heavy and smoky, like summer. The long, hot summer. Your belly is damp, my love. Anthony took a deep swallow of his drink and clenched his jaw against a pain that he had not been able to get used to after almost a year of trying.

It was worse when he drank, for the drunker he became the sharper grew his images.

Hurt me, darling, Lisa said. Her teeth were tight together and she half smiled. Hurt me with your hands.

225

My dear child, said Anthony, do you know why you want to be hurt? It's to expiate your guilt feelings about cheating on your husband.

Am I sleeping with Sigmund Freud or with Anthony Cooper? asked Lisa and rolled over so that he could bite her shoulders.

Who's sleeping? demanded Anthony and began to handle her.

Sometimes you make me feel like a whore, said Lisa. And I love it. A very good, expensive French whore from whom you're going to get your money's worth.

Anthony flicked his cigarette towards the empty fireplace in Nathaniel's living-room.

Dumb, he thought. Lisa was as dumb as they come. Goddamn her. And I never could abide stupidity in a woman.

He fixed a fresh drink and as he sat down again he reflected that the whole thing was a damned good joke on him. Dumb or not, hopelessly naïve and unschooled as she had been, it was still Lisa who came to plague his dreams at night and who appeared in the bottom of his glass when he drank. And for quite a while after she had gone he had not realized that it was going to be like that. He had thought, Good riddance. Her and her school-teacher husband and her two obnoxious children and her belly that will soon be distended and ugly and her breasts that will begin to sag like overripe pears. I'm well rid of that one and damned lucky not to have had any more trouble about it than I did.

It was dark in Nathaniel's living-room and Anthony thought vaguely of getting up to put some lights on.

I must be getting drunk, he thought. Shouldn't get drunk, Anthony. Don't want to have a hangover in the morning, Anthony. Balls, Anthony. You're nothing but a phony and a coward, Anthony. Ought to take a walk, Anthony. Good for an over-active libido, walks. Like cold baths and basketball.

He got to his feet with an effort and picked up a fresh, unopened bottle of Nathaniel's Scotch.

Got to take a little walk, he thought. A little constitutional before retiring to my dear Aunt Margery's little pink-ruffled guest room.

He went out of the front door and walked carefully across the

226

street. He went past his own house that already had a closed, veiled look even though he had left it only a few hours before, and made his way down the path that led to the gardener's cottage. It took him long, fumbling minutes to find the proper key on his ring, but at last he managed to open the door and walked into the house.

A darling little place, he thought. Just like something out of *Hansel and Gretel*. How Goddamned cute can you get. Hansel and Gretel. God, she was dumb. Clichés rolled off her tongue with every breath she drew. A magnet, huh? Christ.

Anthony sat down in an arm-chair and he drank directly from the bottle now, not bothering to get up and find a glass in the little kitchen.

Man, he told himself, that's when you've had it. That's when you're really a drunk, when you start drinking it right out of the bottle. Funny. But with Lisa around beer had tasted good. Just beer and nothing else.

Liquor is a weakness, said Lisa. It doesn't solve anything to get drunk, Anthony. Not a single thing.

But my dear child, I'm essentially a very weak man, said Anthony. All the Cooper men are weaklings. Take my Uncle Nathaniel, for instance——

I don't want to take your Uncle Nathaniel, for instance or any other way. I want to take you.

How do you want to take me?

Like this, said Lisa and began to touch him the way he had taught her.

Poor Uncle Nathaniel, said Anthony. Doesn't know what he's missing.

Shut up, said Lisa as she rolled over on top of him. Just shut up and lie still. Who do you belong to?

And then lower and more savagely as she moved faster and faster on top of him.

Who, Anthony? Who do you belong to?

Whom, corrected Anthony, to make her angry and stronger, and then at last, just before the end, To you, my darling. I belong to you.

But he hadn't, thought Anthony and tried to make his smile

triumphant as he sat in the dark in the little house where Lisa had lived. He hadn't belonged to her any more than he had ever belonged to anyone. He was his own man, always had been, and he hadn't changed. Anthony leaned his head against the back of the chair and grinned drunkenly in the dark.

No, my dear girl, not to anyone. The only person I've ever belonged to is me, and I'm never going to be any different. Thank whatever gods there be, or something. I am the master of my soul.

But then, why were there the moments of aching? The moments of impotent rage towards people who didn't matter? Like Polly Sheppard, for instance.

It hadn't taken Polly long to forget that Lisa Pappas had ever existed, reflected Anthony. Within a matter of days after Chris and Lisa had left Cooper Station, Polly was back to normal. Good old civic-minded, community-spirited, busy-body Polly who, as Lisa had confided to Anthony, had been Lisa's best, true, good friend.

Friends like that you can live without, Anthony had warned. Polly Sheppard is nobody's friend but her own.

Don't you dare say a thing like that, insisted Lisa angrily. Polly and I have been friends for years. You don't know what she's had to put up with, Anthony. Did you know that Jim Sheppard used to run around on her all the time?

Anthony smiled and kissed her neck. That was his Lisa all right. Here she was in his bed, doing what all Cooper Station would have considered as "running around", and her voice was full of outrage at the defections of Jim Sheppard.

No, I didn't know, he said.

Well, he did and it was just awful for Polly. She thought she was going to die from it.

My dear child, people don't die from the effects of infidelity.

How would you know, Anthony. Honestly, I think you're the most cynical person I've ever known.

Seeing someone like Polly Sheppard in a true light does not constitute being a cynic, said Anthony.

Well, you can be wrong, can't you? And you're wrong about Polly.

But Anthony hadn't been so far wrong. The night of the town meeting he had questioned Lisa.

And what did your good true friend Polly have to say about all this? he asked.

What could she say? demanded Lisa. It wasn't her place to speak up.

I thought it was an open meeting, said Anthony. At an open meeting everyone has the right to say whatever he wishes. What did Jim have to say?

Nothing, admitted Lisa. But it was too late to say anything anyway. They offered the money and before anyone could say anything, Chris jumped at it.

I thought he would, said Anthony.

What do you mean by that? asked Lisa.

He supposed that he could have told her. If she'd known about the money then perhaps she would have hated him instead of believing herself in love with him, and then everything would have been easier for her. But Anthony could not tell her and he didn't even know why. What difference did it make? He was through with her anyway, so why not make a clean break of it? Now what did he mean by that? He'd already told her it was finished and she'd accepted that, so why worry about what she might think? But still Anthony did not speak and he would not admit that it was because he wanted Lisa to think well of him in the future. As the years passed, he wanted her to remember him as the great love of her life, as the sophisticated older man who had been everything to her. He did not want her to think of him as the man who had paid off her husband in order to get rid of her. It all smacked too much of a bad novel or a second-rate movie.

At least she left with a few illusions, thought Anthony. She left thinking that I was really sorry to see her go and that Polly Sheppard was still her friend.

He ought to get up and go back to the house. Margery and Nathaniel would be home shortly and they'd start wondering what had happened to him. If he knew his Aunt Margery, with her Goddamned cloying maternal instinct, she'd peek into his room to see if he were properly covered and find him gone.

229

Well, let her. Anthony took another drink from his bottle of Scotch, then he went into the bedroom that opened off the living-room. He sat down on the edge of the bed and against all the strength of what little will he had left, he remembered the day he had been with Lisa for the first time on this same bed. He remembered her nakedness and the goldenness of her legs and shoulders where her summer tan had already started, and he remembered the way she had fought to try to keep from feeling when he touched her and the way she had finally given in to him as he had known she would.

Dumb little thing, thought Anthony drunkenly. So she'd been a good lay. What the hell did he care that she was gone? He had a full third of his new novel finished and Kent Purdom, his agent, had sent him a wildly enthusiastic telegram.

"Come home, my boy," the wire had read. "You're as good as new and we'll have another best-seller on our hands."

Well, Anthony was going tomorrow and damned glad he was of it, too.

Back to the penthouses and the air-conditioned bars and the sleek, smooth, smart girls who didn't fall in love with you, nor look at you with enormous eyes while you talked nor hang on to you when it was over with stories about being pregnant. And when the sleek ones got to be too much for you, you could always go to a whorehouse or get a fancy call girl who knew all the perversions and loved the extra money that practising them brought in. Those girls didn't scream and pant and moan and faint. They practised their art coolly, with precision, while you watched and reluctantly admired them for the master craftsmen they were. Even if they didn't excite you particularly, you still had to admire them. After all, what was sex anyway but just another appetite to be appeased, like hunger? So you might as well be a gourmet about it and get the best money could buy.

But the sleek, smooth girls did not have hair that smelled of the sun and the whores did not sob your name against your shoulder. The sleek girls, when they wanted it at all, wanted it coldly and neatly with a good strong condom between you and them and you certainly didn't spend time discussing philosophy with a whore. The sleek ones laughed at sophisticated comedies and the whores laughed at vulgarisms and whoever heard of a girl who laughed over nothing anyway.

God, but it'd be good to get back to the city, Anthony told himself. He'd had enough of the country to last him a lifetime. He was going to be all right once he got back to civilization. Lisa was all right already. All she'd needed was to get away from him and her world had straightened itself out in a hurry.

He took another drink from the bottle and leaned back on the bed.

Oh, yes, Lisa'd gotten over him just fine. He didn't like to remember the night the ache had gotten the better of him and he'd picked up the telephone.

Hello, my love, he'd said to her.

Anthony?

My dear child, have you already found someone else who calls you my love?

Anthony, it's one o'clock in the morning. What do you want?

I want you to come live with me and be my love. That's Sheridan or somebody. I forget.

Anthony, are you drunk?

Only a little, my love.

Oh, for heaven's sake, Anthony. Go back to bed and sleep it off. You're going to kill yourself if you go on like this.

Will you come?

Anthony, go back to bed.

But my bed is too big and too cold.

I've got to hang up, Anthony. Chris has to be at school early in the morning and I don't want to disturb his sleep. Good night, Anthony.

Good-bye, my love, said Anthony after he had hung up.

Well, if Lisa was so Goddamned well adjusted these days, he would be, too. It wouldn't take long, once he was back in the city. He'd sober up and finish the damned novel and become a human being again.

Anthony turned his face against the uncovered pillow on the bed and even after all this time it seemed to him that it still smelled of Lisa.

What a horse's arse I've turned out to be, he thought angrily.

231

But still, he buried his face in the pillow.

Good-bye, my love, he said silently. Good-bye to summer and your little round belly. Your silly laughs at nothing and the soft places between your thighs. Your frowns at the Russian novelists and your wondering how the hell to spell Nietzsche and your nervous fingers ripping at the wet labels on beer bottles and the way you looked in a hot, perfumed bath and your little lame brain that it was exciting to put new creases in, your big eyes and your silly Tell me a story, Anthony.

It was almost one o'clock in the morning when Margery and Nathaniel found him. They had searched their own house and Anthony's before thinking of the cottage. He was snoring and the bottle of Scotch was empty on the floor next to the bed. Margery had turned on a lamp and she stood still and looked down at Anthony.

Why, Nate, honey," she said. "He must have had a bad dream or something. His face is all wet."

Nathaniel picked up his nephew and swung him over his shoulder. He started towards the door with him while Margery picked up his coat, a half-empty package of cigarettes and a lighter.

"Nate, honey, he must've been crying in his sleep," said Margery.

"Don't worry about Anthony," said Nate, panting a little. "He's never shed a tear in his life."

18

SOMEHOW or other, thought Lisa, you never expected people to die during the month of May, for in northern New England, May always seemed like the beginning of everything. Lawns were like heads of newly fuzzed green hair, ready for cutting, and every brook and stream scrambled its way towards the sea in what seemed an absolute frenzy of freedom. In front of the house that Chris and Lisa had rented in Gammon's Landing, Massachusetts, there were two round, fat forsythia bushes that looked almost comical under their heavy load of yellow blossoms, like two cheerful club women in yellow flowered hats. Just beyond the eastern rim of Gammon's Landing was the sea and along the beach front people had started taking down the wooden boards that had protected the windows of their cottages all winter long. Hot-dog stands and shooting galleries sported new coats of paint as everyone got ready for the crowds that would begin to arrive over the Memorial Day week-end. It seemed that the whole world was beginning to stir again after a winter of hibernation and it seemed impossible for anyone to die amidst all the life that pulsed on every side.

But it did happen, thought Lisa, as she packed two bags for herself and Chris. In Cooper's Mills, Irene St. George was dead and Lisa thought how typical this was of her. Leave it to Irene to do everything differently from everybody else. Lisa sighed as she snapped the second bag shut. Now she'd have to start in on the children's things. Thank God for her new friend, Janie Wright. Without Janie, Lisa and Chris would have had to drag the kids up to Cooper's Mills and while Midget and little Chris wouldn't be too much trouble, Linda was still only six weeks old and woke in the middle of the night for a feeding and a diaper change. In one way, though, Lisa was sorry they weren't bringing the children. She would have liked to stop off in Cooper Station and visit Polly Sheppard and show off her new daughter. Still, perhaps it was just as well. In all the months that she'd been in Gammon's Landing, Lisa had received only three letters in reply to the many she had written to Polly, and none of the three had included anything that sounded like an invitation. Still, thought Lisa as she folded the last of Linda's diapers to take over to Janie's, perhaps it was always that way when you moved away from a place. You started a new life in a new house and made new friends and you didn't have time to think about last year or the year before that. Just the same, though, it was funny the way things had turned out with Polly. You'd think after they'd been friends for so long that Polly would have made some attempt to maintain her end of their relationship. Well, she'd just wait and see if Polly showed up for Irene's funeral and, if she didn't, then Lisa would consider their friendship over. It was perfectly all right to make excuses for Polly's not writing, after all she was always busy with a million different things, but a funeral was something else again.

Linda Pappas awoke quickly, with loud demands to be fed, and Lisa laughed as she bent over the crib. Linda's fat little face was red with anger at being kept waiting for more than three seconds and she was soaked clear up to her shoulders.

"Never mind, my love," said Lisa as she picked up the baby, "we'll have you all fixed up in a minute."

She stood in front of the gas stove half rocking Linda in her arms as she waited for the bottle to warm.

My love, thought Lisa. My love. Anthony used to say that all the time.

Lisa did not let herself think of Anthony often any more. But in the beginning, when she and Chris had first come to Gammon's Landing, she had thought of him often. Mostly in

234

the morning, when she was so sick she wondered if she'd ever get through the day. Then she had leaned, retching over the toilet, and cursed him along with Chris and every man ever born. Then, everything had been wrong. Her doctor was a native of Gammon's Landing by the name of Wendell Garrett, and she missed Jess Cameron with a fury that made her feel even sicker than she was. At least Jess had always had soothing, comforting words for her, even when he couldn't stop the morning sickness, and she could talk to Jess. Dr. Garrett, on the other hand, was brusque almost to the point of rudeness.

"It'll pass," he told Lisa when she complained of her illness.

"Is that all you can tell me?" Lisa had demanded.

"Mrs. Pappas, you're not the first woman in the world to have had an incurable morning sickness, and you won't be the last. It passes."

"Goddamn him," said Lisa angrily to Chris. "I never really appreciated Jess until now."

"Gee, baby, I'm sorry," said Chris. "Is there anything I can do?"

"No," mimicked Lisa, "there's nothing you can do. Just leave me to hell alone."

Then she went into the bathroom and threw up again.

Bastards, she thought feelingly. Every Goddamned last one of them.

But, of course, the sickness did pass after several agonizing weeks, and Christopher Pappas silently thanked God for that. Maybe now, Lisa would be a little easier to live with.

"I know none of this has been pleasant for you, honey," said Chris, "but I haven't exactly enjoyed it either, you know."

He slipped his hand under her pyjama top and began to stroke her and Lisa moved impatiently under his touch.

"Oh, for heaven's sake, Chris, cut it out," she said crossly.

But he continued to handle her. "I've missed you, baby," he whispered against her hair.

Lisa sighed aloud and in aggravation. "I don't feel well, Chris," she said.

His hand was still and for a moment he said nothing.

235

"What is it, baby?" he asked at last. "The morning sickness is all gone. So what is it?"

Lisa sat up in bed and reached for a cigarette.

"For heaven's sake," she said crossly. "Is it so damned hard to understand? I'm pregnant, for God's sake. How do you expect me to feel? Like doing cart wheels or something?"

"Not exactly," said Chris and now his voice was impatient and edgy. "But neither do I expect you to act as if I had the plague. Sometimes you act as if you hate me."

Lisa smoked and stared up at the ceiling through the dark.

"I don't hate you," she said.

And that much was true. She did not hate Chris. In fact, in some strange way she loved him more than she ever had. It was comforting to live with a man like Chris. To know where she stood every minute and to never worry what she could talk about and to never feel out of her depth. It was only when he tried to touch her that she felt something stir within her.

You're a fine little animal, my love.

But that's all over, Lisa argued silently. Anthony was fine in bed. Wonderful. But you can't spend your whole life with your clothes off. It's over and done with and a good thing for me it is, too. I never would have been happy with him.

But still, when Chris tried to make love to her, she felt slightly disgusted, as if she were being unfaithful to Anthony and in a way that she had never felt when she was being unfaithful to Chris.

It's crazy, she told herself. I don't owe Anthony one single thing. All I owe I owe to Chris and I should be concerning myself only with his happiness.

Anthony. Her whole body cried out silently for him. Anthony, I need you.

"No," said Lisa to Chris. "I don't hate you. I just don't feel well."

She felt that she should reach out to him, touch him, reassure him, but she could not and she felt guilty and angry with herself.

"For heaven's sake, Chris, I can't help it, and I should think you'd be able to understand how I feel."

"Christ, it wasn't all my fault, you know," said Chris angrily. "You had your fun, too."

For a moment. Lisa felt a fear that was almost panic.

"What do you mean, I had my fun?" she asked.

"I mean as well as I did," retorted Chris.

Lisa breathed easily again. For a frightening moment she had thought that Chris was referring to her and Anthony. But of course, that was ridiculous. Chris had never suspected her for a second. In spite of all the talk that had gone around Cooper Station. In the first place, none of it had ever reached his ears, and even if it had, he would have put it down as part of the vicious plot to get rid of him. He had accepted Lisa's explanation that she and Anthony were simply friends and neighbours at its face value and he had, in fact, been friendly with Anthony himself.

"He's really intelligent," Chris had said of Anthony. "Too bad he's so mixed up."

"What do you mean, mixed up?" asked Lisa defensively.

"Are you kidding?" asked Chris. "That guy's got the weirdest set of values in the world. Hurry up and grab everything today. There's no tomorrow for Anthony."

"Well, Anthony doesn't need the same set of values as you do," countered Lisa. "He isn't a married man with a family. And even if he never wrote another word, he'd still have all that Cooper money to fall back on."

"Maybe," said Chris, and Lisa thought he sounded a trifle smug, "but I sure wouldn't want to live that way."

Lisa almost hated him. "No, you wouldn't," she said sarcastically. "Not you. You've got to do your lousy bit for mankind. What the hell do you care if the kids don't have shoes as long as you can wear that damned white collar of yours and teach school for peanuts?"

Chris looked at her sharply. "You sound just like my old man," he said coldly, knowing that this would reach her as would nothing else. She hated his father and Chris knew it. "Maybe you think I'd be better off in the fruit store at Cooper's Mills," he continued. "Then I could wear a work shirt and an old apron and sell bananas."

237

"Oh, shut up," said Lisa crossly, unable to think of anything to say.

"I will," said Chris in that maddeningly calm way of his. "Just don't go around trying to justify Anthony Cooper's existence to me. He's smart and a nice guy and all that, but he doesn't seem to have much purpose as far as I'm concerned. His novels certainly aren't going to live after him and he's never even had enough ambition to get married and produce a son to carry on his name."

"That's the Greek in you coming out," said Lisa. "You're all alike. Sons, sons, sons. God, I thought your father would die when Midget turned out to be a girl. It's a damned lucky thing for me that I had better luck producing little Chris or he'd think I was worthless for sure."

But after that night she wondered often about Chris's words and of the child she now carried.

What if it's a boy? she thought. What if it's a boy and turns out to look just like Anthony?

She knew Chris. Tolerant and kind he might be, but he'd never stand for another man's son in his home. He'd throw her out on the street and keep Midget and little Chris, and for a moment a picture flashed through her mind of Anthony smiling and welcoming back his love with his baby in her arms. But she didn't even know if he was still in Cooper Station. He might have gone back to New York the way he always said he would, and besides, she did not want to spend the rest of her life with Anthony Cooper.

Yes, Chris would throw her out even if it meant wrecking his career with a messy divorce. And Lisa would fight him, she knew. She didn't have much but she wasn't about to lose what little she had. Not after those lousy years at the university getting Chris educated. Not now, just when they were beginning to get somewhere.

Lisa thought of an eventual return to Irene and Cooper's Mills and she shuddered. She'd wind up like Marie Fennell, just another old bag to be laughed at and joked about and not even pitied.

What if it's a boy and he looks like Anthony?

238

She tried to comfort herself. New babies don't look like anybody, she assured herself. And even if this one looks like Anthony later on, Chris will be so used to him by then, and Cooper Station will be so far behind us, that he'll never even think of it.

But she still had her moments of fear. The day the baby was born, Lisa asked, "What is it?" as soon as she awoke.

"A girl," they told her, and Lisa went back to sleep without even asking to see her.

Thank God, she thought as she drifted off.

And the next day she realized that it wasn't true about new babies not looking like anyone. Linda looked exactly like Lisa. The same pale brown hair and big eyes. The same nose and mouth and chin.

"Baby, why are you crying?" asked Chris.

"Because I'm so happy," said Lisa. "I wanted it to be a little girl all along."

"I guess I did, too," confessed Chris. "I missed too much of Midget's babyhood not to want to watch a little girl growing up." He kissed her gently.

Lisa looked up at her husband and felt a wave of such love go over her that tears formed at the corners of her eyes again.

I'll make it up to you, darling, she thought and put her hand against Chris's cheek. I'll make it all up to you.

Lisa finished burping Linda and put her back to bed.

"And that's that for another four hours, my love," she said to the child.

Everything was done. The only thing left was to drop the children and their things off at Janie's as soon as Chris came home from school and then they could be on their way. Lisa went into her kitchen and made herself a cup of instant coffee, then she sat down and lit a cigarette and wondered why she didn't feel anything about her mother.

Maybe I'm not used to the idea yet, she told herself.

The telephone call had come just that morning, only a few minutes before Chris and the older children left for school. It

239

was the chief of police at Cooper's Mills and he told Lisa that Irene was dead.

"Must've fallen down the front hall stairs, Lisa," he said. His name was Johnny McGrath and Lisa remembered that he had always been kind. Plenty of times he could have locked Irene up for the way she behaved. But he never had. He'd always seen her home, drunk as she was, as if he were seeing home a great lady.

"Here you are, Mrs. St. George," he would say, opening the door of the police cruiser with a flourish and taking off his hat.

"My deepest thanks," Irene would reply grandly. "Good evening, Mr. McGrath."

"I'm sorry as hell, Lisa," said Johnny McGrath. "I always liked your mother. At least it was quick, this way. Her neck was broke and she died right off the bat."

"Thank you, Mr. McGrath," said Lisa quietly. "We'll drive up this evening."

"Got her over to Breton's funeral parlour," said the police chief. "Figured you'd want it that way. Old man Breton took care of your Grandma and Grandpa."

"That's fine, Mr. McGrath," said Lisa. "Thank you again."

"My, she's a cool one," said McGrath to a lounging policeman after he had hung up. "Never said if and or but. Didn't even act surprised, much less broken up."

"Well," said the policeman, whose name was Oscar Roullier, "I don't see how anybody could get broken up over an old drunk like Irene St. George."

Johnny McGrath was shocked. "Well, for Christ's sake, it was her mother!"

"Yeah," said Oscar Roullier.

Lisa and Christopher Pappas arrived in Cooper's Mills at seven o'clock in the evening and went directly to the Pappases' fruit store.

"Hi, Pop," said Chris as he and Lisa entered.

The old man looked up. "Oh," he said sourly. "It's you."

"Who'd you expect?" asked Chris.

"I dunno," said Costas Pappas. "I thought maybe you two had got too fancy living down there in Mass. to bother comin'

240

home to bury her mother." He indicated her with a jerk of his head towards Lisa. "You mother's out back if you care," he said to Chris.

Nothing changes, thought Chris Pappas as he and Lisa walked towards the back of the store. His father and mother would go to their graves with the idea that their only son had somehow failed them by breaking out of the pattern they had set. The store still looked as it had always looked. Junky, overcrowded and slightly dirty. Just like his father, thought Chris wearily. And he knew he would find his mother the same way.

Thank God we got out, thought Chris and squeezed Lisa's arm. We would have died here, and died young, from dirt and boredom and the wanting of something better.

"My son," said Aphrodite Pappas.

"Hello, Ma," said Chris and bent to kiss her yellowish cheek. "How are you?"

"I'm good enough," said Mrs. Pappas, then she leaned away from Chris and looked up into his face. "But you," she said, "you're gettin' skinny."

Lisa sighed. It was what her mother-in-law always said whenever she saw Chris. He could have weighed three hundred pounds and she would still have said it.

"How are the children?" asked Mrs. Pappas by way of greeting to Lisa.

"They're fine," replied Lisa.

She and Chris had something to eat and then went directly to the funeral home to conclude the arrangements that Johnny McGrath had started. When that was over, they returned to the Pappases and went straight to bed and even when Lisa realized that Chris's father and mother had not uttered one word of regret about Irene's death, she still could not cry for her mother.

She lay on her back next to Chris and the smell of spring came through the open bedroom windows, heavy with scent. She moved a little and Chris's hand found her breast.

"I love you, baby," he said against her temple.

Lisa's heart started to pound. She did not respond, but this time she didn't move away.

His mouth found hers and he kept one hand over her heart,

reassured by its beating that she was just as aroused as he. "Be my little French girl," he whispered, stroking her.

Lisa turned her head away. "This isn't right," she said and pushed at his hands half-heartedly. "Chris, don't. This must be a sin. Tonight of all nights. My mother is dead."

"She's dead," whispered Chris harshly into her mouth. "She's dead and we're alive."

"Alive," she whispered. "Alive. Think of the wonder of that."

And then she could not talk at all. She could merely raise herself up to meet him in the agony of giving.

No, she thought sleepily, later, May was no time for dying. And for the first time since she and Chris had left Cooper Station, she went to sleep without a single thought for Anthony.

It was a quick, simple funeral for Irene St. George, with a Low Mass at the Catholic church and no one there besides Chris and Lisa but Irene's old drinking buddies from the Happy Hour Café. They shed their beery tears and left as soon as the Mass was over without going on to the cemetery, for which Lisa was grateful. She and Chris buried Irene alone and when it was over they got into their car and drove back towards Cooper's Mills

"We'll have to stay over another day, I suppose," said Lisa. "I'll have to see what arrangements she made about the house and her things."

Lisa looked out of the window on her side and suddenly she wanted to go home.

"Look," she said, "we could see Mr. LaPlante now, couldn't we? He's always in his office after lunch. He was her lawyer and he must know what she wanted done."

"We could try him," said Chris.

"Let's go," said Lisa. "Then we could go right home. I'm lonesome for the kids."

Maurice LaPlante was a stocky, white-haired French Canadian who smoked small cigars and drank wine at breakfast. Lisa had never liked him but Irene had thought him a fine old gentleman and had said so often.

"You don't find them like Maurice LaPlante any more," she had told Lisa. "He's a gentleman of the old school."

Well, perhaps he was, thought Lisa, to Irene. But most of

Cooper's Mills regarded him as just another old soak who'd seen much better days. In any case, thought Lisa gratefully, her business with him had not taken long. Irene's house and its rooms of stiff, well-kept and little-used furniture now belonged to Lisa.

"The house is in good repair," said Mr. LaPlante, "and the taxes are all paid up-to-date. She was never one to let things go, your mother. Kept her place right up."

"Well, what are we going to do with it?" Lisa asked Chris. "We have about as much use for a house in Cooper's Mills as nothing at all." Chris shrugged and Lisa turned towards the lawyer. "Put it up for sale," she said. "The furniture, too."

Mr. LaPlante put up a restraining hand. "Don't be so quick," he warned. "Take a ride over there and look at the place. Maybe there'll be something you'll want for yourself. Some souvenir. Don't be so quick."

"All right," sighed Lisa. "I'll go."

It was agreed that Chris would go back to the Pappases and repack the suitcases while Lisa went on alone to Irene's house.

"It won't take me long," she told Chris. "We'll be able to get started early."

The house looked as it had always looked. Drab, dark and unfriendly. Lisa took the key from under a loose board in the porch floor and let herself in. Then she went dutifully through every room in the house. She even took note of the loose carpeting on the stairs where Irene must have caught her heel before she fell, and still she felt nothing. No sorrow, no pang of loss. There was nothing for her here. Nothing she needed or wanted. It was as if she had never lived here at all.

"Aren't you even sorry for her?" Anthony had once asked Lisa about Irene.

"No. Why should I be?" Lisa had asked, genuinely puzzled at his question.

"Because she hasn't had much of a life, really," said Anthony. "Why do you suppose she drinks?"

"For the same reason you do, I suppose," said Lisa. "Weakness. And the mistaken idea that there is a solution to anything in a bottle."

243

"Not all of us look for a solution, my love," said Anthony. "Some of us ask only for a measure of solace."

"Maybe so," retorted Lisa, "but I wouldn't want momentary comfort at the price of the next day's bomb of a hangover."

"You're a nasty little Puritan," said Anthony and reached for her.

"That's what you think," replied Lisa.

They had made love then and the subject of Irene was forgotten. It never came up again between them.

Now, standing in Irene's living-room, Lisa found herself wondering. Perhaps it had been true about Irene, she thought. Perhaps she had needed solace more than anyone had ever imagined.

I guess she wanted it all, thought Lisa. The fur coats and the diamond bracelets and the handsome men in an adoring group at her feet. And instead of the Paris trips and the iced champagne, she'd gotten Wilfred St. George and Cooper's Mills and the Happy Hours Café. She felt a sudden kinship with Irene.

Lisa sat down on one of the uncomfortable plush chairs that still, after all these years, made her feel itchy and ill at ease. She lit one of the cigarettes which, in her lifetime, Irene had considered so grossly unladylike.

"For heaven's sake, Lisa," she had said. "Are you going to go about with one of those things stuck in your mouth like a mill-girl? For heaven's sake, Lisa, remember who you are!"

Lisa finished her cigarette and squashed the butt in the same place she had put her ashes. In the dirt around a rather obscene-looking rubber plant that Irene had kept on a stand in the living-room.

Lisa knew who she was all right, she thought as she locked the front door of the house behind her and replaced the key. She was Lisa Pappas, and she wasn't going to waste her life regretting. She was married to a good man who was going places. A man who would never run off and leave her to fend for herself and her offsprings as Wilfred St. George had done. She'd never wind up as a town character as Irene had done because if she wanted something she'd go after it. She wouldn't sit on her behind in a beer joint and wish false wishes that had no hope of coming true.

Her hands felt very strong on the steering wheel of the car as she pulled away from the kerb in front of Irene's house and headed for the Pappases.

She was a happy, contented woman, she told herself. A woman in a hurry to get back to her husband, her home and her children and she smiled a little as she thought of what Anthony Cooper would have had to say about her present state of mind.

"You'll wind up with a passle of brats and memberships in the P.T.A., a select, snobbish bridge club and the Ladies' Aid."

And it was true, thought Lisa. She would go back and join the best bridge club in Gammon's Landing and she would go to every P.T.A. meeting with Chris. Furthermore, she would bake two cakes for the Ladies' Aid cake sale next week and they would bring the best prices of all the cakes there.

So there, Anthony, she thought, as she parked in front of the fruit store. I may be all you said I'd be, but I like it that way.

Less than half an hour later, Lisa and Chris had said their good-byes to Chris's sullen parents and were on their way home. They could have avoided Cooper Station by taking the new turnpike that by-passed the town but they did not.

"Hasn't changed much, has it?" remarked Chris as they drove down Benjamin Street.

"No, and it never will," replied Lisa. "Thank God things worked out the way they did and we got out of here."

"You were pretty upset at the time," said Chris and smiled.

"It just goes to show that things do work out for the best," said Lisa. "I wonder what ever happened to Doris Delaney Palmer. How I hated that bitch."

"She'll go on for ever," said Chris. "Her kind always does. She could ride roughshod over the whole world and wind up without a trace of regret on her face."

Lisa laughed. "You know something funny?" she asked. "I've never been able to picture Doris Palmer as anything but full grown and wearing that iron corset of hers. I can't picture her in bed with anybody, let alone poor Adam Palmer, and it seems almost obscene to think of her having a baby."

"Maybe Adam thought so, too," said Chris, matching her laughter. "And that's why they never had any kids."

They drove past Polly Sheppard's big Colonial-style house and Chris didn't slow down.

"Are you sorry about Polly?" he asked. "I kept thinking she'd show up for the funeral."

"So did I," answered Lisa and sighed. "No, I can't say I'm sorry. I guess we just sort of outgrew each other. You know, Polly was never really too bright in spite of that fancy college education of hers. She had a narrow mind, just like everybody else in Cooper Station."

"Are you sorry about anything?" asked Chris, and for just a moment a chord sounded in Lisa.

Come live with me and be my love.

It might have been fun with Anthony, she thought. For a little while, anyway. New York and a nice apartment and interesting night-clubs and Europe next year. But what about when it was over? And it would have been over soon. Anthony would have tired of her easily as a steady diet. What was it he used to say? You'll never be a gourmet's delight, my love. You're too much. Like too much dessert or a heavy wine with the meat course. Of course, he'd been joking, but just the same he would have wearied.

Lisa looked straight into Chris's eyes just as they were passing the sign that said, YOU ARE NOW LEAVING COOPER STATION. PLEASE COME AGAIN.

"No, darling," she said and squeezed his arm. "I'm not sorry about one single thing."